Fiona looked up at Nate, her eyes suspiciously bright.

"I will never forget you, or what you did for me tonight. But I suspect it's just the latest in a long line of amazing things you've done. Not many people would have stepped forward like that, but you did. You're a hero."

Nate felt his face heat and knew he must be as red as the sirens flashing on the ambulance pulling into the parking lot. "I'm not a hero."

The corner of Fiona's mouth quirked up while she studied him. "The fact that you're denying it just makes you even more heroic."

Now it was Nate's turn to look away. He didn't know how to explain to her that he'd simply reacted—she was in danger, and he'd stepped forward, wanting only to protect her. That wasn't heroic; it was instinctive, pure and simple. Heroes recognized danger and stepped forward in spite of it.

He hadn't stopped to consider the danger, but had rushed right in, his only thought to keep Fiona safe.

Dear Reader,

Most people think of the holidays as a time to spend with friends and family, celebrating traditions and making happy memories. It can be a very joyous time, something to look forward to all year long. But for those people who don't have families or friends, the holidays can be very isolating and lonely, something to dread rather than anticipate.

That's the case for Nate and Fiona. They're both lonely—Fiona by circumstance, and Nate by choice. Neither one of them sees the holidays as something to get excited about, especially when Fiona's life is threatened. But as they deal with the mysterious dangers surrounding Fiona, they both come to realize that there's more to life than work, and sometimes, you really can have it all—a family (complete with a pampered cat), friends and a fulfilling job. And don't forget the Christmas tree!

I hope you enjoy Nate and Fiona's story. As always, thanks for reading!

Lara

KILLER SEASON

Lara Lacombe

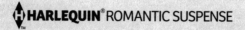

HARLEQUIN® ROMANTIC SUSPENSE

Recycling programs
for this product may
not exist in your area.

ISBN-13: 978-0-373-27944-9

Killer Season

Copyright © 2015 by Lara Kingeter

This edition published by arrangement with Harlequin Books S.A.

For questions and comments about the quality of this book, please contact us at CustomerService@Harlequin.com.

Printed in U.S.A.

www.Harlequin.com

Lara Lacombe earned a PhD in microbiology and immunology and worked in several labs across the country before moving into the classroom. Her day job as a college science professor gives her time to pursue her other love—writing fast-paced romantic suspense with smart, nerdy heroines and dangerously attractive heroes. She loves to hear from readers! Find her on the web or contact her at laralacombewriter@gmail.com.

Books by Lara Lacombe

Harlequin Romantic Suspense

Deadly Contact
Fatal Fallout
Lethal Lies
Killer Exposure

Visit Lara's Author Profile page at Harlequin.com or laralacombe.blogspot.com for more titles.

Chapter 1

Nate Gallagher leaned forward with a sigh, squinting to peer through the foggy glass of the refrigerated case in search of caffeine. It was late, and he still had a few hours to go before he could sleep.

He opened the door, reached in and pulled out a bottle, reading the label with some suspicion. *All day energy!* it proclaimed, the neon-green letters garishly bright against the black background. *Might as well try it*, he decided, tucking the bottle under his arm. He didn't think he could gag down any more coffee—he'd drunk so much of the stuff over the past week, he was in real danger of turning into a coffee bean.

He glanced at the register as he made his way over to the hot-food station. Fiona, the night-shift clerk, had given him the usual smile and wave when he'd walked in, but now she had her nose stuck in a textbook. Every time he came in here, it seemed she was always studying.

"Sociology," she'd replied with a smile, after he had asked her about it one night. "I'm in the master's degree program at the University of Houston. I want to go into education after I graduate."

Nate didn't know much about sociology, but she looked like his fantasy version of a professor, with her sleek auburn hair, wide brown eyes and generous mouth. He could picture her in a tight-fitting business suit that hugged her curves, standing in front of a classroom wearing sky-high heels. Even her usual uniform of jeans and a T-shirt made him take notice, and there had been many times he'd wanted to pull her against him, press those amazing curves against his chest and bury his nose in her hair. He wasn't sure what she smelled like—he'd never gotten that close— but he'd passed many pleasant moments daydreaming about it. Warm vanilla. Roses. Clean citrus. He didn't really have a preference, but he hoped to find out, one way or another.

Not for the first time, he wondered about her story. She had to be smart to be in graduate school. But why was she working here? It wasn't the most intellectually demanding job, and it couldn't pay very well. There had to be some other reason why she'd taken the job.

He hoped she was due to graduate soon—the grave-yard shift at a convenience store was no place for a woman like her. Although he tried to come by a few times a week, he'd be relieved when she completed her degree and would have to quit. Part of him would miss seeing her, but it would be one less worry on his mind.

He stopped at the display of hot foods, surveying his choices with a growing sense of resignation. *Nachos or a hot dog?* Neither option was particularly appealing, but he had to eat something. Breakfast had been a long time ago, and his stomach was threatening to quit if he didn't eat soon.

Nate fumbled with the tongs as he attempted to fish a hot dog out of the warmer, trying to pick one that didn't look quite so desiccated. He'd suffer through this junk tonight, but tomorrow he was going to try to start eating better. He experienced a momentary pang of longing for his mother's home cooking, but she was so angry with him for missing Thanksgiving that she was more likely to smack him with a pan than fix him something to eat.

It wasn't that he wanted to be away from his family, but being a detective meant he had to make certain sacrifices, choices that weren't always popular. His dad seemed to understand that, but his mother? She took it as a personal affront every time he missed a family gathering. Because a big city like Houston had its fair share of crime, he wound up missing more family events than he attended.

"Again?" she'd said, when he'd called last week to tell her he couldn't make it for Thanksgiving. "What have we done, that you would choose your work over your family? That's not how I raised you. Never mind. Stay there and work. That's fine."

Nate wasn't stupid. He knew that when she said "fine"

in a tone of voice that made it sound like she was talking around a mouthful of soap, things were anything but.

Still, he never argued with her. It wouldn't do any good. She would never understand his job, and, truth be told, he didn't want her to. Bad enough he had to live with the images of the dead, the murder victims who haunted his dreams and drove him to keep working, keep searching, trying to find their killers and bring them to justice. Humans were capable of so many atrocities, and he hoped his family never had to see that ugly side of life.

He squirted ketchup onto the stale, dry bun with a mental sigh, deliberately pushing thoughts of his mother and his job out of his mind. He was already exhausted, and thinking about her lectures did nothing for his mood. Hopefully, she would wait to scold him in private at Christmas, so his sister, Molly, wouldn't have to hear it. She didn't like it when they argued—she had Down syndrome and was very sensitive about picking up emotions.

The thought of Molly made him smile. Twenty-one yellow roses would arrive at the house tomorrow, part of his birthday gift to her. They were her favorite flower, and he was unabashedly proud of himself for having thought to send them. Normally, he made a quick phone call between bouts of paperwork, but her twenty-first birthday was a milestone, something to celebrate. The special gesture had cost him a pretty penny, but she was worth it. And hopefully the flowers would help ease the sting of his absence at the Thanksgiving table.

He knew she missed him and didn't always understand why he couldn't be there. But, unlike their mother, at least she didn't punish him for it.

Wiping stray ketchup from his fingers, Nate picked up his dinner and drink, then turned to head over to the register. As he rounded the corner, he clipped the edge of the counter, and the bottle, slick with condensation, slid from his fingers. It hit the tile with a dull thud and skittered across the floor, coming to rest under a display of potato chips.

"Damn," he muttered. He debated leaving the bottle where it was and grabbing another, but a quick glance at the front counter changed his mind. If he left it, Fiona would have to pick it up before going home, and he didn't want her to have to crawl around on the dirty floor to fish it out from under the metal rack. He carefully set the hot dog on the food counter, crossing his fingers that it wouldn't tip over off the wrapper. He'd seen some pretty nasty things in his line of work, but he refused to eat food that had come into contact with the convenience store counter.

Resigned to his fate, he dropped to his knees and bent over, peering under the display in search of the wayward bottle.

Fiona heard the telltale *thud* of a plastic bottle hitting the floor and looked up with a wince. From the sound of things, Hot Guy was going to need a new drink, if he didn't want to wind up wearing his soda. *Maybe that wouldn't be so bad, though*, she thought. *I could help him clean up.* She indulged in a brief fantasy of wiping the sticky liquid off his stubbled cheeks, those impossibly broad shoulders and his flat stomach. Touching the customers wasn't exactly in her job description but, for him, she'd make an exception.

He'd been coming in a few times a week for the past several months. Never at the same time of night, but regularly enough that she'd begun to expect him and even look forward to his visits. She had no idea what he did for a living, but he always looked tired, as if he carried the weight of the world on his shoulders. But despite the dark circles under his eyes and what seemed to be a permanent five-o'clock shadow, he was a handsome man. His deep green eyes seemed to take in everything at once, and even though he rarely met her gaze directly, she had the feeling he always knew where she was and what she was doing.

Being around him made her nervous. Not in a weird or uncomfortable way—it's just that he was almost too handsome to be real. She couldn't help staring when he was in the store, watching the way he moved with a subconscious grace up and down the aisles. She'd perfected the art of spying on him while appearing to study her textbook. He'd asked her about it once, the deep rumble of his voice vibrating through her and making her toes curl. She'd stammered out a reply. He'd given her a smile and a nod, and he hadn't spoken to her since.

Maybe I can get him to talk again tonight. She stuck a stray bit of paper in the book to hold her place, then hopped off the stool. As the only employee on duty, she should offer to help him retrieve his bottle. Although she mopped the floor every night, it was still wrong to make a customer crawl around on it.

She rounded the corner and froze, sucking in a breath at the sight that greeted her. Hot Guy was on all fours, his perfect butt in the air while he dug underneath the chip display. She felt her cheeks heat and knew she should look away, but she couldn't stop staring. *Are those custom-made jeans?* They had to be, the way they molded to him and fit like a second skin. His shirt rode up on his back, revealing a thin stripe of golden skin and a hint of fabric. *Boxers or briefs?* she mused.

She cocked her head to the side, enjoying the view with a silent sigh of appreciation. She really should help him, but seeing as he was already on the ground, there was no sense in both of them getting dirty. Better for her to stand here and…supervise. Yeah, that's what she was doing. She wasn't gawking like a sex-starved woman. She was supervising.

The door chimed, announcing the arrival of another customer, and she reluctantly turned away to head back to the register. At least she'd have the memory of this moment to keep her warm at night.

She rounded the corner, stopping short as a young man came barreling down the center aisle. He was tall and lean, his hands stuck deep into the front pockets of the jacket he wore with the hood pulled up. She frowned slightly, the hair on the back of her neck prickling. It was chilly in Houston, but this man looked *wrong* somehow, as if he wore the jacket to conceal himself rather than to stay warm.

Before she could make sense of his odd dress, he caught sight of her standing there. In one fluid motion, he drew his hand from his pocket, pulling out a gun and pointing it at her chest. "Money. Now."

Fiona stared at the gun, unable to take her eyes from the black, snub-nosed piece. *It's so small*, she thought stupidly. *How can something so small be so dangerous?*

"You deaf?" he asked, grabbing her arm and jerking her forward. "I said I want money." He shoved her toward the register, and she hit the counter hard enough to make her wince, the pain from the blow piercing through the fog of shock. "Give it to me."

Back when she had started this job, Ben, the owner, had given her some training on what to do if the store was ever held up. She was supposed to cooperate, offer no resistance, and do everything she could to get the robber out of the store without hurting anyone. If possible, she was to hit the silent-alarm button, which would alert the police that a robbery was in progress. Fiona had listened dutifully, filled with naive confidence that such a thing would never happen to her. But now that she was faced with the reality, her hands shook so badly she could barely open the register, much less find and press the alarm button.

"Faster," he said, leaning over the counter to monitor her progress as she emptied out the register with numb fingers. He swayed back and forth on his feet, his bloodshot eyes frequently cutting over to the door.

Fiona didn't know whether to hope for an interruption, or pray no one else came in and spooked him enough to shoot her.

His breath wafted over her, the stench of stale beer so strong she almost gagged. She stuffed the rest of the bills into a plastic bag and thrust it across the counter, trying hard not to look at his face. If he thought she couldn't identify him, maybe he wouldn't hurt her…

When he didn't take the bag right away, she glanced up to find him looking at the door again. Was there someone outside? She couldn't see the sidewalk from this angle, but he was staring so fixedly that something must have caught his attention.

She kept her eyes on him, trying to control her breathing as she fumbled with one hand under the counter. Where was that damn button? Her fingers skimmed across the flat surface, searching vainly for the alarm. When she finally found it, she bit her lip to keep from crying out in relief. She pressed it with a quick stab of her finger, then brought her hand back up so he wouldn't see what she'd done.

The man swiveled his head back around and eyed the bag greedily. His fingertips brushed across her skin as he grabbed it, making her shudder. She wiped her hand on her shirt to erase his touch as he placed the bag on the counter and opened it, keeping the gun trained on her while he checked the contents. After a few seconds, he raised angry eyes to her face, thrusting the gun forward with a jerk of his arm. "Where's the rest?"

She shook her head. "There is no more," she stammered, taking a step back when he leaned over the counter, peering into the empty register. A movement behind him caught her eye, and when she looked up her heart skipped a beat.

Hot Guy was slowly creeping toward the counter, a gun in his hand and his finger on his lips.

Chapter 2

She was calm, he'd give her that. Most people didn't respond well to a gun shoved in their face, but Fiona was handling things like a pro.

He moved quietly across the floor, stepping lightly to keep the heels of his boots from clacking on the tile. The last thing he needed was to alert the perp to his presence.

The man was growing increasingly agitated, yelling and waving the gun in Fiona's face. Probably high, if his twitchy, jerky movements were any indication. There was no telling how much money had been in the register, but if he thought Fiona was holding out on him, he was likely to get violent.

As if on cue, the man reached across the counter and grabbed Fiona's arm, jerking her off her feet with a rough tug. He pressed the gun against her temple as he dragged her across the counter. She kicked wildly, sending the lottery ticket display crashing to the floor.

"Where's the rest?" the man screamed, yanking her upright before slamming her back against the counter.

She whimpered, the sound soft and helpless. Nate felt his finger tighten on the trigger, but he couldn't risk shooting the guy when he was on top of Fiona—the bullet might pass through him and hit her.

"Please," she begged, trying in vain to twist away. "There's no more. I swear."

"You're lying!" He slammed her against the counter while he screamed in her face. "Where's the rest of the money?"

This guy was hanging on by a very thin thread, and if Nate didn't act soon, the punk was going to kill Fiona. The thought made his gut tighten as he moved closer, searching for an opening. No way was he going to let her die in this crappy little store. He stepped to the side, trying to find a better angle for his shot.

Fiona caught the movement, and her eyes widened as he approached. "No," she said, keeping her gaze locked with his while she spoke. "Please don't."

Warmth spread through his chest at her brave attempt to protect him. Despite being in very real danger, she didn't want him to get involved, clearly thinking he would only get himself hurt. His estimation of her climbed even higher, and he nodded, trying to silently reassure her while he crept closer.

The perp stepped back, pulling Fiona as he moved. He came dangerously close to bumping into Nate, but he shifted just in time. He turned and pushed Fiona forward, but before she took a step, he saw Nate. With a cry of alarm, he yanked Fiona back against his chest, bringing the gun up to press against her head.

"Drop it," the robber demanded, his voice high and strained. "Drop it or I'll shoot her."

Nate kept his gun up, knowing that if he lowered it, Fiona was as good as dead.

"I'm a police officer," Nate said, striving to keep his voice calm. The last thing he wanted was to antagonize the guy further. "Put down your weapon and let the woman go."

The man's wide eyes scanned the empty convenience store as he took a step back, careful to keep Fiona in front of him while he moved. "You drop your gun first," he hedged.

Nate shook his head. "You know I can't do that," he said. "No one has to get hurt here. Just put down your gun and we can talk."

"I'll shoot her," the man warned, his finger sliding dangerously close to the trigger. "Don't make me do this."

Nate saw the desperation in the other man's eyes, recognized that he was close to the breaking point. Even though all his training screamed against lowering his gun, he couldn't count on the perp to remain in control. Better to break a few rules than to risk watching Fiona die in front of him…

"Okay, okay," he soothed, slowly lowering his hand until the gun pointed at the floor. The man's eyes followed the movement, his body relaxing some as the worst of the danger passed. "Let's just talk," Nate offered, hoping to distract the man enough that he would lower his own weapon.

"I don't want to talk," said the man, vigorously shaking his head like a dog sloughing off water.

"That's okay," Nate replied, careful to keep his voice friendly. "I'll talk, and you just listen. Sound good?"

After a slight hesitation, the man nodded uneasily. It was a start.

"I'm Nate. What's your name?"

The man narrowed his eyes, as if trying to decide whether he should part with this information. "Joey," he finally muttered.

"Joey," Nate repeated, nodding his head. "That's a good name. A good name for a good guy, I'm sure."

Joey huffed out a laugh. "You think I'm dumb? I'm not a good guy, man. Don't you see what I'm doing here?"

Nate tilted his head, pretending to consider the other man's words. "The thing is, Joey, I don't think you really want to be doing this. I think you got yourself in some kind of trouble, and you need the money to buy your way out. I know you don't want to hurt this lady here." He cut his gaze to Fiona, who was staring back at him with wide eyes. She was holding herself so still she could be mistaken for a statue, and her impossibly pale face only heightened the resemblance. He wanted to give her a wink of reassurance, but to do so would only inflame Joey, a risk that wasn't worth taking.

"If she gets hurt, it's on you. It's 'cuz you made me do it." A note of desperation rang in Joey's voice. He was clearly in over his head. He began to inch back toward the entrance, obviously wanting to leave.

A movement in the parking lot caught Nate's eye, and he looked beyond Joey and Fiona to see a squad car braking just outside the store. Thank God, they hadn't come in with sirens blazing…

"Okay," Nate said, taking a half step forward. He held up his free hand, trying to appear nonthreatening. "Let's not talk about people getting hurt. As far as I'm concerned, no one has to get hurt tonight," he continued, deliberately trying to draw Joey's attention so the other man wouldn't realize that backup had arrived. *Keep him distracted, keep him facing forward.*

"You need to put your gun down," Joey insisted, his eyes glued to the weapon at Nate's side. He swallowed hard, his Adam's apple bobbing in his skinny neck.

Nate nodded. "Okay. I can do that. But you have to promise not to hurt this nice lady here." When Joey didn't respond, Nate offered a weak smile that the other man didn't return. "You know I'm a cop. I can't part with my gun unless I know you're no longer a threat."

The two officers who had crept into the store paused at this statement, glanced at each other, then nodded. He was out of the line of fire, at least for the moment.

"Put it down," Joey ordered. He tightened his grip on Fiona, causing her to let out a distressed squeak.

Nate nodded again, remembering from his days in the academy that positive feedback was important in a hostage situation. Keep the hostage taker balanced, always say yes, don't talk about death. The main idea was to avoid antagonizing the hostage taker, in the hope that lives would be saved.

"Okay. I'm going to set it down on the counter. How does that sound?" Nate slowly moved forward while he spoke, causing Joey to move incrementally backward. With every step, Nate was herding them right into the arms of the waiting officers, and the poor guy didn't even know it.

Fortunately, the cops seemed to have caught on. They maintained their position, weapons pointed at Joey, while they silently waited. He prayed they had turned off their radios before entering the store—the last thing he needed was for a call to come through and alert Joey to the fact that they were no longer alone.

Nate placed the gun on the counter and reached out to Fiona. "Okay, Joey. I put down my gun like you asked. Now you give me the girl."

The other man hesitated, so Nate applied a little more pressure. "It's only fair," he said, maintaining his forward motion. "I gave up my weapon. You have the money. Let her go and you can leave."

His fingertips grazed Fiona's arm. It was nothing more than a brush of skin against skin, but he wanted to roar with satisfaction. *Close, so close.*

Joey loosened his grip on Fiona. Hardly daring to breathe, Nate eased his hand around her arm and gently tugged.

"Just let her go," he whispered. "You don't want to take her with you."

Joey gave a jerky nod, then released Fiona with a little shove. In one swift motion, Nate pulled her against him and pivoted to the side, throwing them to the floor between the shelves of the main aisle. He covered her with his body, his whole focus on protecting her while all hell broke loose above them.

She couldn't breathe.

Hot Guy was a solid weight on top of her, pinning her to the floor and blocking her view. Not that she wanted to see, anyway. What she could hear was bad enough.

Male voices shouting, the "pop" of what could only be a gunshot, then a high, pain-filled scream that made the fillings in her teeth ache. Squeezing her eyes shut, Fiona pressed her head against Hot Guy's shoulder, try-ing in vain to block out the horrible wails now coming from somewhere nearby.

It was all too much to process, especially when she had no idea what was going on. She was still adjust-ing to the fact that she no longer had a gun pressed to her temple. She wanted to reach up to touch the still-tingling spot, to rub away the chill of the metal that lin-gered on her skin, but her hands were trapped against her stomach.

"Are you all right?"

His voice was deep and soft, for her ears only. It rumbled from his chest and into hers, a strangely in-timate sensation that only added to her discomfiture.

She nodded automatically, not trusting her voice, not knowing what to say. She'd just had a gun held to her head—she couldn't think right now, much less de-termine if she was fine.

He pulled back to study her face, his green eyes taking in every detail. She fought the urge to squirm, unused to such scrutiny, especially at such close range.

"Are you sure you're not hurt?" He reached up to trace a finger over her temple, right where the gun had pressed into her skin. Fiona caught her breath at the gentle stroke, goose bumps popping out along her arms in the wake of his contact.

"I'm fine," she said, her voice breaking at the end. She winced and cleared her throat, not wanting to sound too emotional. She wasn't going to fall apart just because some thug had held her hostage for a few minutes. She didn't have time—she had to proctor final exams for her adviser's classes soon, and a nervous breakdown was not in her schedule.

But, oh, it felt so good to be pressed up against her rescuer. Hot Guy was everything she'd thought he would be and more—a potent combination of muscle and bone, wrapped up in a very nice package. And his smell—God, his smell! Warm skin, some kind of woodsy smell from his soap and a faint note of musk all mingled to create a heady combination, making her want to press her nose to his neck and inhale deeply.

But that would be too creepy.

He carefully extracted himself and pushed to his feet, then reached down to offer his hand. She took it and had a sudden thrill as he quickly pulled her up. She swayed a bit on her feet, and he placed his hand on her shoulder to steady her. Fiona closed her eyes, enjoying his warm touch.

"I know you."

Fiona opened her eyes at the intrusion to see a uniformed police officer staring at Hot Guy, his eyes narrowed in thought.

Hot Guy stared back, his brows drawn together while he considered the other man. "Steve, right?" he said slowly.

The officer nodded. "And you're—?" He let the question trail off, inviting Hot Guy to supply his name.

"Nate Gallagher. Homicide."

The officer nodded, recognition dawning. "Gallagher. You were the MVP of the last police-fire softball game. I knew I'd seen you somewhere before!"

Nate smiled faintly. "I'm glad you recognized me. I knew I was taking a chance having my gun pointed in your direction."

Steve shook his head. "I'm not gonna lie—I didn't appreciate that. You're lucky we saw what was happening when we pulled in."

Nate shrugged, then pulled Fiona closer to his side. "I couldn't let him hurt her," he said simply.

The officer transferred his gaze to Fiona, as if noticing her for the first time. "Are you all right, ma'am?"

She nodded. Why did they keep asking her that? It's not like they could do anything to help her if she told the truth.

"We need to take your statement," he said, holding up an arm to gesture her forward. She moved reluctantly, not wanting to leave the security of Nate's side. Even though their contact was limited to his hand on her shoulder, she still felt comforted by his presence.

Now that Nate and the other officer were no longer talking, Fiona realized that the robber's moans of pain had stopped, leaving the store silent except for the intermittent crackle of the police radio. As she cleared the aisle and glanced down, Fiona saw the man was unconscious, lying in a small pool of blood.

She swallowed hard at the sight, her instincts urging her to put as much distance between them as possible. He'd been so rough and strong, jerking her around the store, but now, lying on the dirty floor with his face slack, he seemed very small and powerless.

Rationally, she knew the man couldn't hurt her, unconscious and handcuffed as he was. Still, her body refused to move any closer, and she stood frozen in place, panic climbing up her spine to wrap choking fingers around her throat.

Another officer was kneeling by the man, halfheartedly pressing a wad of gauze to his shoulder. The officer glanced up at her and offered an absent nod. She nodded back mechanically, and he frowned.

"Are you all right, miss? You look a little pale."

"I, uh—"

She couldn't get the words out, so she cleared her throat and tried again. "I think I need to use the bathroom."

Fiona turned to the right and practically ran for the bathroom, yanking open the door with such force that it bounced off the wall to slam shut. She flipped the lock and collapsed onto the toilet, leaning forward with her arms wrapped tight around her stomach.

Oh God, oh God, oh God. Her thoughts were a twisted jumble as she rocked back and forth, the events of the past half hour crashing over her anew. She hadn't had time to think or even panic in the moment, but now that the danger had passed, she couldn't seem to escape the flood of emotions that adrenaline had kept at bay.

Fiona pressed her fist to her mouth in an effort to muffle the quiet sobs. She had learned to stifle the sounds of her grief as she cared for her mother during her battle with cancer, but right now Fiona couldn't stop the tears from falling. She ripped a ribbon of toilet paper off the roll and pressed it to her eyes, mopping up the tears before they could drip onto her shirt in a telltale sign of distress. She had to regain her composure so she could talk to the police, and then she could go home and cry in the privacy of her empty house.

She dropped the soggy toilet paper into the trash, then moved to the sink and splashed water on her face. She caught a glimpse of herself in the mirror as she toweled off and froze, her eyes fixed on the red mark that marred her temple. With shaking fingers, she reached up to touch the bumpy spot, feeling the definite imprint of the gun barrel.

So close. Her stomach twisted at the thought of her brains on the floor, and she quickly dropped to her knees in front of the toilet, making it just in time.

"Fiona?" Nate's voice was quiet on the other side of the door, and Fiona wanted to sink into the floor tiles and disappear. How long had he been standing there? Had he heard her crying? Worse still, had he heard her throwing up?

"I'll be right out," she said, trying desperately to sound normal.

"Can I come in?"

God, no! The cloying sweetness of industrial air freshener had combined with the acrid stench of bile, making a new and entirely unappealing aroma that now permeated the small room. The last thing she needed was for Nate to come in and get blasted with the scent of her breakdown.

"Um, not right now," she hedged, wiping her mouth with a wet paper towel and smoothing back her hair. "Just give me a second."

He was silent, but something told her he hadn't gone far. She stared at her reflection in the mirror, silently cursing herself for crying. Why couldn't she be one of those women who was attractive when crying? Instead, she looked like some kind of allergic mess, with swollen eyes, puffy lips and blotchy red skin. That was bad enough, but the fact that she had to step out and face Detective Hottie, who hadn't batted an eye at tonight's events, made her feel even worse.

I can do this. Taking a deep breath, Fiona dabbed at the last lingering wetness on her cheeks and ran her palm down the front of her shirt to smooth out the wrinkles.

Her fragile defenses in place once more, she turned and opened the bathroom door.

Here I go.

Chapter 3

Dammit, she'd been crying.

Nate could tell the minute she opened the door. She walked out with her shoulders back and head held high, her chin thrust upward in defiance and determination. But her eyes gave her away. Red rimmed and slightly swollen, they bore silent witness to her earlier tears.

He turned to follow her, but not before catching a whiff of the bathroom. *Oh, honey.*

She certainly wasn't the first person to lose her lunch after such a stressful situation, but he hated that she'd had to experience it.

Joey was still out cold on the floor near the register, so he quickly steered her in the opposite direction, guiding her to walk the outer perimeter of the store on her way to the door. Not only did he want to spare her from seeing her attacker again, it gave him a chance to swipe a bottle of ginger ale as they walked past the refrigerated cases.

"Here you go," he said, pressing the bottle into her hand with a smile. "Thought you might want this."

She blushed but met his eyes. "Thanks," she said softly, her mouth turning up at the corner. "Guess I wasn't as quiet in there as I'd hoped."

"Don't feel bad," he assured her, reaching up to lay a hand on her shoulder. For some reason, he couldn't stop touching her, a fact that should have bothered him but didn't. "I've seen 350-pound men cry like a baby after having a gun shoved in their face, so a little vomit is no big deal."

She stared at the bottle for a few seconds, then shrugged and twisted off the cap.

"Something wrong?"

She shook her head. "I was just thinking that we're not allowed to eat or drink anything from the store."

"I'm happy to pay for it," he said, reaching into his back pocket for his wallet. She laid a hand on his arm, stopping him.

"Don't worry about it," she said, giving him a small smile. "After the night I've had, I think the store can donate a soda to make me feel better."

"Sounds fair to me," he said, placing his hand on the small of her back to urge her forward again. He wanted to get her out of the store and away from her attacker as soon as possible. He could just make out the faint wail of a siren, which meant the ambulance was on its way. Fiona didn't need to be here when the paramedics loaded Joey onto the stretcher and carted him off to the hospital.

Besides, they needed to take her statement and the sooner the better. He glanced up while they walked, heartened to see surveillance cameras mounted in the ceiling and pointed at the register. Maybe they'd get lucky and there would be footage of the attack—he knew from experience not every security camera was functional.

"Do those work?" He nodded at one of the cameras as they neared the door.

Fiona glanced up, following his gaze. "I think so," she said, frowning slightly. "I've never seen the tapes, but that doesn't mean they don't exist."

They made it to the door before Fiona stopped, a stricken look on her face.

"I need to call Ben," she said, sounding miserable.

Nate felt a pang of jealousy at the mention of another man's name. Was Ben her husband? Her boyfriend? Why did she sound unhappy at the thought of talking to him? More important, why did it matter so much to him?

"Who's Ben?" His voice was deceptively neutral, but he held his breath while he waited for her to respond.

"The store owner," she replied, triggering a wave of relief that had his breath gusting out on a sigh. Fiona shot him a questioning look, which he ignored. He couldn't explain his reaction to himself, much less to her.

"I can call him," he offered. "Do you have his number?"

Fiona looked up at him, relief and gratitude shining in her big brown eyes. "You'd do that for me?"

If she kept looking at him like that, he'd do just about anything for her. "It's probably better if I call him. Part of the job and all."

She glanced down, and he sensed a shift in her mood. "Everything okay?"

Fiona nodded, refusing to meet his gaze. "It's just…" She trailed off, swallowed hard, then spoke again. "You saved my life tonight," she said, her voice wobbly. "You kept that man from hurting me."

Nate shifted, her praise making him uncomfortable. "I was happy to do it. That's my job. Besides, the fact that you stayed calm kept the situation from escalating out of control."

She shook her head. "You really don't get it, do you?"

He frowned, not following her thoughts. "Get what?"

She looked up at him then, her eyes suspiciously bright. "I will never forget you or what you did for me tonight. But I suspect it's just the latest in a long line of amazing things you've done, and you're so quick to dismiss it as your job. Not many people would have stepped forward like that, but you did. You're a hero."

Nate felt his face heat and knew he must be as red as the sirens flashing on the ambulance pulling into the parking lot. "I'm not a hero," he said, reaching up to tug on his collar. When did it get so warm in here?

The corner of Fiona's mouth quirked up while she studied him. "The fact that you're denying it just makes you even more heroic."

Now it was Nate's turn to look away. He didn't know

how to explain to her that he'd simply *reacted.* She was in danger, and he'd stepped forward, wanting only to protect her. That wasn't heroic—it was instinctive, pure and simple. Heroes recognized danger and stepped forward in spite of it. He hadn't stopped to consider the danger, but had rushed right in, his only thought keeping Fiona safe. If anything, his lack of discipline could have easily resulted in a tragedy tonight, something he was sure his captain would point out after learning of the situation.

The EMTs entered the store, and he heard the officers tell them where Joey had been shot and how long he'd been out. Fiona heard them, too, her expression turning distant as she listened to the conversation.

"Do you think he'll be okay?"

Considering the man had held a gun to Fiona's head, Nate really couldn't care less if he recovered. Knowing Fiona wouldn't appreciate that response, he merely nodded. "Most likely," he said. "He got hit in the shoulder, and there wasn't enough blood for the bullet to have clipped an artery. He'll be just fine once they get him patched up, and then he'll get to enjoy all the comforts of the city's fine facilities."

She frowned, clearly not buying his casual reply. "He passed out," she said, raising a brow as if daring him to deny that fact.

Nate shrugged. "It hurts like hell to get shot. Maybe the pain got to him."

Her face softened when she looked up at him. "You've been shot before?"

He inwardly winced, cursing himself for letting that

slip. She was looking at him with stars in her eyes again, and he couldn't bear to mislead her.

"It was my fault," he told her, needing her to understand. "I was a rookie, and I got caught up in the excitement of making a bust. I didn't wait for backup, and I walked right into it."

Her mouth formed a perfect *O* while she raised her eyebrows. "Where were you shot?"

"In a run-down crack house off Westheimer, over in the projects."

She gave him a mock glare, her lips twitching as she fought off a smile. "I meant where were you physically injured." She ran her gaze over his body, searching for a clue. His skin tingled in response, and he found he liked having her eyes on him.

"Grazed my leg," he said, patting his left thigh. He'd been exceedingly lucky—the perp had been high, which had affected his aim.

"Wow," she murmured. "Does it still bother you?"

He shook his head. "Not really. It aches a bit, now and then, but only when there's bad weather coming."

Fiona gave him a mischievous smile. "You sound like a grandpa."

Nate narrowed his eyes and pursed his lips in an exaggerated sneer. "Just stay off my lawn," he said, raising his fist in a weak shake.

Fiona laughed at that, her features relaxing for a moment. Warmth spread through his chest at the sight, and he grinned back at her. She deserved a laugh after her night, and he was absurdly proud to have been the one to lighten her mood.

The clicking sound of gurney wheels locking into place told him the EMTs had loaded Joey and were getting ready to leave. Fiona heard it, too, the smile fading from her face while she listened to the men roll out the door.

"So what happens now?"

Steve chose that moment to join them, and he spoke before Nate could reply. "We need to take you down to the station and get your statement." He held up his arm, indicating Fiona should precede him out the door. "If you'll come with me, please."

She frowned slightly. "What about the store owner? I need to call him and let him know what happened here."

Steve pulled out his notepad and passed it to Fiona. "My partner is staying here to keep the scene secure. You can give him the owner's number and he'll call."

She nodded while she scribbled down a number, but Nate could see the wrinkle between her brows and knew she still wasn't fully comfortable.

"Why don't I come along?" he offered. Fiona's expression lightened, and her apparent relief at his continued company made him want to puff out his chest.

Trying to hide his satisfaction, Nate turned to Steve. "If your partner has things under control here, I could give my statement, as well."

Steve nodded. "Sounds good. Want to follow us back to the station?"

"Sure." Nate addressed his next remark to Fiona. "I can drop you back here when we're done, so you can get your car."

A faint smile lifted the corners of her mouth. "I'd appreciate that."

As Nate watched her walk away with Steve, he was forced to admit his motives weren't entirely altruistic. She needed a ride back to her car, to be sure, but it was the perfect excuse to spend time with her.

And he intended to make the most of it.

Fiona wrapped her hands around the plastic coffee cup, trying to soak up the weak heat leaching through the sides. She couldn't stop shivering, despite the warm mugginess of the room. Houston winters weren't terribly cold, but the heater in this aging municipal building seemed to have only one setting—thermonuclear. It was enough to make the place feel like a muggy swamp. Under normal circumstances, she'd feel bad for the officers forced to work in this humidor. Now, though, she was grateful for the warmth and the coffee, even if it did taste like stale pencil shavings.

On a certain level, she'd always known that working the night shift at a convenience store was a dangerous job. Despite the fact that she spent most of her shift alone, studying at the counter, the clientele who did frequent the store weren't exactly the most upstanding citizens. To be fair, she saw quite a few shift workers, honest people who stopped in on their way to or from work. Generally speaking, though, those who came around were dancing on the thin edge of trouble.

To her mother's way of thinking, it had never been a question of *if* she'd ever get robbed, but *when*. Christine Sanders had been furious and terrified when Fiona had told her about the job. "I won't let you work there," she'd said, drawing herself up in the hospital bed with shaking, painfully thin arms. "I forbid it."

"I'll be fine, Mom," Fiona replied, returning to the bedside with a damp washcloth. She gently laid the cloth across her mother's forehead, and the lines of pain etched into Christine's face softened a bit. "It won't be that busy—hardly anyone needs gas at two in the morning. Besides, I need this job for my research. You don't need to worry."

"I do worry." Her mother's eyes were bright blue, burning with fever and fear. "Those places get robbed all the time, and they're going to see you, a pretty young woman working alone. You make an easy target, Fi."

"Gee, thanks," she said, smoothing back the thin, wispy strands of hair that hadn't succumbed to the chemo treatments. "Are you saying you don't think I can be intimidating?" She narrowed her eyes in a fierce scowl, but her mother only smiled sadly.

"You should pick a different research topic. One that doesn't have you working in the middle of the night."

It was a familiar refrain, one her mother had said countless times before. As always, Fiona was at a loss for how to respond. She'd tried several times to explain her research project—studying the effects of shift work on employee mental health—but her mom wasn't able to look past her job.

"Can't you just interview people during the day? Or find what you need online?"

Fiona swallowed a sigh. "I am doing that, but this job gives me an opportunity to observe people without them knowing about it. They're less likely to be on guard, or to tell me what they think I want to hear."

Christine only frowned. "I'm not going to stop worrying about you. But I am glad you've found something that will keep you occupied after I'm gone."

Fiona rubbed her chest, the memory of her mom's words aggravating the now-permanent ache behind her breastbone.

A late-in-life "miracle baby," Fiona was an only child. Her father, a police officer, had been killed when she was ten. He was shot while responding to a domestic disturbance call, and while the Houston police department had rallied to support Fiona and her mother, they couldn't fill the void left by her dad.

The loss of her father made Fiona feel even closer to her mother. "It's you and me, kid," Christine liked to say. "Together, we can get through anything."

And for thirteen years, they had. Until that unusually cold March afternoon, when Christine's doctor had called to tell her there was an abnormality with her latest mammogram.

Fiona had been twenty-three when her mother was diagnosed with cancer. What she hadn't known—what the doctors hadn't been able to predict—was that it would take her mother five long, agonizing years to die. Fiona had worked a string of part-time jobs while acting as a caregiver, an exhausting schedule that brought home just enough money to pay her tuition and stay afloat. Being a clerk at the convenience store was the best-paying job she'd had yet, which was why she'd decided to stay on after her mother died. She could go to school in the afternoons and work at night, and with the notes she'd compiled so far, she was getting ever closer to finishing her master's degree.

While she wouldn't trade the time she'd spent with her mother for anything, she did feel a sense of longing when she saw couples out together, laughing and having fun, or pushing a baby stroller. She hadn't dated since college and, given her schedule now, there wasn't a lot of room for a man. That was okay, though. She needed to focus on finishing school, and starting a relationship would only delay that.

Despite her self-imposed single status, Fiona could still appreciate a handsome man. Like Nate. She let her thoughts drift, pulling up the image of his face. She liked knowing his name now, though she'd have to get used to calling him Nate instead of Hot Guy. She'd been attracted to him before tonight, of course. Her fingers tightened on the coffee cup as she imagined him in his dress uniform. His golden skin would look amazing against a black starched shirt, and she was willing to bet he had a lot of shiny medals to pin against his broad chest.

Medals probably earned for stupidly brave actions that could have gotten him killed, her practical side pointed out. She remembered her dad and his friends—adrenaline junkies, all of them. And their exploits weren't limited to the job. Her father had had a string of affairs, no-strings-attached flings with the women who liked to hang around the precinct, looking to date a cop. "Badge bunnies," her mother had called them.

The thought darkened her mood a bit, pulling her

back into reality. There was a reason she didn't try to date cops, no matter how sexy they were.

But, her libido responded, he'd been deliciously solid on top of her, and she wished the circumstances had been different so she could have actually enjoyed lying underneath him. It had been a long time—too long—since she'd felt the weight of a man, and unless she decided to throw her plans out the window, she wasn't likely to feel it again anytime soon. And even though she was hesitant to date a cop, maybe they could have a little fun before they went their separate ways? Nate was going to drive her back to the store, so maybe she could trip and pull him down with her...

She shook her head at the wild fantasy as Officer Rodriguez—she just couldn't call him Steve after such short acquaintance—walked back into the room. He caught her gesture and gave her a concerned look. "Everything okay?"

Fiona felt her face heat. "Um, yeah," she stammered, grasping for something to tell him. She settled for holding up the coffee cup. "I was debating taking another sip, but decided I was better off just holding it for the warmth."

He gave her a sympathetic wince. "Sorry about that. We drink so much of the stuff around here, you'd think we could make it better, but no one ever seems to have the time."

"Don't worry about it," she said with a smile. "Bad coffee and police stations are supposed to go together. I'm pretty sure there's a rule about it somewhere, kind of like peanut butter and jelly."

Officer Rodriguez laughed. "I suppose you're right." He sat across from her and tapped the pages he'd been carrying into order. "I just have a few things for you to sign, and then you're free to go." He pulled a pen from his shirt pocket and slid it across the table.

"First up is your statement," he said, passing a stapled collection of pages to her. "Just review it for accuracy, and if you're satisfied, initial at the bottom of each page and sign on the last page."

Fiona started to glance over the text but was interrupted by the appearance of another form. "Next, we need your updated contact information. And finally," he said, handing her yet another piece of paper, "you need to sign this form indicating your desire to press charges against the assailant."

"Do you think he'll be convicted?"

Officer Rodriguez shrugged. "I doubt he'll make it to trial—his public defender will probably try to plead him out."

Fiona nodded. "Good." She grabbed the pen and prepared to sign, but a disturbing thought made her pause. "Will he know my name?"

The officer frowned. "The perp? If it goes to trial, then, yeah. That will be a matter of public record." He watched her set the pen down and rushed to add, "But you don't need to worry. I've never seen a case where the witness was harmed for testifying."

That was reassuring news, but Fiona still felt uncertain. What if he got out on parole? Wouldn't he be angry with her for sending him to jail in the first place?

Her thoughts must have shown on her face, because

Officer Rodriguez offered her a reassuring smile. "In my experience, once the trial is over, the victims are able to move on with their lives."

"So you don't think he'd come after me if I decided to press charges?"

The officer shook his head. "It's not worth it. If he contacted you, he'd be in even worse trouble. Criminals are dumb, but they're not stupid, know what I mean?"

Not really, but his confidence went some way toward calming her nerves. This was the right thing to do—if she didn't press charges, the man who'd attacked her might get away with it, leaving him free to rob again. And the next time, there wouldn't be a police officer there to save the day.

On a sudden burst of conviction, she signed the bottom of the form and pushed it across the table. There. It was done. No going back now.

Officer Rodriguez collected the papers and gave her a smile. "You're doing the right thing, ma'am."

She nodded as he left the room. Now what? She'd given her statement, answered all their questions and signed the necessary paperwork. Was there anything left for her to do here?

"I want to go home," she muttered, swirling the dark brew around the cup.

"That can be arranged."

She jumped at the voice, spilling the now-lukewarm coffee down the sides of the cup and over her fingers. Shaking her hands to dry them off, she turned around to find Hot Guy—*Nate*, she reminded herself firmly—leaning against the doorjamb. His broad shoulders filled the doorway, and his long legs were crossed at the ankle as he regarded her with those mossy-green eyes.

"Sorry." He smiled at her, the expression transforming his face from watchful to beautiful in a heartbeat. "I didn't mean to startle you." He stepped into the room, and Fiona fought the urge to lean back in her chair. He was just so big, his presence impossible to ignore in the interview room. It hadn't seemed like a small space before when Officer Rodriguez had questioned her, but now she felt the walls were closing in on her, the room shrinking down to her and Nate.

"It's okay," she replied, wiping her still-damp hands on her pants. "I'm just a little jumpy tonight." She offered him a weak smile as he took the chair across from her.

"Understandable," he said, leaning forward to place his forearms on the table. With his hands linked together loosely, he could be mistaken for a man at rest. But as Fiona took in his pose, she could tell by the set of his shoulders and his alert gaze that he was anything but relaxed.

Why was he here? She was happy to see him, but she really did want to go home. Officer Rodriguez had made it sound as if she could leave soon, but with Nate settling in across from her, she now wondered if there had been a delay—maybe there were more forms to fill out, more questions to answer.

"When can I leave?"

"Should just be a few more minutes. I came to keep you company while they're wrapping things up, and then I'll take you back to the store so you can get your car."

She shivered, dread washing over her at the thought of going back to the store. She didn't want to be there, at least not tonight. She wanted to go home and soak in a hot bath, to wash the events of the night off her and rebuild her defenses before facing the store again.

Nate noticed her reaction, his eyes narrowing slightly while he watched her. "Is there someplace else you'd rather go?"

"I'd rather you take me home." She felt her face heat as the boldness of her words registered. "Um, I mean... I don't feel up to going to the store now, if that's okay."

His lips twitched, his eyes warming as he took in her blush. Rubbing a finger along his lower lip, he nodded. "That's fine. I'll take you anywhere you want to go." His voice, deep to begin with, seemed to drop another register. Fiona lifted her gaze from his mouth to his eyes, seeing a flash of heat there. Was he flirting with her? No way. She mentally shook her head. Handsome men like Nate didn't bother to give her a second look. The stress of the evening was making her hallucinate, had her hearing and seeing things that weren't there. All the more reason to retreat to her house and regroup.

She opened her mouth to respond but was interrupted by a sharp rap on the door as Officer Rodriguez returned. He caught sight of Nate and drew up short, surprise registering on his face. "Oh. I didn't know you were in here."

Nate leaned back and propped his hands behind his head. "They finished up with me, so I thought I'd keep Ms...." He trailed off, cut his glance to her and raised a brow inquisitively.

"Sanders," she supplied helpfully.

He winked at her, making her heart thump double time. Then he looked back to Officer Rodriguez. "Like I was saying, I decided to keep Ms. Sanders company. She was looking lonely."

The other man looked at Nate, then swiveled his head to look at her before turning back to Nate. Fiona blushed again, feeling suddenly shy in the face of his perusal. "Uh-huh," he said, his tone making it clear he didn't buy Nate's story for a minute.

Fiona cleared her throat, interrupting the men's impromptu staring contest. "Can I go?"

Officer Rodriguez gave her a small smile. "Yes, ma'am. Thanks for your help tonight."

She stood, collecting her purse and the half-empty cup of coffee. "Thank you," she said. "I really appreciate what you guys did for me."

Nate got to his feet, as well, and placed his hand on the small of her back to guide her out of the room. The barrier of her shirt was no match for the heat of his skin, and she felt his touch like a brand. He steered her past Officer Rodriguez and into the main room, which was surprisingly busy given the lateness of the hour.

Fiona paused at the doorway, taken aback by all the activity. Nate leaned forward to whisper in her ear, the gesture intimate despite the crowd. "It's okay—just keep moving."

"I didn't expect it to be so busy in the middle of the night."

He shot her a grin while he walked her to the door. "Lots of trouble happens after dark, trust me." A rude shout accompanied his words, and Fiona's eye was drawn to the man in a cage on the far side of the room. He staggered to his feet and lumbered over to the bars, screaming obscenities at the officers seated nearby. The police officers didn't even blink, but kept their heads down while they focused on their work.

"What's wrong with him?"

Nate followed her gaze. "Probably just drunk," he replied, shrugging as if the matter was of little consequence. "It's a full moon, which usually makes for a crazy night."

She glanced up at him to gauge if he was pulling her leg. He wasn't. His expression showed no trace of humor or sarcasm. "You're serious about the full moon, aren't you?"

He held the door for her as they stepped into the chilly night air. "Oh, yeah. It's a well-known fact that the crazies come out in force on a full moon. A few years ago, it was a full moon on Halloween." He shuddered as he unlocked the car door for her. "Took me weeks to get over that."

Fiona smiled while she climbed in. "I can imagine," she said, picturing him on patrol, a shiny badge affixed to his chest.

Just like Dad's.

The unsettling thought left her as soon as she caught a whiff of his enticing smell when he settled behind the wheel of the car. Her muscles relaxed, her body instinctively recognizing she was safe in his presence even if her mind was reluctant to surrender. Her hands began to lose the cold numbness that had settled over her after the attack, and she let her head rest on the seat back, taking a deep breath for the first time that night.

The car started with a low rumble. "All right," Nate said, flashing her a quick smile as he worked the gearshift. "Let's get you home."

Chapter 4

Nate frowned as he pulled into the driveway of the small, old house. Fiona lived here? He glanced up and down the street, noting the lack of lights and the general air of abandonment. The homes in this part of town appeared to be decently maintained, but there was an overall feeling of neglect, as if this once prosperous neighborhood had been left behind.

"This is it?"

She nodded. "It was my parents' house. I inherited it after my mom died."

He noticed the omission of her father. Either he'd died long ago, or he hadn't been in the picture. "How long have you lived here?"

"I grew up here, but I've only had it to myself for two years."

Not that long, then. "You took care of your mom, didn't you?"

Her head jerked up and she met his gaze for a moment, her eyes wide. Then she nodded. "How did you know?" she asked quietly.

He shrugged. "You seem like the type of person who takes on a lot of responsibilities."

Fiona nodded, bowing her head to stare at her lap. Great. He'd upset her. *Real smooth, Gallagher.*

Searching for something, anything, to say to change the subject, he fired off another question. "Any problems in the neighborhood?"

Fiona frowned, and he realized he had entered into cop mode and was interrogating her. He smiled to soften the question. "I don't see any streetlights, so I'm wondering if there have been any issues with burglary or vandalism."

She shook her head, and he caught a whiff of her scent. Lemons, underlain by a soft sweetness that was appealing. He'd been too focused on keeping her safe before to really register her smell, but now it wrapped around him like a silk rope. He found himself leaning forward, wanting to get closer to the source.

"I haven't heard of any problems, but I'm not around much. Between classes and work, I'm usually only here to sleep."

He huffed out a laugh. "Sounds like my life."

"Being a police officer must be pretty demanding."

"It can be."

An odd expression crossed her face, as if she wanted

to say more but couldn't find the words. He decided not to press her—she'd already had a rough night.

They were silent for a moment while Nate continued to study the house. It looked decent enough, he decided, even though the grass was a little long and the shutters could do with a fresh coat of paint. The garage door appeared to fit securely, and the front door looked solid. There were a few windows facing the front yard, and he wondered how many were in the back, and what the backyard looked like. Was there another house behind hers, or was it an easement? What kind of fence enclosed the property? Wood, or something easy to climb in a hurry, like chain link? Did she have a lock on the gate?

His musings were interrupted by the sound of Fiona clearing her throat. "I should probably head inside. I'm sure you're tired and want to get home."

"Let me walk you in."

"Oh, no, that's really okay," she stammered, apparently taken aback by his offer.

"I insist," he said, quietly but firmly. "You've had quite the adventure tonight, and I just want to check the house to make sure everything is okay." When she paused, he smiled. "You'd be doing me a favor—I'll sleep so much better knowing that you're safe."

She laughed, and the rich sound made his heart thump against his breastbone. "Fair enough," she told him, opening the car door. "Truth be told, I'll sleep better too, knowing you've gone through the house."

He was pleased to see her pull a small flashlight from her bag as they walked up the front steps, and some of his worries eased when he saw she had two dead bolt locks securing her door. Of course, the bad guys could always come in through a window...

She flicked on a light as she walked in, illuminating the small living room. A floral-print couch sat along one wall, the middle sagging a bit from years of use. Crocheted doilies decorated the end tables and coffee table, and a faded recliner completed the tableau. The room had a preserved feel to it, as if Fiona hadn't bothered to redecorate after inheriting the house. Or maybe she couldn't bring herself to change it.

She gave him a shy smile as he completed his perusal. "It's not much, but like I said, I grew up here."

"No siblings?" It was something he'd meant to ask earlier after hearing about her mother, but he hadn't wanted to upset her further.

"No. I was an only child. Mom was forty-five when she had me—I was a bit of a surprise."

He opened his mouth to respond, but a *thud* from the next room interrupted him. Moving quickly, he drew his gun and pulled Fiona over to the front door. "Go wait in the car," he whispered. "Lock the doors and get low." He spied a portable phone on one of the end tables and grabbed it, pressing it into her hand. "Dial 911. Tell them there is an intruder in your house, and an officer is on the scene and requests backup."

"Nate—"

"Go." He ignored her as he pushed her through the door and closed it quietly behind her.

He moved through the living room and into the kitchen, clearing the small space before heading down the hall that presumably led to a bathroom and bedroom. It had been months since he'd had to draw his gun in the line of duty, and tonight he was holding it for the second time. What where the odds? He shook his head as he stepped softly down the hall. *When it rains, it pours.*

More important, though, why was Fiona in danger yet again? He didn't believe in coincidences, and tonight's activities made him think she was being targeted. But who would want to hurt her? She didn't seem the type to have enemies, but then again, he didn't know her all that well.

Yet.

He approached the doorway to the bedroom cautiously, focusing hard to pick up any stray sounds from the room. There was a soft rustle from somewhere within the room, faint at first, but then louder. It took him a few heartbeats to realize the noise was coming toward him.

"Don't move," he commanded. "Houston police. Come out with your hands up."

The noise stopped, as if the source was considering his words. Then the sound started up again.

Nate moved back, retreating down the hall a few steps before assuming a shooting stance, his gun up and pointed at the doorway. He took a deep breath. "Last chance," he warned. "Put your hands up or I will shoot."

A high-pitched meow answered him, followed shortly by the appearance of a massive gray cat. The portly feline saw him and drew up short, clearly surprised to find an intruder in his home. Nate could only stare back, baffled. *This* was the source of the noise? Not a burglar but an overweight cat?

Feeling sheepish, Nate lowered his gun. The cat, deciding he was of no consequence, plopped down in the middle of the hall and began to lick his nether regions with a vigor that belied his size.

Holstering his weapon, Nate decided to check the bedroom, for form's sake. He sidestepped the bathing feline and poked his head into Fiona's bedroom, grateful, if mildly embarrassed, to find it empty.

Marshaling his pride, he returned to the front door and pulled it open to find Fiona, leaning against the doorjamb with a smile playing on her lips. "All good?" she asked, her eyes sparkling.

He swallowed, determined to remain serious. "Everything seems to be in order."

She stepped past him into the house, treating him to another whiff of her lemony-sugar scent. "I take it you met Slinky?"

"Ah," he hedged. That massive fur ball was named Slinky? "I met your cat, but I don't know that I'd associate him with the word *slinky*. He seemed rather stocky to me."

Fiona shot him a mock glare. "He's just big boned. Besides, I named him when he was a kitten. He'd contort himself into such impossible positions—Mom and I got a real kick out of watching him play."

The cat in question chose this moment to enter the living room, his belly swaying ponderously with each step. He rubbed against Nate's legs on his way to Fiona, apparently forgiving him for the earlier intrusion. She knelt to scratch behind his ears, and the cat plopped down and rolled to his back, exposing his stomach for her touch. Fiona obliged, and he closed his eyes into slits of blissful appreciation, emitting a loud purr. Nate could sympathize—he wouldn't mind having her hands on him, either.

He cleared his throat, trying to distract himself before he let *that* particular line of thought go too far. "Well. Everything seems to be in order here, so I'll just head out."

Fiona rose, offering him a shy smile. "You don't have to go," she said. His heart leaped into his throat—was she really offering what he thought she was offering?

A blush spread across her cheeks, and her eyes went wide. "Um, I mean," she stammered, apparently recognizing her double entendre. "It's late. You're welcome to stay on the couch if you don't want to drive home. That's what I meant to say."

He was tempted to take her up on the offer, but there was no way he would get any sleep on that lumpy couch knowing she was only a few feet away, warm and soft in her bed. Better for him to drive home, take a cold shower and come back tomorrow morning so he could take her back to her car.

"That's a kind offer, but I think I'd better leave. Wouldn't want to put you out." Nate winked at her, which only deepened her blush from a soft pink to red. Something in his chest relaxed at the sight of her, and he felt a strong urge to pull her close and wrap his arms around her. He hadn't meant to embarrass her, and he certainly didn't want her to feel uncomfortable around him.

"What time should I pick you up in the morning?" he asked, hoping a change in subject would put her at ease.

"How about nine thirty? Or is that too early for a Saturday?"

"That's perfect. I'll see you then." He smiled at her, studying her carefully for any sign of distress. She seemed to be okay, but he knew from experience that the shock of a traumatic experience sometimes took a few hours to set in. He didn't want to leave her alone to process everything that had happened tonight, but at the same time, he didn't want to crowd her.

Fiona walked him to the door. The dark circles under her eyes revealed her fatigue, but her expression was otherwise untroubled. Maybe her breakdown in the bathroom had been enough to release the stress from her attack. He hoped she was that lucky.

"Thank you again for everything you did tonight." She laid her hand on his arm, and he felt the heat of her touch through his shirt. "You saved my life tonight. There's no way I can repay you for that." A sheen of tears formed across her eyes and she blinked hard, clearly determined not to cry.

His heart turned over in sympathy at the sight of her tears. "Shh," Nate whispered, and pulled her close. He knew he shouldn't hold her, but he couldn't stand by and do nothing while she was upset.

He buried his nose in her hair, breathing deep. "You don't ever have to thank me for tonight," he said, keeping his voice low as he spoke in her ear. "I'm just glad you're okay."

She nodded. "Me, too," she whispered shakily.

He released her, holding her at arm's length so he could meet her gaze. "You're safe now. And I'll make sure you stay that way. Trust me?"

"Okay." She offered him a shy smile.

She leaned forward the barest inch, and he felt himself move in response. Her warm breath wafted across his chin, and the mood shifted, the air between them becoming heated and electric. She licked her lips, a subconscious invitation that hit him low in the belly.

His pulse thrummed in his fingertips as he reached up to cup her cheek, tilting her head so he could have better access to her mouth. Fiona closed her eyes at his touch, emitting a soft sigh that made him want to roar with satisfaction. He settled for bowing his head and running his lips across hers in a teasing caress that did nothing to bank his desire.

Fiona made an inarticulate sound of frustration, and Nate chuckled, happy to know she wanted this as much as he did. He ducked his head again, intending to kiss her properly, but Slinky apparently had other ideas. The cat butted him hard in the legs, making him sway on his feet and altering the angle of his approach. Before he could tilt his head, his nose smashed into Fiona's, sending a spike of electric, white-hot pain into his brain.

"Ouch!" She pulled away from him, cupping her nose while she blinked back tears.

Nate massaged his own nose. "I'm so sorry," he said. "Your cat caught me off guard." He glared at the offending creature, who had wandered a few feet away and was batting at a stuffed mouse under the coffee table. "Guess he doesn't like me very much."

Fiona shook her head. "He just wants attention. He's here alone most of the time, so when I get home, he knows it's time to cuddle."

Lucky bastard. Nate offered her a smile and nodded, refusing to acknowledge that he was jealous of a cat. "Well, I'd hate to make him wait any longer."

"I suppose you're right. It is pretty late." Were his ears deceiving him, or did she sound disappointed?

He'd love to stay and find out, but he didn't want to take things too fast. The woman had been attacked tonight—the last thing she needed was a horny cop sticking his tongue down her throat. Better for him to go while she still wanted him to stay. They could pick things up again later.

"Try to get some sleep tonight—or what's left of it. I'm sure Slinky will be good company for you."

That earned him a laugh. "He definitely will. Be careful getting home."

"Yes, ma'am. Lock the door behind me."

He waited until he heard the locks click before walking back to the car. He sat behind the wheel for a few moments while Fiona shut off the lights in the living room. A few seconds later, the light in her bedroom went on. He was half tempted to sit in her driveway all night and keep watch over her, but the logical side of his brain told him that was crossing the line. He barely knew her, for crying out loud! Sure, he felt curiously drawn to her; he had from the first time he'd seen her.

And, yes, the more he learned about her, the more he wanted to know. But sleeping in his car was just a bit too stalkerish for his taste. Besides, if Fiona were to look outside her bedroom window and see a strange car in her driveway it would likely terrify her—definitely not something he wanted to do.

"Get a grip, Gallagher," he muttered as he put the car in gear and backed out of her driveway. "You're going to see her in a few hours."

And he was going to count every minute until then.

Joey leaned against the cinder-block wall of the holding cell, trying to arrange his body into the least painful position possible. His shoulder hurt like hell—the drugs they'd given him at the hospital were starting to wear off, and the growing pain was making it hard to think.

"Can I get some meds to take with me? You know, for later?" he'd asked.

The nurse had merely rolled her eyes and shook her head.

Her reaction had pricked his temper, making him sit up a little straighter. "Hey, I'm a person, too! I deserve to be treated with a little respect!"

"How about you give him something to shut him up?" The big cop standing behind the nurse shot him a dirty look. "You'd be doing me a favor."

The nurse gave him a smile as she turned to leave. "Wish I could help, but you know it doesn't work that way."

"Yeah, just my luck." The cop watched her walk out

of the room, his eyes glued to her backside until she was out of view.

Joey shook his head. "You're pathetic," he muttered.

"What was that?" The big man's head swiveled around, and he fixed his gaze on Joey. "You got something to say to me, punk?" His eyes gleamed with anticipation in the fluorescent light, as if he was just looking for an excuse to get physical. Joey recognized the look. It was one he often saw before a fight broke out.

Part of him wanted to goad the other man. After all, a police officer would get into big trouble for beating up an unarmed, handcuffed, already injured man in his custody. But Joey was smart enough to know that the real world didn't work that way. Cops protected their own, and if it came down to his word against the boys in blue, there would be no contest. And while he desperately wanted the satisfaction of mouthing off, it wasn't worth the bruises. So, for the first time in his life, Joey listened to the voice in his head that told him to shut up. "Nah," he replied, shaking his head. "Not to you."

"That's the first smart thing you've done all night," the cop said, his tone smug.

He'd brought Joey back to the station then, and it had taken some time to get his mug shot and for them to finish all the paperwork. Then they'd led him to this cell and taken the cuffs off, leaving him alone for the first time in what felt like days.

The cinder-block wall was cool against his skin, and he pressed his forehead to it, appreciating the distraction from his aching shoulder. He was in a ton of trouble, but the impending charges of armed robbery and assault didn't bother him. No, what scared him the most was his uncle's reaction.

Uncle Sal was not a forgiving man. He ran Houston's largest illegal gambling operation, and he'd acquired his power by combining sheer brutality with an astonishing lack of mercy. He didn't offer credit, nor did he offer second chances. What he did offer was better payouts than the competition. It was enough of a temptation to keep people coming back for more, even though they lost more often than they won. And when they didn't pay up? Usually a visit from one of Uncle Sal's enforcers was motivation enough. Especially because the people who required a second visit never required anything again.

Joey shivered at the thought of his uncle's face when he heard about this. It was enough to make him want to crawl under a rock and disappear, but that wasn't an option.

He'd set out to rob the convenience store because the owner, Ben Carter, owed Uncle Sal. So far, the enforcers had been busy going after other clients, and Ben had escaped their attention. It was only a matter of time until they met with Ben, but in the meantime, Joey had seized the opportunity to prove himself to his uncle. He'd been dying to show that he could be an important part of the family business, and collecting on this debt would be a great way to start.

It was supposed to be a simple job. He'd go in, get the money and leave a message so Ben would realize what had happened. But everything had gone to hell, and now he was stuck here, trying to figure out how he was going to explain the situation to his uncle.

Maybe he could play dumb, he mused. Act like he didn't know Ben was the owner of the store and that he'd done it for money. But no, Uncle Sal would be angry that Joey hadn't come to him for help first. And he couldn't pretend he was high. Sal would kill him if he thought there were drugs involved.

His best bet was to hope they threw him in jail long enough for his uncle to forget about him. Sal had a memory like an elephant, but out of sight, out of mind, right?

The jingle of keys interrupted his thoughts. "You got a visitor."

Joey stood, certain he had misunderstood. "What?" No one knew he was in here, so who on earth would be trying to visit him?

"You heard me." The cop sounded bored. "Approach the door, then turn around and put your hands behind your back."

Joey did as he was told, wincing as the movement pulled the stitches in his shoulder. Cold metal circled his wrists, and he heard the click of the handcuffs locking into place. Then the guard opened the door and gestured him out.

His thoughts whirled as the man led him down a long hallway. Who was waiting for him? Not his mother—she'd been gone for years, off to who knew where. And his brother was in the army, trying to make a life for himself. His friends didn't know he was here, and he definitely hadn't called Uncle Sal. Maybe this was some kind of mistake?

They stopped in front of a white door, and the guard opened it and led him inside. He pushed Joey into a chair, then locked his cuffs to a ring on the table, effectively trapping him in place.

"Thank you, Officer. That will be all."

Joey turned to find an older man standing in the far corner. He wore a dark suit with a crisp, white shirt and held a leather briefcase in his soft hand. He smelled like money, and Joey distrusted him on sight.

The guard frowned but stepped outside, shutting the door behind him. Moneybags moved to take the chair across from Joey, unbuttoning his suit jacket as he sat.

"Do you know who I am?"

Joey eyed him up and down, giving him the evil eye. Normally, that look was enough to make people uncomfortable, but this guy appeared immune to the implied threat. "No," he said finally, injecting the word with as much contempt as he could muster.

"My name is Richard Beck. I am an attorney, and I am here to represent you."

"Why?" Joey's suspicion deepened. A sharp-dressed lawyer just happened to show up looking for him? No way. This was not a coincidence, and he wanted to know who was setting him up and why.

"It's what my client asked me to do." If he was bothered by Joey's attitude, he didn't show it.

"Who's your client?"

"Your uncle."

Joey felt the blood drain from his head, and his limbs went numb. Oh, God. He knew. *I'm a dead man.*

He willed himself to sit up straight, knowing that this lawyer would probably report his reactions to his uncle. And while Joey knew he was in deep, he still had his pride. He refused to give in to the urge to whimper like a child.

"How does Uncle Sal know I'm here?"

"He has his sources."

Of course. Naturally, Uncle Sal had eyes and ears everywhere. Hell, he probably had some cops on the payroll, which would explain how he'd gotten the news so quickly.

"And he's sent you to help me?" The thought gave Joey some measure of comfort. If Uncle Sal was truly angry, surely he would have left Joey in jail to rot rather than send some high-priced professional to bail him out. Maybe things weren't so bad after all?

Richard eyed him thoughtfully. "In a manner of speaking."

What was that supposed to mean? Evidently sensing his confusion, the lawyer went on. "Your uncle is unhappy with your actions tonight. He's asked me to post bail for you, under the condition that you do exactly as he requests."

That didn't sound so bad. "What's he want from me?"

"The owner of the store you tried to rob tonight has some documents in his possession. These are sensitive photos that your uncle would like to possess. Unfortunately, Ben Carter thought to use blackmail in exchange for debt forgiveness. Your uncle did not agree to those terms."

The lightbulb clicked on in Joey's head. So *that's* why Sal's goons hadn't gone after Ben yet! They were trying to get the pictures back so his uncle wasn't embarrassed. "What does he want me to do?"

"If you can retrieve the photos, your uncle is willing to overlook tonight's transgressions." The lawyer's tone made it clear he didn't think Joey's chances of success were high. "If not, he will make sure you are dealt with appropriately."

Joey ignored the shiver that ran down his spine at the implied threat. He had no illusions that Sal would go easy on him simply because they shared bonds of blood. "Does he care how I do it?"

Richard shrugged. "He would prefer you keep things quiet, if possible. But make no mistake—he wants those photos, at any cost."

Joey nodded. He could do this. How hard could it be? "Okay. When's he want them?"

"As soon as possible. Do you think you can handle this request?"

"Oh, yeah." He felt his confidence return with every passing moment. This was his second chance, and he was going to make the most of it. Show Uncle Sal he wasn't a screwup, that he could be trusted. He was tired of being treated like a child. He was going to fix this, and his uncle would be so grateful he'd have to acknowledge that Joey was an important part of the family.

"You really think you can get me out of here?" He

eyed the lawyer up and down. "They caught me red-handed. Gonna be pretty hard to argue I'm innocent."

Richard Beck gave him a small smirk. "Don't trouble yourself with the details. I assure you, I will do my job." He stood and walked over to the door, but turned back before opening it. "Let us hope you can say the same."

Big Sal reached for his phone with a halfhearted curse, shaking his head to clear the fog of sleep. Sylvia, his wife, stirred in the bed next to him.

"Who is calling you this late?" she asked, her annoyance clear despite the sleepy tone of her voice.

He glanced at the lighted display. "Richard," he said.

Sylvia turned over with a huff. "Doesn't he ever sleep?"

Sal chuckled softly. "I pay him too much for that."

He climbed out of bed and grabbed his robe on the way out the door. Although Sylvia knew Richard was his attorney, she didn't know the finer details of the services Richard provided for him. And he planned to keep it that way.

"Yes?" he answered, sliding into his robe as he walked to his study.

"It's done."

"He knows what to do?" Joey had already screwed things up tonight. He wouldn't put it past the kid to do it again.

"I was very clear," Richard assured him.

"Humph." Under normal circumstances, Sal would have been confident in Richard's communication skills. But Joey wasn't the sharpest tool in the box, as he'd proven time and time again. He didn't really think the kid would be able to get this job done, but he had to give him one last shot. He owed it to his sister—God rest her soul—and maybe Joey would actually surprise him.

Stranger things had happened before.

"I will post his bail tomorrow morning, after the initial hearing," Richard was saying. "Will there be anything else?"

Sal shook his head, then remembered the other man couldn't see him. "Not right now. I appreciate you taking care of this."

"My pleasure," Richard replied smoothly. "May I ask a question?"

Sal's curiosity perked up. Usually, Richard didn't want to know any more details than necessary. What had changed? "Of course."

The attorney hesitated, as if choosing his words with care. "If I may, sir. This young man doesn't seem to be the most capable choice for the job at hand. Are you sure you can trust him?"

"He's family," Sal said flatly. "I don't have another choice right now."

"Very good, sir," Richard said. "Good night, then."

Sal hung up the phone and stared out the back window, overlooking the perfectly manicured garden and the Olympic-size pool. It was a full moon tonight, the light so bright he could see every ripple of the water, every silvery shimmer as a light wind stirred the surface, creating tiny little waves. It was a beautiful pool, but he'd never been in it. He'd never had the time.

His doctor was always after him to lose weight and

move more, and swimming would be a great way to exercise. Wasn't it supposed to be a stress reliever, as well? He could definitely use some of that. If those pictures were leaked to the wider world, he was in for a hell of a lot of pain. His thoughts drifted to Sylvia, fast asleep in their bed. She was not a forgiving woman. But worse than that was the thought of what Isabella would do to him. If she knew they had been seen together, that there was photographic evidence of their association…

He shuddered involuntarily, the jolt of fear leaving a bad taste in his mouth. It wouldn't come to that. He would give Joey a few days to get the pictures back. And if the kid failed, well, he'd be able to deal with his nephew with a clear conscience. Plus, there would still be time to get the photos back before they leaked.

It was a good plan, overall. It should work.

It has to work, he amended silently.

He simply couldn't face the consequences of failure.

Chapter 5

Fiona woke up early, anticipation creating a fizzing sensation in her chest. Nate would be here in a few hours, and she wanted to look good. He'd only ever seen her when she was in the middle of her shift, when her hair was flat and her makeup stale. And the way she'd looked last night after throwing up… She shook her head, her vanity demanding she pretend that had never happened.

Would she still feel that insistent tug of attraction this morning? Or had that just been the adrenaline of last night, drawing her to her rescuer and making him seem larger than life? It was possible. She knew from her classes that when two people shared an intense situation, their emotions ran high and they often became aroused. Psychologists thought it had something to do with wanting to celebrate life after escaping an imminent threat. And while Fiona liked to think she wasn't ruled entirely by her hormones, she couldn't deny that she wasn't immune to basic biology.

But she had noticed him when he had first started coming into the store. So perhaps last night had only given her the courage to act on those latent feelings?

She thought back to the barely there kiss they had shared the night before. His lips had been so warm, and surprisingly soft against her own. It hadn't been a passionate kiss, far from it, but there was so much promise contained in the brief contact that she yearned for more. Her skin warmed at the thought, and she sighed. If such a short caress could trigger this kind of response, imagine what a real kiss would do.

Slinky pushed up against her leg, vying for attention. She bent down and picked him up, nuzzling into his soft fur. "And you," she said teasingly. "You're the reason I'm so frustrated this morning."

He purred in response, clearly unfazed by her chastisement. He shifted a bit in her arms and bumped her nose, making her wince. It still ached a bit from Nate's accidental head butt last night. As if he sensed her pain, Slinky turned his head and licked the tip affectionately. "Gee, thanks," she said, setting him down on the bed. He walked over to her pillows, kneaded one into an acceptable shape and settled down for a nap.

"Must be nice," she muttered. After the events of last night, she really wasn't ready to return to work. But her car was still there, and she did need to talk to Ben. Maybe it was time to quit. She could continue to work on her research in other ways. It would take a bit longer, but at least she wouldn't have to worry about getting robbed at gunpoint.

The thing was, she didn't *want* to quit. This job pushed her work to the next level, and her professor loved it. "You've really managed to capture something special here," he'd said at their last meeting. "Your direct observations of these shift workers enhance the quality of your research, and make your project shine."

Could she really walk away from such a promising avenue for her work? There were so many repercussions to think about. The better her thesis research went, the better her dissertation would be. And a strong project would make her a more competitive candidate for one of those ever-elusive faculty positions. The work she did here and now had the potential to affect her entire career, something she couldn't dismiss just because she'd had an unnerving experience last night.

No, I can't stop, she decided. But taking a few days off wouldn't kill her. And maybe she could get to know Nate a little bit better in the meantime.

He seemed like a nice guy, from what she had seen. But then again, so had her father. So had his friends. And they'd all turned out to be cheaters.

"How did you stand it?" she'd asked her mother, years later. "Knowing he was with those other women."

Her mother had merely looked at her, sadness and understanding in her eyes. "I loved him," she said simply.

Fiona shook her head. "But what about your self-respect?"

Christine had smiled then. "It wasn't about that. It never was. I loved your father, and he was so good to us. No one is perfect."

That much was true, but still, Fiona couldn't bring herself to understand why her mother had stayed. Her father had put his relationships with those other women above his relationship with his own family. That was something Fiona couldn't forgive and refused to overlook. And while her father had never brought his girlfriends around, she'd known about them just the same. The lipstick on his clothes. The unfamiliar perfumes that sometimes clung to his skin. And the arguments her parents used to have, always behind closed doors, their voices muffled and low. Fiona had sat, her ear pressed to the door as she'd strained to make out their words. And she'd heard everything. Her mother's accusations. Her father's confessions. She'd been too young to understand at the time, but she'd figured it out eventually.

Sometimes, she wondered what would have happened to her relationship with her father if he hadn't died. Would she have been able to hold her tongue? Or would she have pulled away from him, her disappointment in his actions overshadowing her love for him? Was it really her place to judge? After all, he hadn't cheated on *her*. Her parents' marriage was between the two of them, something separate from their relationship with her. Still, she couldn't help but feel betrayed that her father would look outside their family for fulfillment. As if she and her mother weren't good enough for him.

It doesn't matter now, she told herself. Rehashing the marital problems her mom and dad had experienced wasn't a good use of her time, especially this morning. And it wasn't exactly fair of her to assume that Nate would betray his family in the same way, just because her father had. She had to find a way to keep her father's actions from affecting her own, especially when it came to relationships.

Thirty minutes later, the doorbell rang. The sound made her stomach flutter, and she took a deep breath to calm her nerves. "He's the same guy from last night," she muttered. "One kiss doesn't change anything." It was true, but her body didn't seem to realize that.

She opened the door and smiled up at him. He looked even better in the light of day, if such a thing was even possible. His mossy-green eyes warmed as he looked down at her, and an answering smile tugged at the corners of his mouth. "How's it going today?" His voice was a deep rumble that thrummed through her, making her skin tingle.

"I'm okay. A little tired, but otherwise fine."

His brow furrowed slightly. "Did you have trouble sleeping?"

Yes, but not for the reasons he thought. Truth be told, that almost-kiss had wiped all thoughts of the robbery from her mind, and she'd spent the night tossing and turning, imagining a scenario where Slinky hadn't cut things short between them. "I didn't have nightmares, if that's what you're asking."

"There's no shame if you did," he said, his tone reassuring. "Like I told you last night, you had a hell of a scare, and it may take some time to recover."

Her chest warmed. He really seemed to care about her well-being in the aftermath of the robbery, which was sweet, considering they really didn't know each other that well. "I'm okay," she told him, trying to sound convincing. She didn't want him to worry about her or feel sorry for her. There would be no second kisses if he pitied her, and while she wasn't yet sure how much further she wanted to explore this thing between them, she definitely wanted to keep her options open.

"Do you want to come in for a cup of coffee?"

Nate tilted his head to the side. "Actually, I was wondering if you maybe wanted to grab a bite of breakfast on the way back to your car?"

Fiona nodded before he had finished asking the question. "That sounds great! Let me grab my jacket."

A few minutes later they were on their way. Fiona settled back into the passenger seat and inhaled, smelling remnants of coffee and the faint hint of Nate's soap. "So..." Nate said, trailing off. "How's Slinky this morning?"

Fiona smiled. "Well rested, as usual. Not much gets to him."

Nate huffed out a laugh. "That must be nice."

"I have to admit, there are times I wish I could embrace his philosophy of napping away my problems."

"It would be a heck of an approach," Nate agreed.

"Do you have any pets?"

"No," he said, sounding somewhat wistful. "My parents have a dog, but I don't get to see him too often."

"Aw, that's sweet. What kind of dog is he?"

"A golden retriever. His name is Parker. They got him my last year of high school, so he's getting a little up there in years."

"I bet he's still excited to see you, though."

Nate nodded. "Oh, definitely. That tail gets to going back and forth, and anything within striking distance is susceptible. Sometimes, I think he's happier to see me than my own mother."

Fiona slid him a glance out of the corner of her eyes. "You're kidding, right? I'm sure your mother is overjoyed to see you." What kind of mother didn't want to be near her own son, especially one who had turned out to be such a great guy?

He lifted one shoulder in a shrug. "I'm not so sure. I have to miss a lot of family functions due to my job, and she doesn't always understand. She tends to take it personally."

"I'm sorry to hear that," she replied, not knowing what else to say. "Do you have any siblings?"

"My sister, Molly. She's about nine years younger than me. In fact, it was her birthday yesterday."

"Where does she live?" Probably out of town, since he hadn't mentioned getting to see her.

He hesitated before responding. "She's on the other side of Houston with my parents. I sent her some flowers, but didn't get a chance to drop by."

Something about his answer made her think he didn't want to talk about it, so she didn't press. "Ah. Sorry about that."

"Not your fault," he responded quickly. "The day

was already a bust in the family-visit department. Par for the course."

He sounded matter-of-fact about it, but there was something in his tone that made her think he wasn't immune to his mother's censure over missing out on family moments.

"What about you?" he asked. "Didn't you tell me last night you're an only child?"

"Yep, that's right." Her stomach did a little flip, and she was inordinately pleased he'd remembered. "Like I said last night, my parents were on the older side when I was born—they didn't even think they'd be able to get me, so a sibling was completely out of the question."

"What was it like, growing up like that?" He sounded genuinely curious. "I mean, Molly and I lived in each other's pockets when we were kids—we pretty much had to, as our house was small."

"Did you fight a lot?" Fiona could only imagine how annoying that could be. No privacy, no space to truly call your own. She'd never had to share like that, and as an adult, it sounded like a recipe for disaster.

"No," he replied. He took a deep breath, as if bracing himself for a hit. "Molly has Down syndrome, so she's very loving and happy. There's not a mean bone in her body."

Fiona wasn't sure how to respond to this revelation. He was clearly sensitive about the issue, and she didn't want to say anything that would offend him. "She sounds lovely."

Nate smiled, and she saw his eyes soften. "She's the

best. But what about you? Weren't you lonely growing up without a sibling?"

"Well, no. I mean, I didn't know anything different. I had friends at school, and that was nice. But I always liked having time on my own. I'm not sure what I would have done with a sibling." She had to admit, though, the idea of having a brother or sister was appealing, especially now that she was grown. It would have been nice to have had someone to talk to Mom about, and she could have definitely used the help taking care of Mom after she got sick.

"That makes sense." Nate pulled into the parking lot of a small diner. "It's not much to look at," he said, cutting the engine. "But they make the best pancakes in the city."

Fiona's stomach growled. "I have to admit, I'm so hungry right now I'll eat just about anything."

He held the door open for her with a smile. "Let's hope it doesn't come to that."

They had just sat down in a booth when his phone rang. He gave her an apologetic glance. "I have to take this, it's work."

"No problem," she said, using the opportunity to peruse the menu. Eggs, pancakes or waffles? Why not a combination?

Nate's voice was a low murmur in the background, and she tried to ignore him, wanting to respect his privacy. He wrapped up the call quickly and tucked the phone back into his pocket. Then he cast her a guilty look, one that had her clenching the menu a little tighter.

He's got to go, she realized, her stomach letting out a howl of protest.

Confirming her suspicions, he laid his menu on the table. "I'm so sorry to do this," he began.

Fiona merely nodded. "It's okay," she said, trying to hide her disappointment. "Duty calls, right?"

A look of relief passed over his features. "Unfortunately, yes. Can I take a rain check?"

"Sure thing."

"Great. Let's get you back to your car."

Five minutes later, Fiona waved goodbye as Nate drove away. He'd been all apologies on the drive over, and he'd seemed to really feel bad about having to cancel their breakfast plans. While she didn't think he'd blown her off, it was hard to shake her disappointment. First an almost-kiss, now an almost-date. Were they doomed to never truly connect?

Shaking her head, she walked toward the doors of the store. First things first. Talk to Ben and get a few days off. Then she could think about Nate and decide if her crush was worth exploring.

Ben Carter thrust a hand through his hair as he surveyed the piles of papers on his desk. Where were those damn photos? He'd looked at them again just the other day but had gotten distracted before he could return them to the store safe. He had to find them now, though—last night's robbery attempt had been a little too close for comfort.

"Thank God, she didn't let him back here," he muttered. While it seemed the robber had only been after money, if he'd taken the pictures, too, Ben would have been out of luck.

There they were—buried under a stack of invoices. He scooped them up and fell into his chair, feeling light-headed with relief. These were his safety net, his protection against the wrath of Big Sal. It was a dangerous game he played, that was certain. As far as he knew, no one crossed Big Sal and lived to talk about it. But Ben wasn't interested in bragging. He just wanted to be out from under the other man's thumb.

After all, it wasn't really his fault. He'd made those bets based on bad advice, advice he was convinced Sal had somehow controlled. The man's influence knew no bounds, so it stood to reason he had his fingers in every sports-related pie in the city, if not the region. The guys who made their living off sports probably gave Sal a kickback or two so they could stay in business. How else could they continue to do what they did, making money off the backs of hardworking guys like Ben?

Most people paid up, figuring there was no other way. But not Ben. He was too smart to blindly do as he was told. Besides, if the result of his bet had been truly based on chance, he would have settled up, no questions asked. But he couldn't shake the feeling that he'd been played, and he refused to pay a cheater.

No matter how brutal the man was.

He pulled a manila envelope from his desk and slid the photos inside. It was time to find a new hiding place, one that wasn't as vulnerable as the store or his home.

A knock on the door distracted him. "What?"

Fiona poked her head inside. "Hey, Ben. Got a minute?"

"Sure, come on inside."

She stepped in, glancing around his office. "Wow. Reorganizing?"

"Something like that." He put the envelope with the pictures on top of another stack of papers. "I'm cleaning up, trying to impose order in here. I've got a lot of papers to take home." He gestured to the pile. Better to sneak the pictures out in a collection of files; it would draw less attention than if he walked out with a single envelope.

"So how are you?" Did he sound appropriately concerned? Hopefully so. It would raise her suspicions if it seemed he didn't care she'd been robbed at gunpoint last night.

"A little shaky. Last night was…" She blew out a breath, her cheeks puffing. "Intense," she finished.

"I can imagine." He'd gotten the story from the police and had promised his full cooperation in their investigation. Fortunately, it seemed like an open-and-shut case, and he'd given the cops no reason to look closer at his own personal affairs.

"You did the right thing," he said, belatedly realizing she was waiting for him to say something.

"Thanks. Listen, I came to ask a favor."

"What's that?"

"I'd like to take a few days off. I'm not ready to come back to work yet—it's still too fresh." She shivered, and for the first time he noticed the dark circles under her eyes. She really did look shaken up, poor kid.

"That's fine. Take the whole week," he said, feeling suddenly generous in the wake of finding the pictures again.

"Really?" Her face lightened with relief. "Thanks so much, Ben. I really appreciate it."

He waved away her gratitude. "It's the least I could do. You had a quite a scare last night. We're lucky it worked out the way it did."

Fiona nodded, her expression sobering again. "Yeah, no kidding."

A flicker of movement caught his eye, and he turned his attention to the security cameras that covered the store and the entrance. A tall figure was approaching the door, and something about his body language made the hair on the back of Ben's neck stand up.

Fiona stood, and Ben rose with her. "Say, can you help me with something before you take off?" He gestured to the stacks of paper on his desk. "I need to get these to my car, and I could use a little help. Do you mind?"

"Okay." She held her arms out, and he placed the stack with the manila envelope in her arms. Better to get that out of the store now, in case this new guy turned out to be a threat.

"I'll be right behind you," he promised, shooing her out the door.

He waited until she was gone before locking the door, then he turned his attention to the cameras again, his stomach twisting into knots. Whoever was coming, he looked like a man on a mission, someone who was looking for something and wouldn't stop until he found it.

Was it one of Big Sal's minions, sent to collect? He studied the video feed, concentrating hard as the man approached the door. Fiona walked out as the man walked in, and Ben held his breath, waiting to see if the man would notice her. But no... He let his breath out in a gust of relief as they passed each other without a second glance. The photos were still safe; he still had the advantage.

Belatedly, he realized the man was walking purposefully through the store heading in the direction of his office. His heart began to pound as the man approached, and he cast his eyes around the office, searching in vain for an escape that wasn't there. He was trapped, but at least the door was locked. It was a solid barrier between him and trouble, and hopefully Big Sal's man would give up and walk away once it became clear Ben wasn't going to open the door.

He glanced at the phone on his desk, debating his options. If he called the police, the guy would be forced to leave. But did he really want to draw police attention to the store again, after last night's events? Two calls in less than twenty-four hours was quite a coincidence, one that would draw additional scrutiny to the store and, by extension, him. He couldn't afford to have the police poking around in his personal business, so he was just going to have to wait this guy out.

As if on cue, there was a sharp pounding on the door. "I need to talk to you, Ben. Open up."

For a split second, Ben debated keeping silent and

pretending he wasn't there. If he didn't respond, maybe the guy would think he wasn't in the store and would just leave.

He glanced up at the monitors again and caught sight of the worried expression on Kevin's face. The clerk on duty was a young man, still in high school, and he didn't want the kid to become a target of this man's rage.

"Talk through the door," Ben yelled back. "I don't want to see you."

"Too bad," the guy replied. "You don't have a choice."

"Oh, yeah?" Ben scoffed, feeling a little cocky. Who did this guy think he was? No way was Ben going to open the door just because he said so. Besides, what could the man do to him from the other side of the door? "Just what are you going to do about it?"

No sooner had the question left his lips than a fierce blow landed on the door, followed quickly by another and then another. The door began to bow in under the stress of the assault, and Ben took a step back, a sense of horror rising in his chest as he watched the once seemingly solid barrier splinter into pieces before his eyes.

After a few more kicks, the door finally gave way. A tall, lanky man stood in the doorway, glaring at Ben. He stepped into the room, his boots crunching on the shards of wood as he walked.

Ben moved behind the desk, pressing himself against the wall in an effort to appear smaller. The man advanced until he was only a few inches away, then leaned forward, thrusting his face into Ben's. Ben turned his head and winced, trying to escape the unpleasant sensation of the man's hot breath against his chin.

"As I was saying," the guy said, grinding out the words from between clenched teeth. "We need to talk."

Chapter 6

Fiona stepped outside and narrowly avoided bumping into a tall man who was entering the store. "Sorry," she muttered automatically, dodging to the side just before their bodies made contact. He kept walking, not bothering to respond. She glanced up but wasn't able to catch a glimpse of his face before he walked inside. There was something about the way he moved, though…why did he seem familiar?

Shaking off the unnerving sensation, she walked over to her car, which was parked next to Ben's. She stood there for a moment, waiting for him to join her. *Where is he? He said he'd be right behind me.*

Her impatience only grew when her stomach growled. She still hadn't eaten anything, and while she didn't fancy a breakfast of doughnuts and coffee, it was better than nothing, and she didn't think she could wait any longer to eat. Her head was already starting to hurt, and her body cried out for caffeine.

She cast a last look back at the door, but when Ben didn't materialize, she made her choice. Fishing her keys out of her pocket, she dumped his files in the passenger seat of her car and went back inside in search of food.

As soon as she stepped inside the store, she knew something was wrong. The atmosphere felt heavy and tense. She glanced at Kevin, who was standing behind the counter, and his wide eyes and nervous glances toward Ben's office made it clear the problem was inside. She took a step in Kevin's direction to ask what was going on, but then she heard the angry voices coming from the direction of the office.

"I told you, I don't have them!" That was Ben, and he sounded defiant but a little bit scared. Who was he talking to?

She glanced around the store but didn't see the tall guy who'd entered shortly after she'd stepped out. Was he back there in Ben's office?

"Stop lying to me!" That must be him, the stranger who had given her the willies. Hearing his voice now only made the feeling of dread worse, and she stepped back, wanting instinctively to get away from him. There was something about the situation that reminded her of last night, but she couldn't quite put her finger on what it was.

"Get out!"

"Not until you give me what I want!"

"What should I do?" Kevin's voice was a panicked whisper.

Fiona shrugged, uncertain. It sounded like a terrible argument, but should they call the police over two men yelling at each other?

The two of them stood there, frozen, as the argument raged on. Then they heard a loud bang, followed by renewed yelling.

"I'm calling the police," Kevin announced.

Fiona nodded her agreement. It sounded like things were escalating, and better to be safe than sorry. Hopefully the police would arrive before true violence erupted. Her stomach sank at the thought, and her legs started to tremble. *No, not again!* Her heart pounded at the thought of being attacked again. Some small, logical voice in her head pointed out that she was not involved in this argument and wasn't a target. But her emotions had already shaken off the yoke of reason and were taking over her body.

"Go on," Kevin said. "Get out of here. You've been through enough already, what with last night."

She took a step back but then stopped. "Be careful," she told Kevin. "Maybe you should wait for the cops outside."

Kevin nodded. "I will. Now go home."

Fiona turned and retreated back to her old car. It took a couple of tries for the engine to turn over, but it finally caught and she was able to head out. Part of her felt guilty for leaving Kevin alone to deal with the situation, and she was definitely worried about Ben. But she couldn't bring herself to stay. Although Nate's presence had distracted her when they were together, now that she was alone she felt shaky when she thought about last night.

"Guess I'm not as okay as I thought," she muttered to herself. She reached up to rub absently at her temple, where the gun had left an impression in her skin. It was smooth now, but her fingers filled in the remembered details. *So close.*

Too close. Being on the wrong end of a gun wasn't anything she'd wish on even her worst enemy. How long would it take for her to forget the cold press of steel, the sheer, abject terror that locked her muscles so she was unable to move, to defend herself? She'd never felt so powerless in her life—her limbs had literally been paralyzed, totally unresponsive to her brain's signals.

She took one hand off the wheel and shook it, the motion helping to remind her that she was fine now. There had to be some way to move past this, to forget about the events of last night and get back to her normal life.

Maybe she could include it in her dissertation? She could write a chapter about shift workers and crime. She couldn't be the only person who'd been robbed or assaulted because she was working in the middle of the night when most people were asleep. Her mind started in on a list of questions she could ask her interview subjects, how she could steer the conversation to such a potentially sensitive topic. The last thing she wanted was to further traumatize the people helping her with her research, but this topic would give her a much deeper understanding of the lives of these workers and the risks they took on a daily basis.

She pulled into her driveway feeling much calmer. Now that she had a plan, she could try to dissect her own experiences with a little more clinical detachment, a little less emotion. And if her interview subjects knew she herself had been the victim of an armed robbery, they might be more willing to share their own memories.

She headed into the house and made a quick stop in the kitchen for a granola bar, finishing it in a few bites as she walked down the hall to her bedroom. Slinky lifted his head as she walked into the room, and gave her a halfhearted greeting before returning to his nap. "That looks like an excellent idea," she said, kicking off her shoes and joining the cat on the bed. A quick nap would help her recharge before she started working on her dissertation. She snuggled up next to Slinky's soft warmth and closed her eyes with a sigh.

She had just drifted off to sleep when a faint noise snagged her attention. Probably just the tree branches scraping against the side of the house. She really needed to get them trimmed…

She rolled over with a yawn, ready to surrender back into relaxation. But she heard it again, more insistent this time. It sounded like it was coming from her back door, and while the tree closest to the house was a bit overgrown, its branches didn't extend down to reach her door.

Fiona sat up, focusing. Yes, she heard it again. She

climbed out of bed and started down the hall. Was there a stray animal outside? With Christmas only a week away, the weather was definitely turning chilly. Maybe some lost pet was looking for a warm place to stay. She could take in a temporary lodger for the night—she already had cat food, and if it turned out to be a dog, she could always run to the store and grab a few cans of dog food. Slinky wouldn't be terribly happy, but she couldn't leave a defenseless animal to the mercy of the weather.

With that in mind, she turned the corner and froze in her tracks. The dull brass doorknob of the back door was wiggling, as if someone or something on the other side was twisting it. She heard a faint click, and then the knob began to rotate freely. *No dog can do that*, she thought numbly. Then her brain kicked into gear. *Run!*

She scrambled back down the hall and made it to her room accompanied by the squeak of the door hinges as the back door was pushed open. Oh, God, someone was in her house! She shut her bedroom door, trying to be quiet about it, and turned the lock. The door wasn't very strong, but hopefully it would buy her a few minutes to escape.

Moving quickly, she jammed her feet back into her shoes. Keys, keys—where were they? In her purse. Which was on the kitchen table.

She bit her lip to hold back a cry of frustration. But wait! She had a spare set in her desk. Precious seconds ticked by as she rifled through the drawer, shoving aside papers, pens and the general crap that had accumulated over the years. There, tucked in the far back corner, she found them.

The keys jangled noisily as she pulled them free, but the sound was drowned out by a crash from the living room. Whoever was in the house was looking for something and not being very subtle about it. She didn't have many valuables, but hopefully they would have their hands full trying to get the TV through the doorway.

Fiona shoved the keys into her pocket and grabbed her gym bag off the floor. She dumped the contents on the bed, then reached for Slinky. He let out an indignant protest as she shoved him into the bag and zipped it closed.

"Sorry, baby," she whispered. "But I'm not leaving you behind."

It took some effort, but she managed to shove the window open. Then she scrambled outside and skidded across the lawn to the car, pressing the key fob frantically to unlock the doors. She climbed in and shoved the gym bag over to the passenger seat, feeling a prickle of guilt over manhandling her cat so rudely. Slinky started howling incessantly, a mournful, haunting cry that would have broken her heart if she hadn't been so scared. She got the key into the ignition and turned, but the engine didn't respond.

"Come on, not now!"

She tried again, but a grinding sound was her only reward. She pumped the gas pedal and twisted the key again.

Her front door flew open, and a tall figure appeared in the doorway. Fiona felt her heart stop—it was the man from the store, the one who had been arguing with Ben! Why was he here now?

He saw her, and his mouth twisted in anger. She heard him yell but couldn't make out the words. He started in her direction, and she twisted the key again, desperate for the car to start. Whoever this man was, he clearly meant to hurt her.

Slinky's cries took on a more piercing note, as if he could sense the danger heading toward them. "It's okay," she said, unsure if she was trying to calm the cat or herself.

The engine finally caught, and Fiona slammed the car into Reverse and stepped on the gas. They shot out of the driveway and right into her neighbor's mailbox, which fell over with a crash. She shifted into Drive and moved forward, tearing down the road and away from her house.

"I'm sorry, Mr. Huffnagel," she said, wincing as she caught sight of the destroyed mailbox in her rearview mirror. The intruder was standing at the end of her driveway, his features twisted with rage as he watched her drive away.

Slinky had calmed somewhat, his pitiful howls subsiding into a keening meow. "I know, sweetie." Fiona placed her hand on the bag, patting him through the fabric. "I'm sorry. I'll let you out soon."

Her heart rate began to calm as she put more distance between them and the burglar. She had to report this to the police, but she didn't want to talk to just any detective. Nate would know what to do and could help her.

Breathing deeply, she steered the car in the direction of Nate's station and forced herself to slow down. The man couldn't catch her on foot, and she hadn't seen a strange car in front of her house. She was safe, at least for now.

So why was she still shaking like a leaf?

Chapter 7

"Gallagher!"

Nate glanced up at the shout of his name. Charlie, the desk sergeant, stood at the entry to the squad room, his head swiveling on his long neck like a giraffe in search of a tasty morsel.

"What have you got?" He stood and walked over to the door, not wanting to shout this conversation over the heads of the other officers seated nearby.

"There's a lady who says she needs to talk to you. Fiona Sanders. Know her?"

Nate nodded, his heart thumping hard at the mention of her name. Fiona was here? He quickened his pace, eager to see her again. He'd meant to call her after getting settled in to work but hadn't had a chance. Now that she was here, though, maybe she'd agree to have dinner with him. He owed her at least that much after bailing on her this morning, and if they were away from her cat, he'd be able to finish what they'd started last night. He smiled to himself, the anticipation of kissing her, really kissing her, warming his blood.

His eagerness died when he entered the lobby and caught a glimpse of her face, his stomach sinking with the realization that she wasn't paying him a social call. Her cheeks were pale, her brows drawn, and the dark circles under her eyes looked even more pronounced than they had this morning. She was carrying a gym bag, and as he approached, he saw the bag squirm. What was going on?

"Fiona?"

She glanced up, relief flashing across her face when she saw him. "Nate," she breathed, stepping forward to meet him.

He placed a hand on her shoulder, resisting the urge to pull her into his arms. "I'm here. What's wrong?"

She glanced around, clearly uncomfortable. "Is there someplace we can talk?"

"Of course." He guided her through the maze of desks to an empty interrogation room. Not wanting her to feel pressured, he pulled a chair around the table so he could sit next to her rather than across from her. "Want to tell me what's going on?"

She set the bag on the table and unzipped it. Slinky poked his head through the opening, his eyes wide and his ears flat against his head. "It's okay, baby," she crooned to him, running her fingers over his fur. The cat swiveled to take in the room, his gaze focusing on Nate for a moment.

"Hey, buddy," he said, offering his hand for the cat to sniff. Unless he missed his guess, Fiona had left her home in a hurry. The fact that she'd brought the cat revealed she didn't intend to go back. What had happened?

Slinky dropped back into the bag, apparently unimpressed with the interrogation room and the company. Fiona made sure he was settled, then turned to face Nate.

"Someone broke into my house today."

The news hit him like a punch to the gut. Who would do that? And why? From what Nate had seen when he'd taken her home the other night, she didn't have many valuables. Of course, that didn't mean she was safe from robbery—burglars couldn't necessarily tell what treasures may or may not lurk inside a home.

Before he could get a question out, Fiona went on. "I was home when it happened. I heard a sound at the back door and thought it was a stray animal, but when I went to investigate, the doorknob started to turn."

Nate's blood ran cold. He'd worked several home-invasion cases in the past, and the home owners who were inside at the time of the robbery were invariably shaken and scared. And for Fiona to have to endure such a stressful event hours after being robbed at gunpoint? "I'm so sorry," he said. "Are you okay?"

She nodded. "I ran back to my bedroom, grabbed the cat and climbed out the window."

That was smart on her part. Once again, she'd kept

her cool under pressure, something he admired. "Did the burglar see you?"

"Yeah." She looked down and rubbed her hand up and down her arm as if she was cold. "He did. He heard me trying to start my car and came running out."

"Did you get a good look at him?"

"Not enough to draw you a picture, but he's the same guy from the convenience store earlier this morning."

Nate frowned. "Wait, back up. What guy from the store this morning?"

She gave him a funny look. "Kevin called the police about it. I figured they would tell you since you were there last night."

"Nope—not my normal kind of case. Why don't you fill me in?"

Fiona took a deep breath. "He gave me a funny feeling, like he was up to no good, you know?" She told Nate how this stranger and her boss, Ben, had gotten into a screaming match.

"I didn't stick around to see how it was resolved." She looked down again, and a faint pink blush stole across her cheeks. "I just couldn't stay, not after last night. It was too intense for me."

Nate reached out and gathered one of her hands in his own, giving it a gentle squeeze. "You don't have to apologize for that. And you did the right thing—you left at the first sign of trouble. That's the best way to stay safe."

She let out a weak laugh, but gave his hand an answering squeeze. "Doesn't seem to have done me much good. Why did that guy come after me? And how did he know where I live?"

"I'm not sure about his motive, but as for finding you, that's a matter of public record."

"Great. *That* makes me feel safe."

Nate chuckled. "I know. If it makes you feel any better, we can look into having your records taken down as a matter of protection. In the meantime, sit tight. I'm going to grab my partner. I'd like him to hear your story, if you don't mind."

Fiona shook her head. "Fine with me. The more the merrier, right?"

She turned her attention back to Slinky, and Nate quietly left the room. When he was safely on the other side of the door, he exhaled heavily. What was going on here? Fiona seemed like the type of woman who lived a quiet life. Why had she been the victim of two violent attacks in as many days?

Was this some kind of con? Perhaps Fiona and the robber from last night had cooked up this scheme, and when things had gone south, someone had come after her to collect. He dismissed the thought almost as soon as it entered his mind. He'd seen the actions of the robber last night. The man hadn't known anyone else was in the store, and he'd still gotten violent with her quickly. Those weren't the actions of a partner in crime. Furthermore, Nate had seen Fiona in the aftermath, had held her close to his body and felt the subtle, involuntary tremblings of her muscles in response to her adrenaline surge. That wasn't a reaction you could fake. No, whatever was happening here, he doubted very much that Fiona was involved.

He headed back into the squad room and caught Owen's eye. His partner stood and walked over without hesitation. "What's up?"

Nate gave him the basic rundown. "Will you listen to her story? Maybe you'll catch something I missed."

Owen snorted. "I doubt that, but, yeah, I'd be happy to."

Together, they entered the interrogation room. Fiona turned as they opened the door and gave Owen a nod.

"I'm Owen Randall." He held out his hand with a reassuring smile, and Nate watched as Fiona's shoulders relaxed a bit.

She took his hand with a small smile. "Fiona Sanders."

"I understand you've had quite a few scares lately," Owen said.

"You could say that," Fiona replied, her hand absently moving in the bag. A faint purr rose from the depths of the fabric, and Nate bit back a smile. The cat was resilient, he'd say that much.

"Would you mind telling Owen what you told me?" he asked. "I'd like him to hear the details from you."

"Sure." Fiona launched into her tale again, and Nate took a seat and listened. People rarely told a story exactly the same way twice, and if they did, it was a sign it was a well-rehearsed lie. That wasn't the case here. The basic events were identical, but Fiona used different words and slightly different descriptions when talking that told him she hadn't practiced this on the way over.

It was another sign—not that he needed one—that she was a true innocent in all of this.

Unfortunately, she didn't recall any new details. But that was something he could continue to ask her about.

"And you didn't recognize the man who broke into your house?" Owen asked.

She shook her head. "I had seen him earlier at the store, but I didn't see his face then, either."

"So how did you know it was the same man?"

She gave him a wry look. "He was wearing the same clothes and had the same build."

Owen smiled at her. "Fair enough."

"Do you think there's a connection here? The store gets robbed last night, then this morning a man gets into an argument with Ben."

"Maybe," Nate hedged. "Did you overhear any of the argument?"

She nodded. "He said he wasn't going anywhere until Ben gave him what he wanted."

"And what was that?" Owen asked.

Fiona shrugged. "I don't know. I didn't hear that part."

A niggling suspicion tugged at Nate's awareness, and he stood. "I'll be right back," he said. "Just going to check on something."

It took only a moment to log in to the system, and what he found there made his stomach drop. He stared at the computer screen for a moment, refusing to believe his own eyes. But the information didn't change.

"Fiona," he began, once he was back in the room. "Is it possible the man who argued with Ben this morning and later broke into your house is the same man who tried to rob the store last night?"

She stared at him, confusion taking over her features. "No. I mean, how could that happen? The guy who tried to rob the store is in jail, right?"

Nate shook his head. "I'm afraid not. He posted bail early this morning."

"What?" Her voice rose as the color in her face faded. "How is that possible? He held a gun to my head! Why was he allowed to go free after doing that?"

Nate and Owen shared a glance. "The judge set a high bail. Usually, that's enough to keep guys like this in jail until their trial. But in this case, his attorney posted for him and he was allowed to walk out."

"Where did a guy like that come up with that much money? And if he's that rich to begin with, what's he doing robbing a convenience store?" Fiona's confusion echoed his own, and Nate found himself nodding in agreement.

"That's a good question," Owen said. "It's something we should take a look at. If you'll excuse me a moment?" He stood and left, apparently heading back to his desk to do a little digging.

Nate shot him a grateful look. He didn't want to leave Fiona in the room alone for too long, and he knew Owen didn't miss a trick when it came to investigating a mystery. If there was something fishy going on, Owen would find it.

"Oh, my God," Fiona muttered, more to herself than to him. "What if it really is the same man? He knows where I live! I can't go back there as long as he's after me."

"Don't worry about that," Nate assured her. "We'll get you a hotel room or something."

"No." Her rejection was quick and automatic, a knee-jerk response that made his eyebrows rise of their own accord.

"No?" he repeated, drawing the word out. He felt like a foreign-exchange student trying to puzzle out the meaning of a tricky new phrase. Surely she didn't mean that. After all, she'd just claimed she couldn't stay at her home until they figured out what was going on. Why would she reject his suggestion?

"I can't afford a hotel," she clarified, sounding miserable. "Can I just stay here?"

"You mean in a holding cell? Absolutely not!" The very idea was ludicrous. Did she actually think he'd leave her in a bare-bones holding cell until they found the man who had broken into her home? "Do you have a friend you can call?"

"Not really." She shifted in her seat, as if she was uncomfortable. "A lot of the people I went to school with moved away, and I lost touch with those that are still here, while I was taking care of Mom. I can't very well call them out of the blue and ask to crash on their couch."

"And you don't have any family." It wasn't a question. They wouldn't be having this conversation if she had a place to go.

Fiona shook her head. "No," she said, very softly.

Nate's heart twisted as he looked at her, so small and

alone. At least she had Slinky, but even the company of a cat wasn't enough to provide emotional support in tough times like this.

"I have an idea," he said. "Give me a minute. Owen or his girlfriend may know someone."

He found Owen at his desk, typing away at the computer. "Anything turn up?"

Owen tilted his head. "Maybe. I have the name of his attorney—Richard Beck. Haven't found much about the guy yet. Looks like he doesn't have many clients."

Nate studied the screen. "There's got to be some kind of connection we haven't seen. No way does a selective lawyer like that stoop to doing public defender work."

"No kidding. I'll keep digging."

"Thanks, man. Say, Fiona doesn't have anyplace to go tonight. She's too scared to go home, and she can't afford a hotel."

"She can stay at Hannah's apartment," Owen said, his gaze never leaving the screen.

Nate frowned. "I didn't know she still had her own apartment. Isn't she staying at your place pretty much full-time?"

"Yeah. But it's cheaper for her to pay rent than to break her lease. It's only through the end of the year, and then we're officially moving in together."

"Congrats, man. That's awesome." Nate clapped his partner on the shoulder, feeling genuinely happy for him. Owen had experienced several rough months after his former partner had died, and for a while, Nate worried that the other man was too mired in grief to ever really function again. But meeting Hannah had changed him and brought him back to life. Hannah had endured her own troubles, and it was great to see both of them happy. They certainly deserved it.

Owen smiled, his eyes warming as they always did at the mention of Hannah. "Thanks. Feels like a big step, but we're really excited about it."

"You should be. She's a great catch."

"You don't have to tell me that."

"Are you sure Hannah won't mind Fiona staying in her apartment for a couple of days?"

"I'm sure it'll be fine. But I'll give her a call, just to check."

"Thanks. I'll go let Fiona know."

"Speaking of…" Owen said, halting Nate's getaway. "Is there something going on between you two?"

Nate cleared his throat. "Uh, no. Not really."

Owen raised his brow. "If you say so."

Walk away, Nate told himself. But curiosity got the better of him. "Why do you ask?"

Owen turned back to the computer, but not before Nate saw his mouth curve up. "Just a vibe I picked up."

"From her or from me?" *Stop talking!*

"Both."

"Oh, really?" He tried to sound cool. Was it working? The last thing he wanted was for the guys to start razzing him about his love life. Usually, he was the one doing the teasing.

"Better get back in there," Owen said, a smile in his voice. "Wouldn't want her to be lonely."

"Yeah. Well. I do need to let her know about the apartment." Nate waved his hand in the direction of the interrogation room. "So, you'll let me know what Hannah says? And if you find anything about the attorney?"

"Will do, partner. I'll be there in a few minutes."

Nate walked away, feeling a little sheepish. He liked to think he was pretty suave when it came to women, but if Owen had picked up on his attraction to Fiona after only a few minutes, he must look like a lovesick puppy.

Owen is a detective, though. He took some consolation from the thought. As a cop, they were trained to pick up on details and signs that other people overlooked. So, maybe he wasn't being as obvious as he thought. Maybe Owen was just putting those detective skills to work.

He stepped back into the room and was struck anew by how small and fragile Fiona looked, sitting alone with only her scared cat to keep her company. Suddenly, he didn't care if the guys in the squad gave him crap about his love life. He didn't care if he broadcast his attraction for this woman for all the world to see. All that mattered was keeping her safe.

Pushing aside the urge to wrap his arms around her, he took the chair across from her and smiled. "Good news. I think I have a place for you to stay until we can get to the bottom of this."

"Really? That was fast." She sounded hopeful and a little impressed, which did wonders for his ego.

"Owen's girlfriend, Hannah, doesn't really stay at her place anymore. He said you can crash there."

"Will she mind if Slinky is with me?" Fiona's hand clutched the bag protectively, the gesture telling him as clearly as any words that if her cat wasn't welcome, she wouldn't be going.

"I'm sure it will be fine."

"Okay." Her grip relaxed, relief stealing across her face. "Where does she live? Should I just follow you over?"

"First things first," Nate said, standing and gesturing for her to do the same. "I'm sending a team out to your place to gather evidence, and I'm going to need to take your fingerprints to exclude them from the analysis. Let's take care of that, and then we'll get you set up at Hannah's place."

"Okay. But can we hurry? I want to get Slinky out of this bag and settled." She cast a concerned glance down at the cat in question. "He's still pretty freaked-out."

Nate couldn't help but smile. Even in the midst of her own problems, Fiona was more concerned with her cat than herself. "Yeah. I think that can be arranged. Come on."

He guided her out the door, his hand landing on the small of her back as if it had always rested there. Fiona looked up at him with a shy smile. "Thank you for helping me," she said softly.

"Thanks for letting me," he responded, his protective instincts flaring to life in the wake of her unnecessary gratitude. "Try not to worry. I'll keep you safe." He looked back at the gym bag on the table and added wryly, "Both of you."

Fiona had to admit, being around Nate did her a world of good.

After running from her home, Slinky in tow, she didn't think she'd ever feel safe again. But there was something about Nate and his calm, confident demeanor that she found soothing. First, he'd helped her through the attack last night to the point that she'd been so focused on him she'd forgotten to be scared in the aftermath. Now, he was helping her deal with the insecurity that came from her home being invaded. And the best part was that he didn't even realize he was doing it.

Did he have this effect on everyone, or was it just her? *It doesn't matter*, she told herself. *Just enjoy it.*

Her life was in such turmoil right now, it was probably best not to question any relief that came her way. And if that relief came in the form of an attractive man? Well, who was she to complain? Looking at Nate was a nice distraction, one she should appreciate while she could.

She pulled into a spot next to Nate's car and turned off the engine, then let out a sigh. Staying in an unfamiliar apartment wasn't ideal, but it was better than going home. She shuddered at the thought of her house and the memory of the man who had invaded her space. He hadn't just broken her things, he'd shattered her peace of mind.

Fiona had grown up in that house. It was filled with memories—some happy, some sad—but they were *hers*. To have a stranger violate that sanctuary was disturbing on a psychological level, one that hit her harder than the physical damage he had inflicted.

But the worst part of this whole mess was the fact that she had no one to talk to, no close friends or relatives to lean on for support. Her mother was gone, and while Fiona missed her so much her heart physically ached with the loss, part of her was glad her mom wasn't here to stress about the situation. Christine had always been a champion worrier, and knowing that her daughter was in trouble would only upset her. Still, it would have been nice to hear her mom's voice and feel her touch once more. Even though she was a grown woman, there was something about being around her mom that made Fiona feel everything was going to be okay, no matter how bleak the situation.

A soft tap on the passenger window made her jump, and she turned to find Nate leaning down with an apologetic expression.

"I'm sorry," he said as soon as she climbed from the car. "Didn't mean to startle you. I thought I'd carry up Slinky for you."

"That'd be great. Thanks." Truth be told, her arm ached a little from carting him around earlier. For all his positive qualities, he was not a small kitty.

She pressed the button to unlock the doors, and Nate reached in and grabbed the bag. As he pulled it out, a pile of folders slid off the seat and onto the floorboards and parking lot.

"Crap," he muttered. "My bad." He set the bag on the ground and began to scoop up the papers. Fiona rounded the hood and stooped to help.

"It's okay," she said. "They're not even my papers. Ben asked me to carry them out to his car earlier, and in all the excitement I left without giving them to him."

"Do you know what they are?"

She shook her head. "No clue."

Nate finished collecting the pages and studied the

re-formed pile thoughtfully. "You said Ben and this other guy were arguing about something the other guy wanted, something Ben wouldn't give him?"

Fiona nodded. "That's what I heard. But like I said earlier, I have no idea what he wanted."

"I believe you. But don't you find it odd the same man showed up at your house not long after the argument?"

"I suppose," she replied slowly. "You think there's a connection?" *Why didn't I think of that earlier?*

Nate shrugged. "I think it's a possibility we can't ignore. For all you know, Ben told the guy you have what he wants, which is why you're now a target. And if this is the only thing Ben has given you...?" He left the question dangling, and Fiona nodded in the affirmative.

"Then we should definitely look at these papers. See if there's anything that jumps out as suspicious."

"Good idea."

He shot her a grin that made her stomach flip. "Thanks. You want to carry the papers while I get the cat?" He handed her the stack and turned to collect Slinky's bag.

Fiona eyed the pages with distaste. Would Ben really set her up like that? It was possible—she didn't know him well at all, so she couldn't rule it out. But he had asked her to carry the files out to his car, implying he was going to take them back. And he couldn't have anticipated that he'd get into an argument with the mystery man, so she had to believe he hadn't planned this to happen.

But even though this hadn't been premeditated on Ben's part, Nate was probably right. The only reason the stranger had come after her was because Ben had pointed him in her direction. The realization left a bad taste in her mouth, and she wanted nothing more than to head back to the store and shake him until his bones broke. How dare he betray her like that! What kind of man put innocent people in danger to save his own skin?

Her rage must have shown on her face, because when Nate caught sight of her, he stopped dead in the hallway. "Are you okay?"

"Fine," she muttered. "Just thinking about Ben."

"Don't. He's not worth your anger. And trust me, we have a lot of questions for him."

"If you can find him. It wouldn't surprise me if he's skipped town by now."

"It's possible." Nate sounded unconcerned. "But my guess is he's still here. I'll send out a guy to check. If he did saddle you with something important, he's not going to leave it with you for long. He'll want it back, and the sooner the better. Don't be surprised if he reaches out to you in the next few days."

Just the thought of talking to Ben made her blood boil. "I don't ever want to hear from him again. I can't believe he did this to me!"

"I know," Nate soothed. "But if he does call, you need to let me know so we can bring him in for questioning."

"If you say so," she replied.

They came to a stop at a door halfway down the hall, their feet making a crunching sound on a colorful coir welcome mat. Nate lifted his hand to knock, but before he made contact with the door, it opened to reveal a slender, dark-haired woman. "Nate!" she said, pulling him into the apartment. "So good to see you!" She stood on her tiptoes and planted a kiss on his cheek, then leaned in for a full-bodied hug. "It's been too long."

Nate returned her embrace, the muscles in his back contracting as he squeezed her against him. "I know. I've missed you, too."

The woman turned her attention to the doorway. "Please, come in," she said, gesturing Fiona forward. "I'm Hannah." She stuck out her hand, and Fiona set the papers on an end table so she could return the gesture.

"Nice to meet you," Fiona said. "Thanks so much for letting me stay here."

"Oh, it's no problem at all. I'm hardly ever here anymore, and it's silly for the apartment to stay empty all the time."

Nate rubbed Hannah's back affectionately, and Fiona tried to ignore the spike of jealousy triggered by his casual touch of another woman. She had no claim over him, and one kiss didn't give her the right to feel so possessive.

Slinky, apparently sensing he was now in a domestic setting, chose this moment to let out a yowl of frustration. "Oh, you poor thing!" Hannah exclaimed. "That must be your cat." She took the bag from Nate and crossed the room to set it on the couch. Then she unzipped the bag and pulled the fabric back. Slinky poked his head through the opening, his nose twitching as he glanced around.

"I set up a litter box in the bathroom," she said, before turning back to face the bag. "He should feel right at home.

"Hey there," Hannah crooned, extending her hand for the cat to smell. Slinky gave her a cursory sniff, then slowly climbed out of the bag, carefully feeling out each step before fully committing a paw to the act.

"He looks like he's navigating a minefield," Nate murmured, his breath warm on her neck.

Fiona jumped. When had he moved to stand behind her? "Sorry," he said, placing his hand on her lower back in an echo of his earlier gesture. "Didn't mean to startle you."

"It's okay." She kept her gaze on Slinky, not trusting herself to look at Nate. His hand felt entirely too nice, a warm weight against her body. And that was with her clothes separating their skin—what would it feel like if he touched her without any barriers between them?

"He's so adorable," Hannah said, interrupting her thoughts before they could get any more inappropriate. Fiona refocused on Slinky to find that he was now vigorously rubbing his cheek against the coffee table. Apparently satisfied with the new digs, he was wasting no time in claiming everything within sight as his own personal property.

Fiona smiled, happy to see he was settling in so well. Knowing her sweet boy was okay went a long way to making her feel better. "I really can't thank you enough for letting us both stay here." She blinked hard, trying to push back the sudden tears pricking her eyes.

Hannah stood and walked over, then pulled Fiona into a warm hug. "I'll let you get settled," she said. "I made a quick trip to the grocery store after Owen called me, so you should have enough supplies to hold you for a couple of days. I'm sure Nate can show you around the area if you need to spend more time here." She released Fiona, then turned and hugged Nate. "See you soon?" she asked him.

"You know it," he replied. He walked her to the door, giving Fiona a chance to get her emotions back under control. What did it say about her life that she had to rely on the kindness of strangers when she found herself in trouble? Could she be any more pathetic? Her despair settled in her stomach, making her feel suddenly queasy. She swallowed hard, willing her body to behave itself. The last thing she wanted was to vomit in Hannah's apartment.

Nate turned back from the door, and his eyes widened when he caught sight of her face. Great—she must look truly scary.

"You okay?"

Fiona nodded vigorously. "Yep. Just fine." Her pride kept the tears in check, but for how much longer?

Nate studied her thoughtfully for a moment. "Come on, let's get out of here."

"What?" Her voice was a high squeak, betraying her nerves. "We just got here."

"I know, and we'll come back. But I have an idea."

"What about Slinky?" She couldn't leave him alone in an unfamiliar setting. He needed her, and truth be told, she needed him. After today's scares, she wanted nothing more than to curl up with his furry warmth and forget about everything, if only for a few hours.

Nate tilted his head meaningfully, and she turned to find the cat stretched out on the sofa, bathing himself in preparation for a nap. *Traitor.* "I think he'll be okay on his own for a little bit," Nate said drily.

"I guess you're right. Just let me run to the bathroom first."

She found it just off the hall. It was small but cheerfully decorated with bright colors. As soon as she stepped inside, she noticed that Hannah had the same shower curtain that was in her bathroom at home. The familiar sight made her smile and eased the knot in her stomach a little. It seemed she and Hannah had some things in common, and in another life, they probably would have been friends.

Fiona tried not to wince when she caught sight of herself in the mirror. *Not exactly a sight for sore eyes…* Her hair was falling out of its ponytail, and her skin was so pale she looked sick. She made a face, then settled into damage control. The elastic band reluctantly surrendered its grip on her hair, and she used her fingers to comb through the tangles. Hannah's brush was sitting on the counter, but Fiona didn't feel comfortable using it. The woman was already letting her invade her home—sharing a brush was going a little too far, in Fiona's mind. Once her hair was smooth, she pulled it back into a ponytail again. It wasn't the most glamorous hairstyle, but it was practical and got the job done.

Next, she splashed cold water on her face. The shock of it made her gasp, but when she looked in the mirror again, she was pleased to see her cheeks had turned slightly pink. She still wasn't the picture of health, but she no longer looked like death warmed over. Good enough.

She took a deep breath and realized the fluttery, panicked feeling in her stomach had subsided. Was it the routine of grooming that had helped or Nate's promise of a distraction? Either way, she was glad the uncomfortable sensation had passed.

"Okay, I'm ready," she called as she walked back into the living room. Nate stepped from the kitchen, wiping his hands on his jeans.

"I was just setting out a bowl of water for Slinky," he said, sounding a little self-conscious. "In case he gets thirsty later." She followed his gaze to the lightly snoring ball of gray fur on the couch, and her heart seemed to swell in her chest. He had remembered her cat and thought to provide for him even though they wouldn't be gone long. It was a small but sweet thing, and a wave of tenderness washed over her. Even though Nate wasn't trying to score points, the gesture melted something inside of her.

He walked over to her, and, before she could talk herself out of it, Fiona rose up on her tiptoes and pressed a soft kiss to his mouth. "Thank you," she whispered.

Heat flared in his eyes. "If that's the thanks I get for putting out some water, I'd be happy to do it again. I noticed Hannah has a lot of bowls in her cupboard." He took a teasing step in the direction of the kitchen, a sly smile curving his lips.

Fiona laughed at his antics. "Maybe later. I thought we had somewhere to go?"

"That's true," he said, grabbing her hand and tugging her toward the door. "And I think you're going to like this."

"I'm sure I will," she murmured, happy to be near him, to be touching him. She felt as if she was standing at the top of a tall hill, a little giddy with the realization that just one small shove would send her over the edge, plummeting deeper into like and maybe, just maybe, even into love.

She stole a glance at Nate as they walked to his car. Did he feel it, too? Or was she alone in wondering if this was the start of something between them? More important, could she afford to take that chance? She already felt emotionally vulnerable in the wake of the robbery and her home being invaded. Could she open her heart to another risk, knowing it might get broken?

Her mom would know the right answer. Christine had always been able to find the perfect words for any situation, a talent she had not passed on to Fiona. But no matter. There would be time to worry about it later. Now, she just wanted to enjoy herself.

Sal pulled his nephew's information up on the screen and pressed the button to dial his number. Even though Joey had only gotten his assignment this morning, he wanted to check in and see if any progress had been made.

"Hello?" The kid's voice wavered a little, and Sal's hand clenched into a fist. He was clearly nervous, which meant he hadn't gotten the pictures back yet. Great.

"I'm calling for a status update," Sal said, forgoing the normal conversational pleasantries. He didn't want this call to last any longer than necessary, and since the sound of Joey's voice grated on his last nerve, he needed to keep it short.

"Um." Joey stammered for a moment, hemming and hawing and not really saying anything of substance. Sal bit his tongue to keep from screaming at him to get to the point. "I'm still working on it."

"What does that mean?"

"It means I'm working on it." A note of petulance crept into the kid's voice, and Sal's palm tingled with the urge to slap him.

"Would you care to rephrase that?" he said, his tone dangerously calm.

Apparently, Joey wasn't as dumb as he looked. He gulped audibly and began stammering again. "I talked to the store owner this morning. He doesn't have the pictures anymore. He gave them to the lady clerk at the store. So I went to her house."

"And?"

"She got away before I could ask her anything."

"I see." Sal ground his teeth until pain shot through his jaw. Of course. Could this kid do anything right?

"But I haven't given up," Joey hastened to add, apparently sensing his uncle's impatience.

"Good. I need those pictures back. The sooner the better." Once again, the thought of Isabella's wrath sent a cold trickle down his spine. He knew the kind of people she associated with, and he understood all too well the risks he'd assumed by getting involved with her. But the offer from the cartel had been too good to pass up.

He'd been looking for an opportunity to expand his

business for years, but the timing had never been right. When Isabella had approached him with the cartel's proposal that he launder money for them in exchange for additional power and influence over the region, he'd jumped at the chance. And when Isabella had made it clear she was amenable to enjoying his company on a personal level, as well... He was only a man, after all.

The only condition the cartel had made was that their arrangement remain a secret. He'd agreed without hesitation, never thinking that would be a problem.

Until now.

"I'll get them back," Joey promised. "I can do this."

The kid sounded so eager to please that for a moment Sal almost felt sorry for him. Then the reality of his situation slammed back into him, making his gut clench.

"You have twenty-four hours," Sal informed him coldly. "If you can't get the pictures by this time tomorrow, you'd better start running and pray I don't catch up with you."

He hung up, cutting off Joey's sputtered reaction. The kid might be family, but this was a cutthroat world, and if he couldn't keep up he wasn't going to make it very far. Better for him to learn that now. Besides, at this point, Sal had to focus on his own problems.

The last thing he wanted was to send some of his guys to retrieve the photos. If more people learned of their existence, it would increase the chances the cartel would catch wind of the situation. He wasn't stupid— he knew there were likely people working for him who were also on the cartel's payroll, reporting back to the organization so they could monitor his actions. It was only a matter of time until the deadly group found out, but he wanted to control when and how they learned of this lapse.

Maybe he could redirect their focus to Ben. After all, it was his fault the photos even existed in the first place. Perhaps he could spin this to his advantage, whatever the outcome. If Joey didn't manage to get the pictures back, Sal would simply tell the cartel about Ben. A well-timed suggestion that Ben thought he could use the photos to gain the upper hand over the cartel wouldn't go amiss, either. The organization would be forced to act, and by eliminating Ben, they would be doing him a favor, as well. It just might work…

Sal nodded, satisfied for now. He didn't trust the cartel and knew very well that his contingency plan could backfire in his face. But he wasn't going to let some two-bit convenience store owner take down his empire. Not without a fight.

Chapter 8

Nate was having trouble keeping his eyes on the road.

Fiona was a distracting presence in the passenger seat. She didn't mean to be—he knew that much. She sat quietly, apparently content to let him take her where he wanted to go. It was humbling, that show of trust, especially after all she'd been through in the past twenty-four hours. The very last thing she needed right now was for him to get into an accident. He should be focused on driving safely, but his eyes kept drifting over to watch her, as if he was a compass needle and she his true north.

Every red light was an exercise in torture, and he had to practically sit on his hands to keep from reaching over and hauling her out of the seat and onto his lap so they could finish what she'd started back at Hannah's apartment. He knew she hadn't meant to tease him. She wasn't that kind of woman. She was just trying to thank him for taking care of her cat. But his body couldn't tell the difference between gratitude and lust, and her soft, sweet kiss had left him wanting more.

Get a grip, he told himself sternly. One thank-you kiss did not an invitation make, and he would do well to remember it.

Shaking off the fantasy, he pulled into the parking lot and cut the engine. "Ready?" he asked, turning to face her.

She regarded the logo of the big-box store with a healthy dose of skepticism. "I suppose." She climbed out of the car and waited for him to round the hood so they could walk together. "So, if you don't mind my asking," she said, "what kind of fun did you have in mind for us here?"

Nate didn't bother to hide his smile. "This is only phase one of my plan. I thought you could buy some basics to get you through the night—toothbrush, deodorant, that kind of thing. The forensics team should be finished with your house tomorrow, and I can take you back to collect some more of your things then."

"I really appreciate that. I didn't have time to grab anything before I left. I didn't even think about it until we got to Hannah's." She sounded a little rueful, so he reached out to give her shoulder a squeeze.

"Of course, you didn't stop to think. You were running on instinct. You don't need to feel bad about that."

She nodded, but he could tell the reminder of her earlier scare had dampened her mood. Wanting to get things back on track, he stopped her just inside the store. "Okay, here's the plan. You go grab the toiletries and other items you might need to get you through tonight. I'm going to break away and pick up a few things of my own. I'll meet you at checkout lane sixteen. Sound good?"

Fiona gave him a small smile, her expression indulgent. "All right," she said. "This is all very mysterious, but I'm willing to give you the benefit of the doubt."

"That's all I ask." He trailed his hand down her arm, then headed left as she turned right.

It took him only a few moments to gather his supplies, and he raced through the self-checkout line, not wanting Fiona to see what he was buying. Then he walked back and waited for her at their prearranged spot.

"Ready to go?" he asked as she finished up.

She raised a brow at the bag in his hand. "Do I get to see what you bought?"

"Eventually. But now it's time for phase two of my plan."

"Do any of these phases involve food? I haven't really eaten anything today." She sounded so plaintive, he had to swallow hard to keep from laughing.

"That can definitely be arranged. Can you give me twenty more minutes?"

She narrowed her eyes at him but finally nodded. "I suppose," she said slowly. "But if I don't find food soon, I'm going to have to eat your jacket."

He brushed a hand over the smooth leather of the sleeve. "Might be a little tough," he warned.

"But I'm sure it's well seasoned," she said with a grin.

"I do wear it everywhere," he admitted.

Five minutes later, he pulled into the parking lot of their second destination. "This is our last stop, and then we'll head back," he promised.

Fiona stared out the windshield, her eyes wide. "What are we doing here?"

"Isn't it obvious?" he teased. "We're buying a Christmas tree."

She blinked hard, her eyes suspiciously bright. "I haven't had a Christmas tree since my mom got sick."

Nate's heart broke for her. He'd meant for this to be a fun distraction, but it seemed he'd inadvertently brought up some painful memories. "How long ago was that?"

"Seven years. She died two years ago, but she'd been sick for five years before that." Her voice was quiet, but she didn't sound as if she was crying. That was a good sign...

"We don't have to do this," Nate said, reaching for the keys. "Let's go grab a bite to eat, instead."

"No." Fiona leaned over and placed her hand on his arm, preventing him from starting the car again. "I'd like to get a tree. It's been too long. I think it's time I started celebrating the holiday again."

"You're sure?"

She nodded. "Positive. Let's go find one."

It took longer than he'd thought it would, especially since he assumed she'd simply pick one after her stomach started audibly growling. But she was determined to find the "perfect" tree. The problem was that she couldn't really describe what constituted a perfect tree, so Nate was left grabbing specimen after specimen, holding it upright while Fiona circled around it, inspecting every branch and needle. She'd shake her head, he'd put the tree back, and the cycle would continue. On and on, until Nate started second-guessing the merits of this particular plan.

Maybe a movie would have been a better idea, after all. He took a deep breath, trying to keep the exasperation from showing on his face. Fiona hadn't decorated at Christmas for the better part of the past decade. The least he could do was be patient while she selected the tree that was going to break her slump.

Finally, she nodded her approval. For the life of him, he couldn't see what made this tree stand out from all the others, but it was the one she wanted and so it was the one she would have.

Her face beamed as he secured the tree to the top of his car. "Do you think it's getting smashed up there? What if it falls off while we're driving? Are you sure Hannah won't mind us bringing a live tree into her apartment?"

Nate tied the last knot and then turned to face Fiona. Taking her hands in his own, he met and held her gaze. "The tree won't be on its side long enough to get smashed. And I secured it tightly, so there's no danger of it falling off. Besides, I'm going to drive carefully. And Hannah won't mind—before we got there, she told me she was sorry she hadn't put one up herself."

Fiona nodded. "Okay. Let's get going!" She practically jumped into the car, her excitement palpable.

He climbed into his own seat, feeling pleased with himself. Taking Fiona out to get a tree had been a split-second decision, an idea that had popped into his mind when he'd seen how upset she was back at Hannah's apartment. If he'd known how happy it would make her, he'd have suggested it right away.

"Where should we put it?"

His chest warmed at her use of the word *we*. It made him feel like part of a team, like they were actually a couple. He knew he was skipping ahead a few weeks, but it gave him something to work toward.

"What about the corner of the living room, by the bookshelf?" he suggested. Truth be told, he didn't care where the tree went. He was just happy Fiona was looking forward to decorating it.

She was quiet for a moment, considering his words. "That could work," she admitted. "But what about in front of the window? That way, people can see it and enjoy it from the parking lot."

"Sounds good to me," Nate said. He had to admit, he was starting to get excited about decorating the tree, too. Her enthusiasm was contagious, and it was a nice change of pace for him. Normally, his evenings were spent working, either in the office or while he was at home. His job was important, not just because it gave him a way to help people, but because the better he did at work, the better he'd be able to provide for Molly once their parents were gone.

It wasn't something he liked to think about, but Fiona's circumstances made him more aware of the fact that his parents were getting older, and one day they would be gone. Molly was a well-adjusted young woman, but she still had special needs that prevented her from living on her own. Once their parents died, Nate would need to step into their shoes and make sure his sister was provided for and had the care she required. He couldn't do that if he didn't excel at his job, and to make things more difficult, he couldn't explain the necessity for his workaholic behavior to his mother. It was easier for her to think he was just really busy. If she knew the truth, she'd feel guilty about the situation, and he wanted to spare her that. Guilt was a pointless emotion, and it couldn't change anything.

"How are we going to get this up the stairs?" Fiona's question broke into his thoughts, and he was grateful for the distraction. If he thought too long about his sister and the future of his family, it made his stomach clench into knots.

"I figured I'd carry the tree upstairs while you look after the bags."

"That sounds fair."

It took only a few minutes to get the job done, and in the end, he managed to avoid poking himself in the eyes with the pine needles. Slinky watched them from his spot on the couch, his big green eyes following their every move as they worked to get the tree into the stand Nate had bought. Fiona stood back, surveying their progress.

"Just a little more to the right," she directed. "There… perfect!" Her eyes were bright with anticipation, and she motioned for him to stand next to her. He obliged, releasing his hold on the tree so he could walk over to her. "Doesn't it look wonderful?" she asked.

Nate had to admit, it did look good. The tree was

small, but it was already filling the apartment with a fresh, woodsy scent. And even though it was undecorated, it was still a pretty, festive addition to the living room.

"Ready to decorate it?"

Fiona smiled up at him. "Do we have any ornaments?"

"Check the bags."

She dove for them like a little kid on Christmas morning, oohing and aahing as she pulled out several boxes of brightly colored glass bulbs and strands of lights. "I wasn't sure what you'd like," he said, coming to sit next to her. "So I picked up a variety of decorations."

"This is wonderful," she assured him, placing her hand on his knee for a moment. Her touch was warm through the fabric of his jeans, and he breathed in deeply, enjoying the way her lemon-sugar scent mingled with the pine of the tree.

"I'll let you get started on organizing the decorations. I'm going to order some pizza."

She closed her eyes and moaned. "That sounds really good right now. Mushroom and sausage?" She sounded so hopeful, he couldn't help but nod in agreement.

"I can live with that." He pulled his phone out of his pocket and retreated into the kitchen. Hannah had a collection of magnets on her refrigerator, each one from a different restaurant, and all promising fast delivery service. After locating the information for the pizza place, he called in their order. Then he opened the fridge, in search of something cold to drink. He fished out two cans of soda and straightened up, but before he could head back into the living room to rejoin Fiona, his phone rang.

"Gallagher."

"Is she all settled in?" Owen asked, not bothering with the preliminaries.

Nate glanced into the living room and saw that Fiona had taken the decorations out of the bags and was busily sorting them into some kind of order. "So far, so good. Did you find out anything regarding that lawyer?"

"Not much more than what I already told you. We seem to have hit a wall, at least for tonight."

"Maybe not." Nate eyed the stack of papers still on the end table. "Fiona's boss, Ben, gave her a pile of papers from the store today and asked her to take them out to his car. But our John Doe aggressor showed up before Ben could take them back, so she still has them."

"You think that's why the guy came after her today?"

"Could be. We haven't had a chance to look through them yet."

"Seriously?" Owen sounded genuinely surprised. "It's not like you to sit on a lead like that."

Nate shrugged, even though his partner couldn't see the gesture. "I suppose. I just thought Fiona had been through enough today, and I wanted her to have a break before we got back into it."

Silence greeted his reply, and it lasted so long that Nate wondered if his phone had dropped the call. He pulled the phone from his ear to check, but no, his partner was still on the line. "You still there?"

"Yeah." Owen's voice held a new note, one he'd never heard before. "I'm here. Just processing."

"I didn't know I'd said something that requires processing."

His partner responded with a short laugh. "If you say so, buddy. I'm glad to hear you're taking a break from work."

"It's not really a break," Nate hedged, but Owen cut him off.

"You don't have to make excuses to me. I know how hard you work. Just enjoy the moment."

It was Nate's turn to laugh. "I never thought I'd hear you say that." He propped his hip against the counter edge and let his eyes roam around the kitchen, taking note of the little touches here and there that personalized the space and screamed "Hannah." She had done wonders for Owen—he was a changed man, and it gave Nate hope that he too might find someone who fit him as well as she and Owen fit each other. "It's good to hear you happy."

"Thanks, man. I'm a lucky guy."

Maybe I am, too. He cast another glance at Fiona, smiling a little at the expression on her face. "We'll take a look at the pages in a bit, and I'll let you know if anything comes of it."

"Okay," Owen replied. "I'll keep my phone on me, just in case."

"Thanks." Nate disconnected and slipped the phone back into his pocket. He grabbed the sodas again but paused before walking into the living room, content to just watch Fiona for a moment.

She had finished setting everything out and was now engaged in petting Slinky. He couldn't hear the big cat from where he was standing, but Nate was willing to bet all the money in his bank account that the furry guy was purring his heart out. He looked up at his mistress with adoration, blinking slowly at her as she leaned forward to press a kiss to the top of his head. It was a cozy picture, and seeing her with her cat made his stomach flip with a sense of anticipation and wonder. If she was this affectionate and loving to her pet, what would she be like with the man she fell in love with? Or her children, for that matter? If Slinky was any indication, she'd make a great mother.

Whoa. Where did that come from? Nate had never thought about kids before. Well, maybe he had, but only in the abstract, maybe-one-day sense. Normally, when he thought about the future, he was focused on how he was going to provide for Molly and how he wanted to find a woman who would understand how important his sister was to him. But he'd never before thought about having kids of his own, and certainly not while staring at a woman he was attracted to.

"Nate? Is everything okay in there?"

Shaking himself free of his thoughts, Nate walked into the living room. "All good. The pizza is on its way and should be here soon. I brought you something to drink." He handed her one of the cans, and she smiled up at him.

"Thanks. I appreciate it."

"How's he doing?" He gestured toward the cat as he settled into the recliner opposite the couch. "He seems pretty calm. Much better than when he was in the station earlier."

"He's never enjoyed being in a carrier, and I'm sure the bag smelled bad. I keep my gym stuff in there." She wrinkled her nose in sympathy and scratched behind his ear, causing Slinky to close his eyes in pleasure. If Nate didn't know better, he'd swear the cat was smiling. "You can't really blame him for being upset."

"I'm just glad he's happy now. I know how important that is to you."

A tender expression stole across her face, and she gave him a soft smile. "It is. And thank you for caring enough about him to ask."

Nate took a sip of the soda, unsure of what to say next. He couldn't very well tell Fiona that he was really more concerned about her. Oh, sure, he liked animals. And Slinky was fine, as far as cats went. But his primary concern was Fiona. Since the way to her heart seemed to run through her cat, he was just going to have to bond with the big, fluffy fur ball if he wanted to get closer to her.

It wasn't the most arduous task he'd ever faced. From what he'd seen, Slinky seemed to be a pretty easygoing cat, so it shouldn't be too hard to make friends with him.

As if reading his thoughts, Slinky opened his eyes and stared at him, his wide, green gaze surprisingly intense. "You doing okay, buddy?" Nate asked him. The cat responded with a dismissive flick of his tail before closing his eyes and laying his head down on his paws. Well, then. So much for the direct approach. Maybe he could buy the cat's affections with treats or something.

"So how does your family decorate the tree?" The

change in subject threw him, and Nate blinked to re-align his thoughts.

"Uh, what do you mean?"

Fiona gave him an indulgent smile. "When I was growing up, we'd start at the bottom and work our way up, saving the star on top for last. What did you guys do?"

"Oh." He thought back to childhood Christmases, and the excitement he'd felt when his dad had brought the box of decorations down from the attic. He and Molly would grab ornaments at random and run to place them on the tree, heedless to any kind of design or balance. The finished product was invariably lopsided in the decorations department, but it was theirs and they'd always loved it.

"We didn't really have a system," he said. "Molly and I just put ornaments wherever, and Mom and Dad were content to let us. Our trees never looked like the ones in the catalogs."

"That's okay. It sounds like you and your sister had fun, and that's the whole point." Fiona reached for an ornament and passed it to him before taking one for herself. "Shall we get started?"

"You go ahead. I'll get the music going."

It took him a moment to figure out Hannah's stereo equipment, but soon the festive sounds of Christmas carols filled the apartment. He turned back to find Fiona busily stringing lights on the tree, singing quietly under her breath as she worked. She was so beautiful, lit by the soft glow of the lights she had draped around her shoulders. The domesticity of the scene hit him hard, knocking the breath from his chest. Seeing her here, smiling and happy, waiting for him to join her—it was like a fantasy come to life. He could almost forget the circumstances that had led them here.

At some point, they were going to have to look at the papers Ben had given to Fiona. But not now. He wasn't sure how it had happened, but Hannah's apartment had become their little oasis, a break from the unpleasant realities that waited for them. This was a gift, one he wasn't inclined to squander. Tonight, he was going to focus on the present and let the future take care of itself.

"Nate, are you coming?" Fiona watched him, an expectant expression on her face.

He smiled, his chest warming at the sight. "Yes."

The pizza arrived shortly after they'd finished stringing the lights on the tree. It was hot and delicious and tasted wonderful, especially on her empty stomach. But even better than the food was the way the conversation flowed between her and Nate.

She was no longer nervous to be around him, the way she'd been in the aftermath of the robbery attempt. He was still gorgeous, but his looks no longer intimidated her. Besides, she was more interested in getting to know him, and it seemed the more she learned about him, the more she liked him.

Unless she missed her guess, he seemed to like her, too. After all, he was still here with her, when he could have easily dropped her off at Hannah's apartment and left to go back to work or to do something else. But he had stayed to spend time with her, and, more than that, he'd made it a point to find something for them to do that helped take her mind off her situation and the dangerous stranger who seemed bent on hurting her.

Fiona carried their plates into the kitchen and loaded the dishwasher, smiling to herself at the turn her day had taken. She'd gone from terrified and shaken to feeling safe and content, all in the space of a few hours. And all thanks to the man in the living room.

She paused in the doorway, wanting to watch him for a moment before they started decorating the tree again. Nate had moved to the couch and was sitting next to Slinky, running his big hand gently over Slinky's body. Apparently sensing that someone new was touching him, Slinky opened one eye and regarded Nate with mild interest. But when Nate only continued to stroke his back, Slinky abandoned his suspicion and surrendered to his enjoyment of the attention.

A swell of affection rose in her chest, and tears threatened at the back of her eyes. Underneath his workaholic, professional exterior, Nate had a soft heart, and she felt a burst of pleasure at the realization that she was seeing a side of him that most people didn't know existed.

As if he felt her gaze, Nate looked up and met her eyes. "Ready to get back to it, or are you too full?" he teased.

She stepped into the room, enjoying the easy back-and-forth banter they had developed over the last few hours. "Are you kidding? Now that I've eaten, I've got my second wind. But what about you? You're looking mighty comfortable there, like you could just lie down on the couch and take a nap with Slinky."

He glanced down at the sleeping cat and smiled. "It is tempting. But there's a lot of tree left to decorate. I'd hate to leave the job half-finished."

They settled back into a routine of sorts, hanging ornaments and chatting about anything and everything. It was so nice to have someone to talk to—she hadn't realized how much she missed having a simple conversation with someone. She and her mom used to talk all the time, but after her death Fiona had become so focused on school and her thesis that she hadn't made time for friends. Of course, not that many of her friends from high school were still around, and those who were had moved on with their lives. Taking care of her mom during her illness had left little time for anything else, and making new friends was a lot more difficult than it had been when she was younger. Most of the time, she kept herself so busy she didn't notice the void in her life. But tonight, after spending time with Nate, it was abundantly clear that she had been missing something over the last few years.

She had to wonder, though. As pleasant as this time was, would Nate want to stick around after the situation was resolved? Maybe he was only being nice because he knew she was scared, and once the mystery assailant was caught, he'd go back to his job and she'd go back to her life, splitting her time between the store and writing her thesis. The thought was like a dark cloud blocking out the sun, and she deliberately pushed the idea from her mind. If this was the only time she'd have with Nate, she didn't want to spend it dwelling on how lonely she'd be once it was over.

His phone rang, and he pulled it out of his pocket to check the display. Fiona's heart rate kicked up—was that his partner calling with news about the man who'd broken into her home? But Nate merely frowned at the phone and pressed a button to silence the ringer. He slipped it back into his pocket and caught her gaze.

"Don't you need to get that? We can take a break," she offered.

"Nah. It's just my mom."

"Don't you want to talk to her?"

"Not right now," he said, picking up another ornament. "I'm not in the mood for a lecture."

"Oh." She didn't know how to respond. Nate's attitude toward his family, and his mother, in particular, mystified her. She'd give anything to still have a family that cared about her. How could he take that for granted?

A small knot of worry formed in her stomach, and she bit her bottom lip. Was Nate more like her father than she had thought? Was he the type to always put his job first, at the expense of his family?

"You got quiet," he observed. "Everything okay?"

She nodded. "Yeah. I just…" She trailed off, uncertain. She didn't want to offend him, but maybe she could make him understand why his reaction to his mom's call bothered him.

"You just what?" He sounded genuinely curious, so she decided to forge ahead.

"I don't understand why you didn't take your mom's call. She obviously wants to talk to you. Maybe she has some important news."

"She doesn't." His tone was flat and expressionless.

"But how can you be sure?" she pressed.

"Because she never does. All she ever wants to talk about is what a bad son I am because I don't spend enough time with them." He sounded annoyed, but underneath his irritation Fiona thought she detected a note of hurt.

"Maybe she misses you, but she doesn't know how to express it."

"Maybe," he replied, but she could tell from his voice he didn't believe her.

"Have you tried talking to her about it?"

"No." He sighed, then turned to face her. "Look, can we talk about something else? We were having a nice time. I don't want to ruin it by thinking about my family."

"Sure." She didn't want to upset him, especially after he'd helped her so much today. But she couldn't just drop it—not until she did her best to help him. "I just think you're making a mistake."

"Fiona," he began, a warning note in his tone.

"I'd give anything to have a family," she said quickly, before he could stop her. "You are so lucky to have a mom that cares about you and wants to see you. I'd hate to see you waste that time and regret it later. That's all."

He was silent for a moment, and now that she wasn't talking, she felt the tension that had developed between them. Had she made a mistake? Maybe she had overstepped the bounds of their burgeoning relationship. The closeness they'd developed tonight had made her think they were on their way to being friends, if not more, but perhaps she had ruined that by saying too much, too soon.

She bit her lip, waiting for him to respond. There was more she wanted to say, but this wasn't the time.

Finally, after what seemed like an eternity, he replied. "Thanks for your concern."

She let out her breath, realizing she'd pushed him as far as she dared for tonight. It was time to change the subject. "Is it just me, or do they start playing Christmas carols earlier every year? They started before Thanksgiving this year, which I think is just too soon."

Nate didn't respond right away, and Fiona felt a flutter of fear in her stomach. Was he done talking to her now? Had she wrecked their nice evening after all?

"I know what you mean," he said. "I think the stores start bringing out the decorations right after Halloween."

She felt the tension drop as they both turned back to the tree. "Poor Thanksgiving," she remarked. "It really gets shortchanged in the buildup, and that's too bad. It's one of my favorite holidays."

"Really?" He sounded curious now. "Most people I know are eager to get to Christmas because of the gifts."

"I felt that way when I was a kid," she said. "But once I got older, I realized how nice it is to have a whole day to celebrate food. What other day can you go back for a third slice of pie and no one judges you for it?"

He laughed, and the sound lightened her mood. "I hadn't thought of it that way."

She eyed his trim waist and broad shoulders. "That's

because you've probably never worried about gaining weight before," she said wryly.

He gave her a thoughtful look. "I don't think I can respond to that without getting into trouble."

Fiona grinned back. "Why, whatever do you mean?"

"If I agree with you, I'll sound like an overconfident jerk who spends too much time at the gym. But if I disagree, you won't believe me because as a man, I don't face the same kind of judgment women do when it comes to what I eat. So you see, I can't win this one."

She laughed, enjoying his logic. "It sounds like you've figured out the mysteries of the female brain."

"Really?" He sounded so hopeful that Fiona couldn't help but laugh again.

"No. But you're off to a good start."

"Well, I suppose that's something," he grumbled.

Fiona picked up the star and held it out. "Ready for the final touch?"

"You do it," he said. "This is your comeback tree. It's only fitting you be the one to put the star on top."

"My comeback tree?" She smiled at the expression.

"You know what I mean," he said, the tips of his ears turning an adorable shade of pink. "It's your first tree in years. Finish it off."

She turned back and rose to her tiptoes, but she couldn't reach the top. She rocked back onto her heels, but before she could grab a chair to drag over, Nate stepped behind her. He was so close she could feel the heat of his body through her clothes. "Allow me," he said softly, his voice a low rumble in her ear. Before she could respond, he bent and put his arms around her waist. Then he straightened, lifting her up so she could reach the top of the tree.

It took her a few tries to secure the star to the branch, but, in her defense, being so close to Nate was distracting. His arms were like steel bands wrapped around her waist, strong and unbreakable. It felt so good to be pressed up against him, to feel the solid wall of his chest at her back and the warmth of his breath between her shoulder blades. Goose bumps broke out on her skin as a tingling sensation spread from her center down her arms and legs. She couldn't remember the last time someone had held her like this.

When Nate saw the star was in place, he gradually released the tension in his arms. Fiona slid slowly down his body, her back traveling the masculine planes of his chest and hips and thighs until her feet hit the floor. Still, Nate held her against him, keeping his arms around her to secure her gently in place. She shuddered slightly, the unfamiliar physical contact with a man— with *Nate*—both thrilling and unsettling in equal measures.

"Fiona." His voice was a raw whisper in her ear, low and gravelly. The sound set off fireworks in her belly and her knees trembled a little, threatening to give out. She tilted her head back in acknowledgment, not trusting her voice.

"Turn around," he commanded. He loosened his arms a little to give her room to move, but she couldn't make her body obey. She wanted him, wanted this, but it felt like her brain was no longer in control, and her muscles had turned to jelly in the wake of his touch.

"Turn around," he said again, and this time, he put his hand on her hips and moved her into place. God, was there anything sexier than the way he took charge? Fiona was simultaneously aroused and grateful. It had been so long since she'd been touched by a man—not since college. And while she was certain her body would remember what to do, part of her was still scared. Would he know right away she was out of practice? What if she couldn't satisfy him?

A small voice in her head told her to stop, to simply tell him. Nate was a reasonable man, and he would understand. Better for him to adjust his expectations so he wouldn't be disappointed. But her body overrode her common sense, insisting that if she stopped him now, it would be a waste of a good opportunity.

He placed one finger under her chin and lifted until her eyes met his. They were a dark, mossy green in the light from the tree, and for a moment, she could only stare in wonder at the heat she saw there. He wanted her! The thought sent bubbles of sensation cascading through her veins, and her head began to spin, making her feel tipsy.

A slow, sexy grin spread across his face, and she felt her own lips curve up in return. Her gaze dropped to his mouth and the light dusting of stubble on his cheeks and chin. Before she was aware of having the thought, her hand lifted of its own accord, and her fingertips landed on his chin. She explored the sandpaper roughness, enjoying the raspy texture against her own smooth skin.

"Do you like that?" His voice matched the texture

of his beard, sending another jolt of sensation down her spine.

"Yes," she said simply.

"Guess I'm throwing out my razor then," he replied, swallowing hard as her fingers drifted down the column of his throat. He closed his eyes for a moment, apparently savoring her touch.

"Do *you* like that?" she asked, repeating his question with a smile.

"Uh-huh," he said, making a low humming sound in his throat. "Feel free to touch me anywhere you want."

Anywhere? The thought triggered a flood of images and possibilities as Fiona considered her options. Her confidence grew with each pass of her fingers across his skin, and she smiled as the balance between them began to shift in her favor. Her body was no longer overwhelmed by arousal, helpless and at the mercy of Nate's touch. No, she was back in charge now, and the realization that she could give him pleasure filled her with a sensuous determination to make the most of it.

As if sensing this change in attitude, Nate opened his eyes and regarded her thoughtfully. Without warning, he bent and captured her mouth with his.

This was a proper kiss. No more of that barely there whisper of contact or affectionate peck of gratitude. This kiss was demanding and powerful, sweeping her up in a swirl of sensation and making it crystal clear that there was unfinished business between the two of them. She could sense Nate's impatience and frustration at their earlier, unsatisfactory attempts and his satisfaction at finally, *finally*, reaching his goal.

Fiona felt the same way, pouring all her earlier frustration and pent-up attraction into their embrace. Why hadn't they done this sooner? Why had they danced around this attraction, this force drawing them together? Life was too short to ignore such a powerful impulse, especially one that felt so *good*.

Nate broke the kiss to suck in a gasping breath. "Fiona," he said, before lowering his mouth to hers again.

"Hmm?"

He framed her face in his hands, feathering light kisses across her forehead, her cheeks, down her neck. "We should stop."

"Sure." The word was an automatic reaction; at this point, she would have agreed to almost anything he asked. It took a moment for the meaning of his words to actually sink in. "Wait, what did you say?" Surely she had misunderstood him? He didn't really want to stop, did he?

Nate pressed his forehead against hers, their breath mingling in the space between their lips. "We should stop," he repeated, his voice full of regret.

"Okay," she replied, trying to understand. "But why?" Had she done something wrong? Was he not enjoying this?

"I don't want us to move too fast." He pressed a kiss to her forehead and took a small step back, putting a few inches of space between them. It may as well have been a canyon's distance across, for it cut the link between them just as effectively.

"Ah, I see." Except she didn't, not really. In her admittedly limited experience, guys weren't the ones concerned about moving too fast. She felt his rejection like a sting, sharp and sudden in her chest.

Her thoughts must have shown on her face, because Nate rushed to explain. "Please don't take this the wrong way. I care about you. You know I want you." He gestured impatiently to the front of his pants and the evidence of his desire. "But I don't want to rush into this."

"It's okay," she said. As the fog of arousal cleared out of her brain, she realized he was right. They barely knew each other, and she didn't want to dive into a physical relationship with him before figuring out if they had the potential for something long-term. She had nothing against the idea of a fling, but that approach had never worked for her before.

"I didn't mean for it to go this far," he admitted. "I thought I could stop at a kiss and be satisfied with that."

Fiona smiled. "I know what you mean. I've never felt such an intense reaction before."

He pushed a hand through his hair and let out a sigh. "Me, either. Which is why I don't want to just jump into bed. I think we may have something special here. I'd hate to mess it up before we can find out."

"I agree."

"You do? Really?" He sounded relieved, and she realized he had been worried about her reaction. The fact that he cared put yet another check mark in the plus column of her mental ledger.

"Really," she assured him. "I usually don't get physical this fast, and I think I would have ended up regretting it if we had slept together."

"Yeah. I would have felt bad about it, too."

They were silent for a moment, both of them studying the tree as they searched for something else to say.

Nate spoke first. "You look beautiful standing next to the lights."

She felt her cheeks warm at the heartfelt compliment. "So do you," she said softly.

He laughed, the sound a low rumble in the otherwise quiet room. "No one's ever told me that before."

"Really?"

"Really. It's not exactly the kind of adjective people usually apply to me."

She ran her eyes over his face, the planes of his brows and cheekbones, the way his stubble took on a golden hue in the reflected light from the tree. His expression was open, almost vulnerable as he watched her. He *was* beautiful. And in that moment, she ached to be the one who got to see this unguarded version of Nate all the time.

"I imagine the guys you arrest are more interested in their own problems than coming up with a description of your looks," she teased.

He smiled, his eyes warming. "You may be right."

Slinky chose this moment to jump down from the couch, meowing loudly as he came to stand at Fiona's feet.

"Does he need something?" Nate studied the big cat like he was a mystery he was trying to decipher. "Is he hungry or something?"

"He's ready for bed," Fiona explained. "This is our normal bedtime, and he's just reminding me to get back on schedule."

"I didn't know cats could tell time."

"Oh, yeah. Stick around, and you can catch the morning show where he acts as my alarm clock because he's hungry."

Nate chuckled. "I should probably get going then, so you guys can turn in."

Fiona nodded, but the thought of Nate leaving sent a cold chill down her spine. "Sure," she said, trying to sound casual. She'd known he was going to leave all along, but now that the moment was here, the fear of being alone was rising quickly in her chest like a noxious tide.

Nate looked at her closely. "Are you okay?"

"Yes." She nodded. "Just tired." It was true. The craziness of the day was catching up to her, and she wanted nothing more than to fall into bed and sleep away her bad memories.

"Would you like me to stay?" He sounded genuinely curious, and his question sparked a flare of gratitude in her belly.

"Are you sure it wouldn't be too much trouble?" She didn't want to inconvenience him further, but the idea of having him nearby was comforting…

"Not at all. I can bunk on the couch." He glanced at it, then back at her. "Slinky already warmed it up for me."

Fiona smiled. "He's good at that."

"Go on." Nate gestured to the bedroom. "I'll get settled here. We can start fresh in the morning."

That sounded heavenly, and Fiona closed her eyes in blissful appreciation of the idea. "You really are the best," she said, already taking a step in the direction of the bedroom.

"Get some rest," Nate called after her.

She flipped the light on and closed the door, then thought better of it and left it open a crack. Slinky would need access to the litter box during the night, and she didn't want to have to get up to let him out. It took only a few minutes to slip into the nightshirt she'd bought earlier and to brush her teeth. Then she climbed under the covers, her fatigue overcoming her initial reticence about sleeping in someone else's bed.

What a day. After such a rough start, she hadn't imagined anything good could come of it. But Nate had turned it all around and had given her something positive to focus on. And the way he'd kissed her! Tingles ran through her body as she remembered the feel of his lips against hers, the warmth of his tongue.

She closed her eyes with a sigh and drifted off to sleep, thoughts of Nate keeping her fears at bay.

Chapter 9

Fiona smiled at him, a come-hither look that sent all the blood in his body racing south. Her eyes were dark and sultry, and her auburn hair was tousled around her face, making her look every inch the temptress. She slowly sauntered over, teasing him with every sway of her hips, until she stood just inches away.

It was all he could do not to grab her and haul her up against his chest, but his arms wouldn't respond to his brain's commands. He was paralyzed by this sultry, sexy version of Fiona, and his eyes remained glued to her body, anticipation building in his belly.

She moved like quicksilver, all graceful, fluid lines as she reached out to touch him, to caress him. He felt her hands on his skin and was surprised to realize his shirt was gone. When had that happened? No matter, she was touching him, and that was all he cared about.

"You're wearing too many clothes," he said, the words sounding strangled as he struggled to remember how to speak. She had short-circuited his brain, and he had to concentrate to complete even the simplest of tasks. Like breathing.

She merely laughed, the sound low and husky and oh so sexy. Her teasing fingers flattened against his chest, and she gave him a shove. He fell through the air, the shock of it making his body stiffen and his stomach lurch. But he needn't have worried. He landed on a soft mattress, the linens cool against his heated skin.

Fiona stepped forward to the edge of the bed, her fingers working at the button of his pants. He tried to help her but found he couldn't use his hands. Clever girl that she was, she didn't need his assistance. With a firm tug, she stripped the pants down his legs and off his body.

Her face lit up in appreciation as she ran her gaze up and down the length of him, and a sense of male pride filled his chest. She liked what she saw, and he couldn't wait to see her in a similar state.

She cocked one eyebrow at him and gave him a sexy smile. Then she slowly climbed onto the bed, moving her body over his until she straddled his hips. She bent to take his mouth, putting more weight on his chest. It felt so good, but she was heavier than he had expected. He tried to move a little, to release the pressure on his chest, but she kept leaning forward, her weight making it hard for him to breathe. His arousal quickly turned to panic as his brain cried out for oxygen. But his arms wouldn't work, and he couldn't get her off...

Nate came awake with a start, gasping for air. The pressure on his chest was still there, and it took a moment to identify the source: Slinky. The big cat was stretched out on top of him, regarding him with those big, luminous eyes.

"Uh, hi, buddy." He tried to roll to the side, hoping to move the cat off him and onto the sofa. But Slinky dug his claws in, the sharp spikes piercing the fabric of his shirt and pricking the skin of his chest painfully. Okay, apparently that strategy wasn't going to work.

"You're kind of heavy," Nate said, hoping a more direct approach would work. But the cat merely blinked at him, apparently unconcerned with his respiratory distress.

"Is there a reason you're here with me and not Fiona?"

Slinky's ears perked up at the mention of Fiona's name, but he made no move to get down. With a sigh of resignation, Nate closed his eyes. Now that he had identified the problem, his breathing was coming easier. And while he wasn't thrilled about his new role as Slinky's bed, the cat wasn't too bad. If anything, he made a good space heater and helped to stave off the chilly air in the apartment.

Just as he was drifting off, something thumped his nose. Nate's eyes popped open, and he stared at the cat, who was pretending to ignore him. "That was uncalled-for, don't you think?"

The cat merely yawned, then laid his chin on Nate's chest. Nate let his eyelids drift down again, but kept them open a slit so he could watch the cat. Sure enough, as soon as Slinky thought he was asleep, the big cat stretched out a paw and bopped him on the nose again.

"Hey! What is your deal?" He tried to sit up, which was difficult to do with eighteen pounds of recalcitrant cat glued to his chest. Slinky mewed at him and held on for dear life, so, in the end, he wound up cradling the cat like some kind of large, furry baby.

"Listen," he said, trying to keep his voice down. "You can't just poke at people while they're asleep. It's rude." Slinky mewed at him again, more insistently this time. There was something about the tone of his cry that made Nate think he wasn't just trying to be obnoxious.

"What is it? Are you hurt or something?" He felt a little foolish talking to a cat, but there was no help for it. Slinky looked fine, and Nate didn't feel anything out of place. But what did he know about cats?

Another cry. "I don't know what you want. I don't speak cat."

Apparently fed up with his ignorance, Slinky jumped out of his arms and walked toward the bedroom door. Then he walked back over to Nate, mewing insistently.

"Let me guess," Nate said drily. "Timmy's in the well?"

Then he heard her. A soft whimper came from the bedroom, and he realized what Slinky had been trying to tell him all along. Fiona was in distress.

He moved quickly to the door and pushed it open, trying not to make noise. If she was having a nightmare, the last thing he wanted to do was create a racket that would wake her up and add to her terror.

She was curled on her side, the sheets twisted around her. In the moonlight from the window, he could see tear tracks on her cheeks and his heart clenched. While he watched, she moaned again, then kicked out, trying to fend off an invisible threat.

"No, no!" she cried. She turned away, but the sheets tangled her legs and kept her from going far. "Stay away!"

Nate crossed to the bed and sat on the edge. He reached out to touch her, but thought better of it. "Fiona," he said, his voice low but firm. "It's just a dream. Wake up."

She frowned at the sound of his voice and stilled. He spoke again. "Wake up for me, Fiona."

"Nate?" she said. She sounded so lost and alone, as if she had been abandoned to her fate.

"It's me," he responded. "Wake up for me."

Her eyes fluttered open and she found him, her gaze unfocused. "Nate?"

"I'm here." He allowed himself to touch her then, just a hand on her arm. "You're safe."

The breath gusted out of her in a heavy sigh, and she launched herself into his arms. "I was so afraid," she said, her face buried in the hollow of his shoulder. "He kept chasing me, and he wouldn't stop."

"He's not here," Nate assured her, running his hand up and down her back in what he hoped was a soothing gesture. "And if he does show up again, I won't let him get to you."

"I know." She shuddered in his arms and burrowed closer. "But you weren't there."

"Not in your dream, maybe," he said. "But I'm here in real life, where it counts."

"Yes, you are." She squeezed him, then pulled away. He reluctantly let her go, immediately missing the warmth of her body.

"Do you think you'll be able to go back to sleep?"

She nodded. "Now that you pulled me out of the dream, I hope so."

"Good." He leaned down and pressed a kiss to her forehead. "Try to think about something else. I'm here if you need me."

"Thanks." Fiona curled on her side and closed her eyes, and Nate stood, intending to leave her alone.

"Nate?"

He stopped. "Yes?"

"Would you mind staying? Just until I fall asleep again?"

Her simple request hit him hard, and some primitive, caveman-like part of him sat up and took notice. "Of course," he replied. He'd do anything in his power to protect her, even from the demons that haunted her dreams.

Nate walked around to the other side of the bed and lay down on top of the covers. He reached for her hand, wanting her to know he was here as she fell asleep. Fiona gripped his hand hard and used it to pull herself across the bed until she snuggled up to his side. She let out a deep sigh of contentment, and her body relaxed against his.

"Thank you," she sighed, just before she drifted off.

Nate couldn't talk around the lump in his throat. He settled for wrapping his arm around her, anchoring her in place. Slinky jumped up, shaking the mattress as his impressive weight landed on the bed. He strolled over and curled up next to Fiona, purring contentedly as he settled into place.

Nate closed his own eyes, surprised to find sleep was pulling at him, too. He usually didn't rest well with someone else in his bed. But his own body relaxed, instinctively recognizing the *rightness* of it all. With Fiona in his arms and her cat a warm weight next to them, he felt as though he had his own little family to take care of. It was a potent sensation, the realization of a dream he hadn't known he wanted so badly.

It wouldn't last. It couldn't. He had too many real-life responsibilities to handle, between his job and his own family. There simply wasn't room in his life for anything else, and it wouldn't be fair to pretend otherwise. But that didn't mean he couldn't enjoy this interlude while it lasted. He just had to soak in all the sensations, the smells, the sounds. Tuck them away in his memory so he could pull them out and relive them later, when he was alone again and Fiona had moved on with her life.

He breathed in deeply, taking comfort from her now-familiar scent. *Remember this*, he told himself, pushing aside the aching knowledge that it was only temporary. What was that saying? Better to have loved and lost, or something like that. And while he couldn't say that he loved Fiona yet, he did like her very much. It wasn't a stretch to assume that if they tried to work something out, it wouldn't take long for his like to turn into love.

But that was an issue for another day. Now, he was just going to enjoy holding her in his arms. For however long it lasted.

Joey paced back and forth outside the fast-food place, puffing hard to take the last drags off his cigarette. Things had not gone well this morning, and he had to figure out a way to get back on track.

Uncle Sal had sounded angry, and no wonder. He hadn't exactly made a lot of progress so far. But what he hadn't expected—what had made his guts turn to water—was Uncle Sal's threat.

If you can't get the pictures by this time tomorrow, you'd better start running and pray I don't catch up with you.

The memory of those words made him shiver. He'd known all along that Uncle Sal didn't think highly of him, but he'd never for a minute thought the man would kill his own family.

Maybe he should try to leave now, get a head start to improve his chances of getting away. If Uncle Sal was occupied trying to get the pictures, he wouldn't pay much attention to Joey's absence.

It was a tempting thought, but Joey dismissed it right away. Big Sal had a long reach and an even longer memory. Running away might temporarily solve his problems, but eventually they would catch up with him.

Taking one last pull, he dropped the cigarette and ground the stub under his shoe, taking pleasure in savagely crushing it into nothingness. If only his other problems were as easily handled!

The woman shouldn't have gotten away this morning. He'd done everything right—he'd cased her place before breaking in, and he hadn't made too much noise. The only reason she'd seen him was because she'd gotten lucky. How was he to know she'd be so fast? He shook his head. He should have tampered with her car first, gotten rid of her means of escape. Next time, he'd make sure she couldn't get away.

And there would be a next time.

Even though he had no idea where she'd gone, he knew she had to come back to her place. She'd left all her things behind, and there was no way she was just going to abandon them forever.

Joey had watched earlier in the day as the police had come and searched the house. Probably looking for evidence, but he hadn't left them any. He'd been smart earlier and had worn gloves so as not to leave any fingerprints. They'd stayed a few hours, but once they'd gone, he'd been able to creep back inside the house and take stock of her belongings.

She had some nice stuff, he had to admit. A lot of it was old, but he could still get a good price for the electronics. It might be worth pawning some of it later, if only to pad his pockets. Might as well get some benefits out of this wasted opportunity.

"Not now," he said to himself. He didn't want her to run as soon as she came back home. He needed her to stay so he could talk to her, find out where she'd put the papers. Later, after he'd delivered the goods to Uncle Sal, he might come back and clean her out. But he had to be patient, play the long game.

So he'd left again, but he'd taken care to unlock the back door. It had worked for him once; he could make it work a second time. Besides, she wouldn't expect him to come back. He had the element of surprise on his side.

A cold wind kicked up, making him wince. He huddled into his jacket and grabbed the cold metal door handle, giving it a tug. First things first. He'd grab a bite to eat here, then he'd head back to her place. She had to come back sometime.

And when she did, he'd be waiting for her.

Chapter 10

Fiona woke slowly, reluctantly rising from the depths of sleep to a greater awareness of her surroundings. She was surrounded by warmth and softness, and, for a moment, she wanted nothing more than to stay there forever. But then her body woke up, her stomach rumbling and her bladder doing its part to get her attention. She was going to have to get out of bed after all.

She opened her eyes and smiled at Slinky. He was curled up in a ball, his back resting against her stomach. It was his favorite spot, and she always enjoyed cuddling with him. She smoothed her hand over his body, and he stretched in his sleep before settling back into place with a contented sigh.

Fiona arched her back, then froze as something behind her moved, as well. For a panicked second, she wondered what, exactly, was in bed with her. Then it all came rushing back—her nightmare, waking up to find Nate in her room, his offering to stay until she fell asleep. He must have gotten tired, too, waiting on her.

Waking up next to a man was a new experience for her, one that she wished she could savor. But, at the same time, it was a little awkward. How bad was her morning breath? And her hair—it must be sticking out everywhere. Normally, she didn't care what she looked like in the mornings. The only male around to see her was Slinky, and as long as she fed him, he didn't judge her appearance. But this was Nate. And he probably looked perfect, no matter the time of day.

She slowly turned her head, slitting her eyes open to get a glimpse of him. Yep, it was just as she'd suspected. He was still aggravatingly handsome. The stubble on his cheeks was a little heavier than last night, giving him a bad-boy look. And his hair, though tousled, looked expensively styled rather than like bedhead. She ran her gaze up to his eyes to find that he was regarding her, as well, his own lids half-open.

"Hey there," he said, his voice rough with sleep. The corner of his mouth curled up. "Is it safe to open our eyes now?"

She smiled back. "I wasn't sure if you were awake yet."

"So naturally you squinted at me to keep the full force of your gaze from tearing me out of sleep. How thoughtful of you."

Fiona couldn't help but laugh. Then the realization of what she'd done kicked in, and she clapped a hand over her mouth. "I'm sorry," she said from behind her hand. "I didn't mean to breathe on you."

It was Nate's turn to laugh. "It's okay. A little morning breath never killed anyone."

"I suppose you're right." But she didn't want to test that theory, so she kept her hand where it was.

"Are you hungry? I could fix us something to eat."

At hearing the word *eat*, Slinky lifted his head and meowed. Nate leaned over her and regarded the cat with a raised brow. "I'll even make something for you, buddy."

"That sounds really nice," Fiona said. "Let me run to the bathroom, and I'll come out and help you."

"Take your time," Nate replied, sliding gracefully from the bed. "Go ahead and shower. It'll take me a few minutes to get everything put together. And I'm sure Slinky will be happy to help me."

At the sound of his name, Slinky stood and stretched, then walked over to the side of the bed and sat, looking up at Nate expectantly. "Ready?" Nate asked him, then turned to go. Slinky jumped down, trotting after him and the promise of food.

Fiona watched them leave, a feeling of contentment stealing over her. It hadn't taken Nate very long to fit into her life, and she wondered if he thought the same about her. Or perhaps this was just a moment out of time. Maybe once they returned to their normal routines, the magic between them would dissipate, too flimsy to withstand the rigors of daily life.

She shook her head and climbed out of bed. She had to stop overanalyzing everything. It was a trait that served her well as a graduate student, but it didn't always help in her personal life.

Twenty minutes later, she stepped into the kitchen to find Slinky sitting on the table, watching Nate as he stood in front of the stove.

"So you see," Nate was saying, "you have to wait until just the right moment to flip the omelet. If you flip it too soon, the eggs don't get cooked all the way through and it's too runny. But if you wait too long, it gets burned. It's a matter of timing."

Slinky mewed in response, and Nate shook his head. "No, I told you it's too early. You just stick with your cat food, and leave me in charge of the human breakfast."

Fiona snorted out a laugh and Nate whirled around, his cheeks and the tips of his ears turning a dark pink. "Oh, hey," he said, trying to sound nonchalant. "I didn't hear you come in."

She took pity on him. "I haven't been standing here long." She crossed to the fridge and tugged on the door, bending forward to check out the contents. She reached in and fished out the orange juice, then turned to find Nate's eyes on her. Or rather, her bottom.

Tingles raced through her system, making her feel warm despite her still-wet hair and the cool air in the apartment. "Ah, don't you want to flip those?" she asked innocently.

Nate turned back to the stove with a muffled oath, moving quickly to tend to the contents of the pan. Fiona grabbed two glasses and filled them with juice, then returned the carton to the fridge. She moved to the table and shooed Slinky off. "You know you're not supposed to sit on tables," she chided. He merely blinked at her and sauntered into the living room, no doubt heading for the couch and his morning nap.

Moving quickly, she wiped off the table and set out dishes and the juice. Nate walked over a moment later, the hot pan in one hand and a plate of toast in the other. He slid the omelets onto their plates with a flourish, and she had to admit they looked delicious.

They tasted even better. The eggs were fluffy and soft and practically melted in her mouth. Somehow, he had scrounged up ham, tomatoes and onion, and the ingredients all combined with the melted cheese to create a wonderful concoction that made her stomach celebrate.

"These are so good," she practically moaned. Nate merely grinned, but she could tell he appreciated the compliment. "I had no idea you could cook."

He shrugged. "This is nothing," he said, managing to sound modest. "My real specialty is chicken parmesan."

"I can't wait to try it." The words were out of her mouth before she could think twice, and she immediately wished them back. *Way to make things awkward.*

Nate didn't respond, lending further support to her conclusion that last night had been an anomaly. Time to change the subject.

"Should we look at those papers today?"

He nodded and swallowed. "Yeah, I think that would be a good idea." He forked another bite into his mouth and chewed, his gaze serious. "It's the only thing I can come up with that explains why you were targeted yesterday."

Fiona shook her head, the omelet turning to ash in her mouth. "I just can't believe Ben would do that to me."

"I hate to say it, but people will do almost anything in the interest of self-preservation." Nate swallowed his last bite and leaned back in the chair. "You'd be amazed at how quickly we can get criminals to flip on their buddies if we offer a reduced sentence or some other carrot."

"I suppose you're right. And it's not that I know Ben well at all—I only talk to him at work. We're definitely not friends. But I still assumed he had a basic level of decency, you know?"

Nate's mouth curved in a wry smile. "And that's your first mistake."

Fiona studied him for a moment, chewing a bite of toast. "You sound burned-out."

He lifted one shoulder in a shrug. "Maybe a little bit. In my job, I see the worst of people day in and day out. It's hard not to become jaded with that regular parade of heartbreak."

"But you keep doing it."

"Well, yeah." He sounded surprised, as though there was no other option. "I feel I still make a difference. I'm not going to quit when I can help people."

His answer made sense, and she recognized his attitude. It was the same one her father had had, a belief that he was doing good work and changing lives. And Nate was—she was living proof of that. After all, if he hadn't been in the store two nights ago, the attempted robbery would have gone very differently.

But she couldn't help wondering what this job cost Nate. Helping people was great, but he was paying a high price for his dedication. From what she could tell, Nate's relationship with his family was strained at best. Did he even realize what he was sacrificing? Or did he just not care? Either way, his dedication to the job at the expense of his family was troubling.

Fiona swallowed the last bite of toast. "Why don't you hop in the shower while I clean up here?"

"You don't mind?"

"Not at all. You cooked, so it's the least I can do."

He thanked her with a smile and left. She busied herself clearing the table and washing the dishes, trying to push thoughts of Nate and his family out of her mind. It really wasn't any of her business what kind of relationship he had with his parents and sister. For all she knew, they had been physically or emotionally abusive, and he'd cut them out of his life for a good reason. But, based on what he'd told her about his childhood, that didn't sound right.

Still, just because she would give anything for a family didn't mean he felt the same way. Maybe he was comfortable maintaining an emotional distance from his parents—not everyone needed to have a close relationship with their loved ones to feel happy. Her mom had been her best friend, but it was probably different for sons.

Probably.

She grabbed a towel and began to dry the pots and pans he'd used. She was likely getting ahead of herself, but Nate's disconnect with his family was enough to cool her feelings for him somewhat. Oh, sure, he was still handsome, and she was still physically attracted to him. But she'd always imagined herself with someone who valued family and who wanted to build a family with her. Not a man who spent so much time working that he had no energy left for the people closest to him.

"Doesn't matter," she told herself. "We're not there yet."

"We're not where?" Nate asked, stepping into the room as he rubbed his hair with a towel. He smelled like soap and fabric softener, and Fiona inhaled appreciatively. He removed the towel from his head to reveal his hair, still damp and a little bit spiky after the vigorous drying. It made him look younger, and she couldn't help but smile.

He reached up and brushed his hair into its normal style, then looked at her expectantly. She realized with a start that he'd asked her a question. "Uh, we're not at the station yet," she managed. "So that means you haven't heard any more about the robber from last night." It was true, and it sounded vaguely plausible.

Fortunately, Nate seemed to buy it. "We'll head in after you take a look at those papers." He stepped back into the living room and returned a second later with the stack, which he placed on the kitchen table. "Ready to get to it?"

Fiona pulled out a chair and sat with a sigh. "Sure thing."

It didn't take long to move through the papers. Routine store invoices and work orders weren't the kind of thing people would commit violent robbery to possess, and she said as much to Nate. He nodded. "It was a bit of a long shot, but worth a try."

She reached the end of the stack and grabbed the manila envelope that was left. That was unusual; she'd never known Ben to organize any of the store papers like that. She tore open the flap and dumped the contents onto the table, surprised to see a collection of color photographs tumble out rather than the expected receipts.

Nate reached out and grabbed a picture, turning it over and examining it with a frown. Fiona picked up a second photo.

It was a close-up of a man and a woman locked in a passionate embrace. She didn't recognize either of the people, but then again why should she?

She looked at another photo. The same couple, but this time he had his arm around her shoulders and they were walking side by side. He was an older man, his hair threaded with silver and a little extra weight around his midsection. But he carried himself well, with the kind of confidence that made people overlook physical flaws. The woman obviously adored him—she gazed up at him with her heart in her eyes, apparently hanging on his every word.

"Well," she said, uncertain why Ben would have pictures like this in his possession. "This is unusual. I've never seen these before."

"Hmm," Nate replied, clearly lost in thought. He scrutinized each photo, and when he was finished, he lifted his head and met her gaze. "Your boss is blackmailing someone."

"What makes you say that?" How did he come to that conclusion after looking at a few pictures?

"First of all, see how each shot uses a telephoto lens? You can see their faces and their bodies, but they clearly don't know they're being photographed. That tells me the photographer is being sneaky."

"Sure." She nodded, scanning the pictures again. He was correct—they were all taken from a distance.

"And notice how each photo shows the couple in some kind of intimate position? They're not seen having sex, but you can tell by the way they touch each other that they're physically involved." He lined them all up, showing the couple progressing from a hug to a walking embrace to kissing in the middle of the street, oblivious to passersby.

"Finally," he said, tapping one picture, "see how he's wearing a wedding ring? And she's not?"

Fiona pulled the picture closer for a better look, no longer surprised that he was right. "How did you see all that from a glance?"

He offered her a small smile. "I'm a detective. It's my job to notice details."

"I'm going to start calling you Sherlock."

That earned her a laugh. "Just keep it between us, okay? Owen would never let me hear the end of it."

"I can do that." She turned her attention back to the pictures. "Do you recognize these people?"

He tilted his head to the side. "He looks a little familiar, but I'm not sure where I've seen him before."

"Do you have a book of mug shots we can look at? Maybe you've arrested him before or something?"

"Maybe," Nate replied, sounding distracted. "But as for a book, I can do you one better. We'll scan this in at the station, and there's a program that will compare his face to the collection of images we have on file. If he's in the system, we'll find him."

"Sounds good to me. Shall we get to it?"

Nate stood and held out his arm. "After you."

Nate pushed away from the computer with a sigh. "Well, it's done," he said, turning to face Fiona. "I'm not sure how long it will take for the computer to locate a match, but we should probably find something else to do. Waiting on the program is a bit like watching paint dry."

"So it's not like they show in the movies?" she asked, a teasing note in her voice. "It only takes those cops a few minutes to find their man."

"That's because they're just better at their jobs than I am," he replied soberly before smiling back at her. It was nice to have her around. She didn't seem to take him too seriously, and he enjoyed the banter that seemed to come so easily to them.

"So what should we do now?"

He glanced over at her, pleased that she looked stronger than she had yesterday. "We can stop by your house and you can pick up some clothes," he suggested. Now that she'd had a good night's sleep—after the nightmare, that is—she might not be so distressed by going back to the scene of the break-in. And this time she wouldn't be going alone. He'd be there to make sure she felt safe.

Her face brightened. "That would be nice. Plus, I'd like to check and see if anything is missing."

"That's a good idea." Normally after a break-in, the homeowner was present to tell the investigating officers if anything had been taken. But in Fiona's case, she'd fled the scene and hadn't been able to make a report. While Nate doubted the man had stolen anything, it would still be good to have her confirm it.

He stood and gestured for her to follow him. They found Owen in the break room, preparing a cup of coffee.

"Hey," his partner said, looking up from stirring cream into his brew. "Did you get settled in at Hannah's?"

"Yes," Fiona replied, smiling at him. "And please thank her again—I really appreciate her letting me crash in her home."

"It's no problem. She's happy to be able to help." Owen's face softened at the mention of Hannah, and Nate fleetingly wondered if *he* looked like that when he thought of Fiona. Surely not. They hadn't known each other long enough for that, right?

"Did you get a chance to look through those papers yet?"

That was his cue, and Nate spoke up. "We did, and the only odd finding was an envelope of photos. It's clear they're being used for blackmail, and the male subject looks familiar."

"You scan them in?"

Nate nodded. "Waiting on the program now."

"Want some coffee?" Owen offered, looking at Fiona.

Nate felt a small pang of embarrassment. He should have thought to offer her something to drink, but he'd been so distracted by the job at hand that it hadn't occurred to him. It was further proof he had no business trying to be Fiona's boyfriend.

"No, thanks," she replied. "I definitely don't need any caffeine right now."

"You're obviously not a cop," Owen joked, which made her laugh. "We live on this stuff."

"Gotta keep your energy up to chase the bad guys," Fiona said.

Owen nodded, pausing to take a sip. "True enough."

"We're going to check out her place, pick up some clothes and stuff," Nate said. "Do you mind keeping an eye on the computer and calling me if a match comes up?"

Owen nodded. "No problem. Let me know if you need anything while you're out."

"Thanks, man." Nate put his hand on Fiona's back and guided her out of the station. It felt entirely too good to touch her, and he was quickly getting into the habit of resting his hand at the small of her back. It was a casual gesture, but any contact with her body made his heart thump double time. He flashed back to last night and the way she had touched him, her fingers simultaneously tentative and bold, as if she was hungry to explore his body but felt too shy to really let go. And, fortunately for him, she hadn't. It had been hard enough stopping things before they went too far. If Fiona had truly pushed him, he would have surrendered to the moment. He was a strong man, but there wasn't enough self-control in the world when it came to his reaction to her.

In the end, though, he'd done the right thing. While he wanted nothing more than to tear off her clothes and lose himself in her, he knew she deserved more than some fleeting moments of pleasure. Fiona was the kind of woman who was worth the effort of a relationship— the sacrifices, the time, the little gestures that told her she was important. All the things he couldn't give her right now, thanks to his job and his family situation.

With a mental sigh, he pushed his disappointment to the side. He would have time to mope later. Now, he owed it to Fiona to keep her safe until he and Owen could figure out who was threatening her and why.

It didn't take long to get to her house; for once, Houston traffic wasn't horrible. "Probably a sign of the coming apocalypse," Fiona joked, and he had to agree.

Her home looked a little sad in the light of day, especially with the yellow crime-scene tape bisecting her front door. "Is it okay for us to go inside?" she asked, frowning.

"Absolutely," he assured her. "The evidence-response team gathered what they needed yesterday. They left the tape in place to discourage any nosy neighbors."

"Speaking of neighbors," she muttered. She glanced at the house across the street and winced. He followed her gaze to the jumbled pile of bricks that had once been her neighbor's mailbox. "I really need to apologize to Mr. Huffnagel," she said, sounding guilty. "I tore out of here so fast yesterday that I backed right into his mailbox."

"I'm sure he'll understand," Nate said. "We can stop by when you're done here and explain the situation to him."

"Sounds good," she said. Nate killed the engine, and they climbed out of the car. Fiona eyed the door suspiciously. "So do I just break through the tape, or do I need to reapply it after we're done?"

"You can break it," he replied. "There's no need to put it back up." He took a step forward with her, but just then his phone buzzed in his pocket. He dug it out and recognized Owen's extension. "Go in and get started," he said, waving her on. "I'll talk to Owen and meet you inside in a minute."

Fiona nodded and headed into the house. Nate took a step back and answered the phone. "That was fast," he said, in lieu of a greeting.

"You're not going to believe who came up as a match." Owen sounded excited, and Nate's own adrenaline spiked in response.

"Don't keep me waiting," he said, his fingers starting to tingle the way they always did when he was on the verge of a big break.

"Big Sal." Owen let the name hang in the air for a moment.

Nate combed his memory for the significance of the name. Then it hit him like a punch to the gut. "Big Sal, Houston's gambling king? *That* Big Sal?"

"The one and only." He could hear the smile in his partner's voice and knew he was enjoying this.

Nate let out a low whistle. "That's interesting."

"Isn't it, though?"

"And I take it the woman in the photos isn't his wife?" Nate ventured.

"Definitely not," Owen replied. "And here's the kicker...even though he likes to think of himself as a tough guy, Big Sal is known far and wide for his devotion to his wife. If she saw these pictures, she'd go ballistic."

"Hell hath no fury," Nate said softly.

Owen laughed. "From what I've heard, Mrs. Big Sal is a force to be reckoned with. It wouldn't surprise me at all if Big Sal was afraid of her."

"I wonder how Ben got those photos," Nate mused, thinking out loud. "Do you think he hired someone specifically to follow Big Sal, or did he steal them?"

"That I don't know," Owen said. "But I'd sure like to talk to him about it. I think I'll go pick him up, and when you get back to the station, we can have a little conversation with him."

"Sounds good," Nate said. "Thanks."

"Anytime, partner."

Nate hung up and tucked the phone back into his pocket. Then he walked up the driveway, shaking his head. Somehow, Ben had gotten hold of incriminating photos of one of Houston's most notorious criminals. And, unless he missed his guess, Ben was using those pictures to blackmail Big Sal, probably to get off the hook for a debt owed. The problem was, Big Sal had resources Ben could only dream about, and there was no way the man would take kindly to a little punk like Ben messing up his life.

"No wonder they're coming after Fiona," he said to

himself. "If Big Sal thinks she has the photos, he'll do anything to get them back."

In a way, this was good news. As soon as Big Sal got the pictures, Fiona would no longer be a target. A small, selfish part of him was saddened by this realization, as it meant he'd no longer have an excuse to spend time with her. But then his conscience kicked in, reminding him that getting her out of danger was more important than his pathetic crush on a woman he couldn't have.

"Fiona," he called, pushing open the door and entering the house. "I have good news."

She didn't respond, so he moved deeper inside. "Fiona," he repeated, raising his voice a little. Maybe she had her head buried in her closet and couldn't hear him very well.

Silence hung in the air, and a frisson of unease trickled down his back. Why wasn't she answering him? He started down the hall, but a strange scent stopped him in his tracks. He sniffed cautiously, trying to recognize it. It was slightly sweet, with a pungent tang that made his nose cold.

Chloroform.

His stomach dropped, and he quickly slipped his gun from its holster. "Fiona?" He made his way slowly down the hall, approaching her bedroom. It was a long shot, but maybe she was still inside…

Hope died when he stepped into the room and found it empty. There was an open bag on the bed where she had started packing, but she was nowhere to be found.

He quickly searched the rest of the house, but it was useless. There were no signs of a struggle, which made him think whoever had taken her had sneaked up on her from behind and incapacitated her before she could raise an alarm. But where had they gone?

Definitely not through the front door. He'd been in the driveway the whole time and hadn't seen anything amiss. The back door, then. Nate practically ran onto the porch, his head swiveling from side to side as he looked for any signs of her.

Nothing. His throat tightened, making it hard to breathe. He had to find her!

For the first time, he noticed that her yard backed up to an easement, a grassy alley that ran between her home and the one behind it. The easement stretched the length of the street, and it would have been easy for the assailant to knock her out, throw her over his shoulder and escape through the back door. If he'd parked his car at the end of the grassy strip, he could have dumped her inside and taken off without attracting much notice. Nate certainly hadn't heard an engine start up, and no wonder—the distance from Fiona's house to the end of the easement was easily a hundred yards, plenty of space to muffle sounds and mask a hasty getaway.

Nate cursed a blue streak, but it did nothing to relieve the heavy sense of dread weighing on his chest. How had he let this happen? He'd promised to keep her safe, and he'd failed spectacularly. What kind of a cop yakked on his phone while a woman was kidnapped mere feet from him?

He hastily dialed Owen, his hand shaking so badly it took several tries to get the number right. "She's gone," he said, as soon as his partner picked up. He could hear the thread of panic in his voice, but he didn't care.

"What?"

Nate took a deep breath to stem the rising tide of impatience. Yelling at Owen wasn't going to bring Fiona back, and it wasn't the other man's fault that Nate couldn't speak coherently right now. "Fiona has been taken," he clarified.

Owen cursed. "Did you see who took her?"

"No. But I smelled chloroform in the house. She didn't put up a struggle."

"That's good," Owen replied. "Means she probably didn't get hurt."

Nate hadn't thought of it that way, but the idea was of little comfort. The fact remained that Fiona had been taken against her will, and right under his nose!

"I'll send out the evidence-response team," his partner continued. "In the meantime, you should come back to the station."

"I can't," Nate said. He felt both frustrated and helpless, and he had to do *something*. Going back to the station felt like an acknowledgment of defeat, as if he was giving up on finding her.

"You didn't see who took her," Owen pointed out. "And I'm assuming that means you didn't see where they went. So what do you think you're going to accomplish, running around with no direction or clues to guide you? Come back to the station, and we can work together to find her."

It was a persuasive argument, but Nate couldn't bring himself to accept it.

"Just send the team here, and go pick up Ben. I want to talk to him. Also, dispatch some officers to check out Joey's place."

"You think the guy who tried to rob the store took Fiona?"

"Maybe." Nate tapped his fingers against the side of his leg, trying to think. "I can't afford to overlook the possibility. Not when Fiona's safety is at stake."

"And where are you going?"

Nate ran a hand through his hair, suddenly realizing what he had to do.

"I'm going to pay Big Sal a visit."

Chapter 11

Fiona opened her eyes and immediately wished she hadn't. She was in a dim room, but the small amount of light that illuminated the space pierced her eyes and sent sharp, stabbing pain directly into her brain. She lifted a heavy hand and laid it across her face, wanting to return to the soothing relief of darkness.

Her mouth felt as if it was stuffed with cotton balls, and she tried to swallow. It hurt, and she choked back a moan as the dry tissues of her throat rubbed together painfully.

Where am I?

She squinted from between her fingers, trying to make out the details of the room. She was lying on a small bed, the mattress lumpy and smelling faintly of mothballs, which did nothing to help her aching head.

The carpet had once been beige, but now it looked stained and greasy, and she drew her legs up to make sure she wasn't touching it. The bed probably wasn't any better, but she steadfastly refused to look at it.

There was a small window high in the wall, enough to let in some light but not big enough to serve as an escape route. Not that she could use it—her head was spinning like a merry-go-round, and her stomach heaved threateningly. *Don't throw up*, she told herself firmly.

She took a few deep breaths, which seemed to help a little. What had happened? The last thing she remembered was standing in her bedroom, folded shirt in hand, packing a small bag of essentials. She'd heard footsteps in the hall and had assumed it was Nate, but he hadn't responded when she'd called out to him.

She frowned, having trouble focusing her thoughts. The memories were there, but they were shrouded in fog, making it hard for her to pick out the details and piece them together to form a complete picture. It hadn't been Nate, but who was it?

I never saw his face. Whoever it was, he had come up from behind her and clapped a hand over her face. A horrible scent had flooded her nose—sweet and cloying and vile. She'd gagged, but before she could try to push him away, her vision had narrowed and quickly faded to black.

How long have I been out? Hours? Days? The thought that she may have lost so much time sent a chill down her spine and made her guts cramp. She could be anywhere at this point—there was no way to tell, unless she could get a glimpse of what lay outside.

Determination gave her the strength to roll over onto her stomach, and she drew her knees up and pushed until she was kneeling on the bed. The movement made the room tilt dangerously, but she clenched her jaw and sucked in a breath until she felt stable again. It took a few, painful moments, but eventually she was able to stand on shaky legs, gripping the wall for support.

Unfortunately, the view didn't tell her much. The window was obscured by a tangle of brown vines that blocked her view, and she bit her lip to keep from crying in frustration. All that effort, wasted!

She sank back onto the bed, causing the mattress springs to squeak loudly in protest. Think, she had to think! There had to be a way to get out of here, or at the very least, to summon help. She patted her pockets halfheartedly, already knowing she wouldn't find her phone. That was still in her purse, which was back at the house.

Did Nate even know she was gone yet? Maybe her kidnapper had left some clues, and he was even now on his way to rescue her. It was a nice fantasy, and for a moment she comforted herself with thoughts of Nate breaking down the door, gathering her into his arms and carrying her away from this dingy, dreary place.

"Not likely," she muttered. This was real life, not some adventure movie, and if she was going to get away she would have to do it on her own. But how?

Before she could come up with an answer to her own question, the silence was broken by the sound of footsteps coming closer. Fiona scanned the room for a hiding place but came up empty. There was no closet, and the bed she sat on was the only piece of furniture in the place. She had nowhere to go, no way to protect herself from whoever was on the other side of the door.

Her heart pounded loudly in her ears, almost drowning out the metallic scrape of a key turning in a lock. The door flew open, and a tall figure stood on the threshold, his height nearly filling the space. She blinked and instinctively shrank back, but there was no escaping him. If he'd come here to hurt her, she was totally defenseless.

"Good. You're up." He took a step inside and closed the door behind him, trapping her in the room with him. She swallowed hard, determined not to let her fear get the better of her.

"Who are you? Why did you bring me here?"

The man ran a hand over his head, knocking the hood of his jacket back and revealing his face. Fiona got her first good look at his features and gasped in recognition. It was Joey, the guy who had tried to rob the store! But why had he taken her? Was he upset she had decided to press charges?

"Ben said you have the photos. I need them."

It took her a moment to register what he was saying. Pictures? That was the cause of all of this? He had taken her because he wanted the pictures Ben had handed her? She shook her head, equal parts dismayed and aggravated. Unfortunately, the gesture only served to exacerbate her headache, and she reached up to rub her forehead.

"All you had to do was ask," she said, a little testily. "I would have given you the damn things. You didn't have to kidnap me."

"You ran away from me earlier before I could say anything," he pointed out, sounding a little pouty.

"Because you broke into my home!" Did she really have to explain her reaction to his break-in? What was *wrong* with this guy?

He shrugged, wincing slightly. *His shoulder must still be bothering him*, she realized. That wasn't surprising—he'd been shot only two days ago. Could she use that to her advantage?

"It doesn't matter now," he replied. "Just give me the pictures, and I'll let you go."

Fiona's stomach dropped. "I… I don't have them." She watched him carefully, trying to anticipate his reaction. Would he attack her? Her muscles tensed, and she clenched her hands into fists, preparing to defend herself. He definitely had a size advantage over her, but maybe she could land some good hits before going down…

He took a menacing step toward her, but drew up short before he hit the edge of the bed. "What do you mean you don't have them? Are you saying Ben lied to me?"

Fiona's mind whirred with possible responses. If she sent him back to Ben, it would give her more time to work out an escape. But could she really do that? She didn't like to think she was the kind of person who would deliberately put someone else in danger, but, in Ben's case, she might be willing to make an exception.

On the other hand, what if she told the truth? How would Joey react to the news that the photos he sought were in police custody?

Probably not very well, she thought, eyeing him thoughtfully. If he felt there was no chance of retrieving the pictures, there would be nothing to keep him from hurting her. He was already desperate. Adding hopelessness to the mix would create a volatile combination of emotions that would likely break the apparently tenuous hold he had on his self-control.

In the end, self-preservation won. "I don't know what Ben told you," she said. "But the last time I saw the photos, he was taking them out to his car. He's probably got them at home." There. Let Joey track Ben down and leave her alone.

He glared at her for a moment, digesting her words. "How do I know you're not lying to me?"

She shrugged, trying to look convincing. "Look at me. You know I don't have the pictures on me, and I'm assuming you searched my house while you were waiting for me."

He nodded in the affirmative, which sent a spike of anger coursing through her system. How dare he paw through her things and invade her privacy like that? She wanted to slap him but took a deep breath, instead. *Not now*, she told herself. *Just get him to leave.*

"Well then, you know I don't have them," she concluded. "Ben's the only one who could."

"I guess so," Joey said slowly. He frowned, apparently confused by this new twist.

"If you really want those pictures, you should let

me go and track down Ben. He's the one you want." She tried to sound convincing but not too eager. Joey seemed like a spiteful kind of guy, the type who would deliberately do the opposite of what she wanted just because she wanted it. He reminded her of a confrontational child who misbehaved to test his limits, only Joey was big enough to be dangerous.

"Maybe," he replied. He narrowed his eyes at her. "But I can't just let you go."

"Sure you can," she coaxed.

"No," he said, more definitively. "You'll just run to the police, like you did the other day."

Fiona shook her head. "I won't," she said firmly. "I'll forget this ever happened."

He rocked back on his heels, his head tilted. "I don't think so. You're staying here until I get what I need."

Dammit. Still, it was better than the alternative. "Fine," she said, not bothering to keep the resentment out of her tone. "Then get out of here. The sooner you find Ben and the photos, the sooner you'll have to let me go."

A small smile flitted across his face, as though he had a secret he wasn't willing to share. "Sure thing," he replied, taking another step closer. Fiona pushed back on the mattress, but her back hit the wall and she couldn't put any more space between them.

"What are you doing?"

"I'm leaving," he said. "But before I go, I need to make sure you don't try anything while I'm gone." He reached into his pocket and pulled out a syringe.

Fiona kicked out, panic making her movements frantic and uncoordinated. "Don't touch me," she warned, trying to sound tough.

"Or you'll what?" he taunted. He stood there for a moment, smirking down at her. Then he lashed out like a snake, grabbing an ankle and tugging sharply so that she was knocked flat on the bed.

"Stop it!" She pushed against him, trying to break his grip, but he only tightened his fingers. Moving quickly, he pushed his knee into her stomach and leaned forward, cutting off her ability to breathe and effectively immobilizing her. There was a sharp sting in her thigh, and after a moment, he moved off her.

Fiona curled into a ball, trying to protect her bruised stomach. Gone was the desire to fight him—she just wanted him to leave her alone.

A tingling sensation radiated from the sore spot where he had injected her, quickly extending down her leg and up into her abdomen. Numbness began to set in, and her limbs grew heavy. Joey stood at the edge of the bed looking down on her, his eyes bright with an unnatural gleam that made her think of a venomous spider watching the death throes of its prey. She tried to glare at him, but her facial muscles wouldn't cooperate.

"Sleep tight," he said, his voice taking on a singsong quality that sent a chill down her spine.

Fiona fought to keep her eyes open, but it was so very, very hard. Joey laughed and waggled his fingers in a disturbing little wave, and then she gave up the battle and let the darkness settle over her.

Nate threw the gearshift into Park and forced himself to take a deep breath before climbing out. He wouldn't get anywhere if he went storming into Big Sal's office making demands. Big Sal was the kind of man who fancied himself a gentleman, and from what Nate had heard, he insisted on acting the part.

At least in public.

"Don't underestimate him," Carl had warned. After a career spent working in the vice squad, Carl had been Nate's go-to source for information on Big Sal. And he hadn't disappointed. He'd given Nate a quick but thorough rundown of Big Sal's operation and habits, and while Nate didn't feel as prepared as he would like, at least he wasn't walking into the situation blind.

He walked into the building and was surprised to find a young woman sitting behind a desk. He hadn't expected to encounter a receptionist, and he supposed it was meant to make the operation seem more legitimate.

She looked up from her desk and offered him a polite smile. "Can I help you?"

"I'm here to see Mr. Salvatore."

She nodded. "And your name please?"

"Nate Gallagher."

Her brows drew together in a small frown as she consulted her computer. "I'm sorry, I don't see you on Mr. Salvatore's schedule for this afternoon. Would you care to make an appointment?"

Nate shook his head. "Nope. That won't be necessary." He showed the woman his badge and stepped around her desk. "I'm sure he can make time for me."

"Sir!" She sprang up from the chair and darted in front of him, physically blocking him from moving forward. "You can't just barge in there!"

He lifted a brow as he stared down at her. "Ma'am, I suggest you move. Now," he added, injecting a bit of steel into his voice.

She regarded him with wide eyes. "I can't," she said, her voice soft. "If I let you in there, he'll fire me. And I really need this job!"

There was genuine fear in her eyes, and for a brief moment Nate felt sorry for her. But he couldn't let this unknown woman's situation keep him from talking to Big Sal, especially when Fiona's safety was at stake.

"I'll tell him you tried to stop me," Nate promised. He put his hands on her shoulders and gently moved her aside, ignoring her pleading gaze. "Follow me closely and make a scene, and he won't fire you."

She nodded, biting her bottom lip. "Thank you," she said.

"Let's go." He'd wasted enough time out here.

He stepped forward and pushed open the door, the receptionist hot on his heels. "Sir, you really can't go in there," she said loudly, grabbing his arm for good measure.

Nate shot her a look over his shoulder before turning back. Big Sal sat behind his desk, staring at the doorway with a look of mild surprise. "What is this?"

Before Nate could introduce himself, the receptionist spoke up. "I tried to stop him, sir. But he insisted!"

Big Sal nodded at her. "That's fine, Josie. I'll take care of this."

She let out a quiet sigh of relief before retreating out of the room. Nate shut the door behind her, then walked forward until he stood in front of Big Sal's desk. The man eyed him up and down in a blatant assessment, and Nate returned the favor. They stared at each other for a moment until Big Sal broke the silence.

"And you are?" He sounded bored, but Nate could tell by the way his jaw tensed that his silence rattled the other man. He debated on staying quiet to prolong the discomfort but decided against it. Time was of the essence.

"Nate Gallagher. Houston police."

If the mention of law enforcement rattled the gambling king, he didn't show it. In fact, it seemed to have the opposite effect.

Big Sal leaned back in his chair, a wide smile spreading across his face. "A police officer?" he said solicitously. "Why didn't you just say so in the first place?" He gestured to one of the chairs in front of his desk. "Please, have a seat."

Nate's impatience was building like a summer storm, but he pushed the feeling aside. He could play the game for a few minutes at least.

Maybe.

"What can I do for you?"

"I have reason to believe one of your associates has kidnapped a woman. I'm here to get her back." That sounded diplomatic, right?

Big Sal lifted one bushy eyebrow. "That's quite an accusation. Why would I be interested in kidnapping someone?"

"Because she was in possession of some rather incriminating photos that show you in an unflattering light. The kind of pictures you wouldn't want to be seen by the wider world."

Big Sal's nostrils flared, but other than that subtle tell, his expression remained unchanged. "Oh, really?"

Nate nodded. "Fiona, the woman you took, works at a convenience store owned by Ben Carter. Recognize the name?"

The other man nodded slightly. "Go on."

"For some reason, Ben has the pictures I mentioned. Now, I don't know the whole story, but I'm guessing Ben made a bet with you, one that he lost. And *I'm* willing to bet he tried to blackmail you rather than pay up."

A smile flickered at the corners of Big Sal's mouth. "He wouldn't be the first person to try such a thing."

"He probably won't be the last, either," Nate observed. "And while I normally wouldn't care how you resolve such situations, I do take issue with you kidnapping an innocent woman."

"I haven't kidnapped anyone," the man said, spreading his hands wide. "I would never do that."

Nate barely resisted the temptation to roll his eyes. "Please don't treat me like I'm stupid. Of course you didn't do it yourself—you have people to do your dirty work for you. But the end result is the same. What's that old saying? The buck stops here?"

Big Sal narrowed his eyes slightly. "Normally, I would agree with you. But, as I said before, I didn't kidnap anyone, nor have I instructed any of my associates to do so on my behalf. That's not how I operate my business."

Nate shook his head. "I want to believe you, I really do. But try to see this from my perspective. All the evidence points to you. There's an attempted robbery at Ben's store. The next day, he gives the incriminating photos he has of you to Fiona. Her home is broken into, and she barely escapes the assailant. Now, she's missing. You're a shrewd man—I'm sure you can understand my suspicions here."

Big Sal let out a sigh. "You have my sympathies, Detective. But all I can do is repeat, once again, that I have nothing to do with this woman's disappearance." He stood, making it clear their discussion was over. "Now, unless you have a search warrant…?" He trailed off suggestively. When Nate didn't respond, he smiled. "As I thought. And while I would be happy to continue our talk, I do have an appointment. So if you'll see yourself out?"

Nate rose and fixed the other man with a stare. "We're not done here," he warned.

Big Sal's smile was polite, but it didn't reach his eyes. "I'm a busy man, Detective, and I'm sure the same goes for you. I trust you will not bother me again, unless you have something more than unfounded accusations to discuss."

Recognizing he had lost this round, Nate turned and walked to the door. He knew in his gut that Big Sal was somehow involved in Fiona's abduction, but until he could come up with concrete proof, he didn't have many options.

He gave the receptionist his card on his way out. Maybe, just maybe, she would notice something and call him.

He climbed back into his car with a sigh of frustration. He'd hoped to rattle Big Sal's cage, but the other man wouldn't give him the satisfaction. Hopefully, his visit had at least served to put the gambling kingpin on notice that he was being watched.

Anger filled his chest, and he punched the steering wheel hard, sending pain shooting up his arm. There had to be something else he could do, some clue he was missing.

"Where are you, baby?" he muttered.

There was no response, of course. He hadn't actually expected one. But the silence merely drove home the fact that Fiona was gone.

The past two days had been like a wake-up call for him. Fiona's presence had made him realize how empty his life had been. He'd dedicated himself to his job, all in the name of being able to provide for his sister when the time came. But had that really been the right thing to do? What experiences had he missed by staying so focused on that distant goal? Had he traded the life he could have had now for the one he thought he would have in the future?

For the first time in a long time, he missed his family. And even though he was a grown man, right now he needed a little reassurance that things would work out. He didn't want to expose his parents to the nasty realities of his job, but he could use some unconditional encouragement, the kind only a father could provide.

He tugged his phone free from his pocket and sat staring at it for a moment, gathering up the courage to make the call. Would they hang up on him? He hadn't spoken to them in so long, it was probably what he deserved. He shook his head and started to put the phone away, but the memory of Fiona's face popped into his mind. She'd worn an expression of naked yearning when she spoke of missing her parents and her desire to have a family of her own. She would want him to make this call, and maybe talking to his parents would bring him a little closer to Fiona, if only in spirit.

It was better than nothing.

Taking a deep breath, he began to dial.

Big Sal waited until the detective left his office before sinking back down into his chair. What the hell had Joey done now?

Just when he thought the kid couldn't screw up any worse, he managed to find a new level of incompetence. And now the police were involved.

His mind whirled with the implications of that realization. The police had custody of the photographs, which meant there was no way Joey could get his hands on them. Sal could get them back—he had officers on his payroll, after all—but how many people had seen them? What kind of damage had already been done?

He reached for the phone on his desk and punched out a number, trying hard not to take his anger out on the keypad. The little bastard had better pick up…

After a few rings, Joey answered. "Yeah?" He sounded out of breath, like he'd been running.

"What have you done?" Sal wanted to yell but knew from experience he got better results by keeping his voice deadly calm.

"What do you mean?" Joey's voice cracked. "I'm working on getting the pictures like you asked. It hasn't been twenty-four hours yet. I still have some time!" He sounded scared, and normally Sal would have enjoyed hearing that note of fear in a subordinate's voice. But things had come too far for that now.

"I just had a visit from a police detective. He seems to think I'm involved in kidnapping a woman who works at Ben Carter's store. Why would he be under that impression?"

Joey sucked in a breath. "Uh," he stammered. "She has the pictures."

"No, she doesn't."

There was a pause as Joey digested this information. "How do you know that?"

Sal ground his teeth together, wishing there was something nearby he could hit. "Because the police have them."

"Oh."

The word sounded hollow, and Sal fought the urge to mock him. "That's it? That's all you can say?"

"I didn't know," his nephew replied, going on the defensive. "How was I supposed to know the cops have them?"

Sal shook his head. "Just bring the woman to my office," he said. "I'll handle things from here."

"But, Uncle Sal—"

"No, Joey. You had your chance. You're done. Bring the woman to me, and we'll sort things out."

"You're not mad?"

Sal rolled his eyes. How could a grown man sound so

much like a child? It was repellant, the way his nephew regressed when confronted with any kind of authority. "No, I'm not mad," he lied. "Just come in so we can talk, okay?"

"Okay. I'll see you soon, Uncle Sal." Joey sounded relieved as he ended the call. That was good; it meant he wouldn't be expecting any kind of punishment.

Sal slid his hand into his jacket, running his fingers over the smooth metal of his gun. Normally, he didn't like to mete out justice himself, but in this case, he'd make an exception. Taking Joey out would go some way toward soothing his own anger, and from a practical standpoint, it kept even more people from getting involved in his business.

He leaned back in the chair, considering his next move. Damage control had to be a priority, that much was clear. He had to get those pictures back and hope that once the woman was returned safe and sound, police interest in the case would die down. Especially since her kidnapper would be dead.

Sal mulled over the speech he would give to the police. "He just showed up at my office, and he attacked me. I was forced to defend myself." That sounded plausible. Now he just had to rehearse it enough to make it stick.

He tried out different inflections, wanting it to sound natural. The only wild card was the woman. He was going to have to provoke Joey into attacking him so that she would agree with his version of events. That shouldn't be too hard, though. The kid had a short temper, and he was already feeling unstable.

His phone rang, breaking him out of his thoughts. He reached for it, not bothering to look at the display. "Yes?"

"Salvatore, what is going on up there?" The heavily accented female voice traveled across the line and wrapped around his guts like barbed wire. Oh, God. Isabella.

"What do you mean, *mi amor*?" He tried to play it cool. Maybe this was just a social call? He held his breath, hoping she was calling to chat or to set up another meeting. *Please don't let them know...*

"There are pictures of us? How could you let this happen?" Isabella sounded distinctly unhappy, a fact that did not improve his own mood.

"Calm down," he said, trying to soothe her. "I have everything under control."

"Calm down?" she shrieked. "You dare tell me to calm down?" He winced and held the phone away from his ear as she switched to a rapid stream of Spanish, her words flowing fast and furious.

"I'm sorry," he said, trying to be heard over the sounds of her temper. "I'm not trying to dismiss the gravity of the situation." He spoke loudly, and she piped down, giving him an opportunity to speak. "I'm in the process of getting the photos back, and all the people who know about them are being dealt with."

She was silent for a moment, but he could tell she wasn't assuaged. "This is most disappointing," she finally said, her tone dark. "We will have to reevaluate our relationship in light of this transgression."

Sal bit his tongue to keep from firing back a defensive retort. This wasn't his fault! But if he played that card, he'd be no better than Joey.

"I understand," he said, proud of himself for sounding calm. "But please take into consideration the fact that I am aware of the problem and am taking steps to correct it."

She huffed, as if his assurances held no weight with her anymore. "We will be in touch." Her words were part threat, part promise, and they made Sal's heart skip a beat. Then she hung up, the ring of the dial tone loud in his ear.

Sal put the phone receiver back in its cradle with a sigh. When it rained, it poured.

Time to reconsider his plan. The cartel obviously wanted blood, and he wasn't about to give himself up as the sacrificial lamb to slaughter. But if he handed over Ben and the woman? That might just work. If the cartel had someone to blame, someone to punish, they might be satisfied with stopping there. And if he was the man to take control of the situation and turn over the ones responsible? Well, that could only work in his favor.

His alliance with the organization was probably over, but he was willing to give up the promise of more power and influence if it meant staying alive. And who knew? After a few years, once things had calmed down and he'd shown them he could be trusted, maybe they would approach him again. Either way, he had to salvage what he could now, before it got any worse.

Chapter 12

"Wake up."

A stinging pain spread across her cheek, and Fiona moaned weakly in protest.

"Now."

Another slap, this one harder. She blinked open her eyes, trying to shake off the heavy blanket of sleep that clung to her consciousness. A blurry form filled her vision, and she squinted in an effort to pick out details.

"Time to go."

Fiona shook her head as she attempted to make sense of the words. Go where? What time was it? And where was she?

"Move! I don't have time for this!"

Whoever the blur was, he sounded angry. She struggled to make her limbs obey, but they were too heavy, as if they had been filled with lead.

Something cold hit her face, and she gasped in shock. It took her a few seconds to register what had happened—someone had thrown water in her face. It ran down her neck and chest, soaking her shirt and plastering it to her skin. She shivered reflexively, but it didn't help.

The chill helped chase away some of her mental fog, and her thoughts started to arrange themselves in logical patterns. Her home. Joey sneaking up on her, taking her here. Then the prick of the needle and the heavy weight of darkness slamming down on her.

She looked up to find him standing at the edge of the bed, his arms crossed over his chest as he frowned at her. "We're leaving."

"Why?" Her voice was a croak, and she stuck her tongue out to collect a few drops of water from her lips. It wasn't much, but it was better than nothing.

"You lied to me."

"No—" she began, but he cut her off.

"I went to Ben's, just to see if you were right and he still had the pictures. He was gone, but I searched his house. Nothing."

"Maybe they're in his car," she suggested.

Joey shook his head, his mouth set in a determined line. "Doesn't matter. You're coming with me." He wrapped his hand around her upper arm and tugged hard, dragging her off the bed.

Her head swam at the sudden change in position, and

she wobbled back and forth, trying not to fall. "Where are we going?"

"I'm taking you to Big Sal."

Who? But she didn't bother asking. It was hard enough standing up straight; she didn't have the brainpower needed to figure out where they were going and why.

Joey dragged her down the hall, stopping impatiently every few steps to keep her upright. "Quit stalling!" he snarled over his shoulder.

I'm not, Fiona wanted to protest. Having to use Joey for support was equal parts disgusting and disturbing, and she wanted nothing more than to be able to walk unassisted. But the drugs he'd given her were still in her system, and her willpower was no match for their soporific effects.

He shoved her into the backseat of the car, and Fiona gave up trying to stay upright. She slumped against the door, forcing her eyes to stay open so she could try to figure out where they were and where they were going. So far, she didn't recognize anything. Then, as Joey drove, they moved from a more remote neighborhood into the characteristic urban sprawl that surrounded Houston on all sides for miles around. The problem was that she couldn't pick out anything identifiable yet.

The scenery grew blurry and she blinked, releasing tears that slid down her cheeks. She didn't bother to wipe them away, and they fell on her already-damp shirt.

She had to do something. She couldn't stay at the mercy of Joey for much longer. But what were her op-

tions? She had no weapons; she was still too groggy
to effectively defend herself, and Joey was bigger and
stronger.

But he's hurt. The thought zinged through her brain
like a lightning bolt. He had been shot in the shoulder
while trying to rob the store, and even though it was
a flesh wound, it still had to be painful. If she could
somehow attack his injured shoulder, he'd be in too
much agony to fight back.

And then what? She frowned, not appreciating the
question. But her brain was right—she needed more
of a plan if she was going to get away. Punching Joey
in the shoulder was a good start, but she needed more
options for what came after.

The car jerked to a stop before she could complete
her thoughts. A moment later Joey yanked open the
back door, taking away Fiona's support. He grabbed
her arm and pulled her out before she could fall, and
she was pleased to note she was much steadier on her
feet now. Still, she made herself as limp as possible so
Joey wouldn't suspect anything. She had a better shot
of taking him by surprise if he didn't think she was capable of walking on her own.

He guided her toward a plain-looking building, and
she let her head loll back so she could glance around
without Joey noticing. There weren't any identifying
landmarks, and she couldn't see a street sign. But there
was a gas station on the corner, and a strip shopping
mall across the street. She'd have places to go when she
starting running...

Joey tugged her inside, shoving her past a desk. The

receptionist let out an astonished squeak, pushing to her feet and lifting an arm to try to stop them.

"Sir, you can't—"

"Shut up," he snapped. "I'm here to see my uncle."

The woman held her ground, blocking the door to an inner office. She glanced between them, her eyes growing wide as she looked at Fiona.

"Please help me," Fiona said softly.

"Quiet." Joey shook her hard enough to make her teeth clack together. Then he turned and fixed a glare on the receptionist. "Move. Now."

"I don't think—" she began. Joey stuck his hand into his pocket and pulled out a wicked-looking switchblade that he opened with a smooth flick of his wrist. Her mouth snapped shut, and the woman slid out of the way, her face now an unhealthy shade of green.

Fiona's heart rate spiked at the sight of the blade. It wasn't the first time Joey had threatened her with a weapon, but the knife seemed so much more danger-ous than the gun. One careless gesture, one accidental touch, and he could kill her quicker than she thought. She breathed hard, trying to control her shaking. She didn't want to get herself stabbed by accidentally bump-ing into his knife.

"Don't even think about calling the cops," he warned the receptionist. He turned back to the desk and sliced through the phone cord, then yanked open the desk drawers until he found the woman's purse. "If you're not here when I come out," he said, his tone deadly se-rious, "I'm coming after you next."

The receptionist dropped into her chair like a sinking stone, and Fiona felt a pang of sympathy for the woman. Then Joey jammed the point of the knife under her chin, and self-preservation kicked in.

"Let's go," he muttered, his breath hot in her ear.

He pushed her toward the door, forcing her to open it so they could enter. The inner office was spacious, with a long bank of tinted windows behind a dark wood desk. A large man stood behind the desk, frowning at the door. Fiona felt a shock of recognition when he met her eyes—this was the man from the pictures!

"What the hell have you done?" His voice was thunderous, and behind her, Joey jerked. The tip of the knife dug into her neck, a painful stab that made her cry out in protest. Joey immediately relaxed his hold, and she felt a drop of wetness slide down her skin.

Please don't be a deep cut, she prayed.

"Uncle Sal," Joey started, but the other man cut him off.

"You've really done it this time, Joey." He stepped around the desk and stalked toward them. Joey walked back, dragging her with him, until they hit the wall. The large man kept advancing until he was standing inches away, apparently immune to the threat of Joey's knife. Shooting a contemptuous glance at the man behind her, he took Fiona's hand in a surprisingly gentle grip and pulled her away from Joey.

For his part, Joey didn't try to hold her in place. He let her go, and she was happy to move away from him. Whoever he was, Uncle Sal seemed much more reasonable than his nephew.

Uncle Sal led her to one of the chairs in front of his

desk and gestured for her to sit. Fiona sank into the plush leather cushions, breathing a sigh of relief. She cast a surreptitious glance at the desk, pleased to see a phone within arm's reach. Uncle Sal looked like he had a lot to say to his nephew, and if both men were distracted, maybe she could call the police.

True to her suspicions, Sal turned back to Joey and advanced on the younger man again. "I knew I couldn't trust you with this job," he seethed. "You're nothing but a screwup. Always have been. Always will be. I tried to give you one last chance to prove yourself, but you can't even handle that!"

Fiona leaned forward, positioning herself within touching distance of the phone. Uncle Sal had his back to her, but Joey was still facing her...

Joey's features twisted with rage. "You don't know what you're talking about, old man! I did everything right! Maybe I don't have the pictures, but I have the next best thing." He pointed at her with the knife, and Fiona froze, hoping the older man wouldn't turn to look at her.

"How does kidnapping a woman help me, exactly?" Sarcasm dripped from Uncle Sal's voice.

Joey opened his mouth to respond, but the other man interrupted him. "Let me explain it to you—it doesn't. Your actions have brought unwanted police attention to my operation. As I told you earlier, I had a detective in my office not even an hour ago, demanding to know where this woman is and why I had her taken. This is the kind of mistake we can't afford. And if you had half a brain, you'd know that already!"

"But she's the key," Joey protested. "She can get us the photos!"

Fiona's hand inched closer to the phone. Just a little closer... Her fingers brushed the receiver, and she nearly cried out with relief.

"No, she can't," Uncle Sal said. "Do you remember nothing? The police have the photos. She has no access to them."

Quietly, carefully, she lifted the receiver, holding her breath in hope that they wouldn't hear the quiet drone of the dial tone over the sound of their argument.

"Then we use her to get the pictures," Joey said. "Don't you see? They'll trade the pictures for her."

The older man shook his head. "Just when I think you can't get any dumber," he muttered. "You can't blackmail the police like that. The officer who came to see me is not one who works for me. He will not take kindly to such an exchange."

Fiona's fingers trembled only a little as she pressed 911 on the keypad. She didn't dare lift the receiver to her ear. Hopefully the dispatcher would hear the sound of raised voices and would send out a police car to investigate.

"Nine-one-one, what's your emergency?"

"Please just let me go," Fiona said, hopefully loud enough for the operator to hear. It was a risk, interrupting the men like that. Drawing their attention could backfire in a big way if they noticed the phone off the hook. But it was a chance she had to take.

"If you let me walk out of here, I'll forget all about

this. I won't tell the police what you've done. We can all just forget about it."

Both men looked at her with identical expressions of disbelief. Then Uncle Sal noticed the phone and his face changed, his expression growing hard. He rushed over to the desk and grabbed the receiver, slamming it down so hard the plastic cracked.

"What have you done?" he thundered, looming over her.

Fiona shrank back into the chair, fear rising in her chest. Joey frightened her because he seemed unstable and unpredictable. But his uncle was on another level entirely. This man was used to getting his way, and he knew how to make problems go away. And right now, he saw her as a problem.

"Please," she whispered, uncertain what she was asking. *Please don't hurt me? Please let me go?* Both, if she was being honest.

He drew back a hand and slapped her hard across the face. Bright spots danced before her eyes, and a metallic taste filled her mouth.

"What do we do now, Uncle Sal?" Joey sounded truly worried, like a child who had lost his way in the dark.

The older man shook his head. "*We* don't do anything," he said, turning to face his nephew. "*I* will take care of this." Then he stuck his hand inside his jacket and withdrew a small black gun. Fiona watched in frozen horror as he pointed the gun at Joey. "I always knew you'd wind up dead," he said. "You were just too stupid to make it. I had hoped someone else would take care of this long before now, but, oh well." With a shrug, he pulled the trigger.

Joey jerked back as the bullet hit his chest, a small spray of red darkening the space in front of him. His eyes widened in shock and pain, and the older man shot him again and again until Joey finally fell, limp and unresisting, to the ground.

Tears stung Fiona's eyes. She hadn't cared about Joey—far from it—but she hadn't wished him dead. Uncle Sal turned back to her wearing a calm expression, as if he did this sort of thing all the time. He eyed her dispassionately, and Fiona's stomach dropped as she realized she was in more danger now than she'd been before.

"Time to go," he said, tugging her up.

"Are you going to shoot me, too?"

He smiled, but it didn't reach his eyes. "I haven't decided yet."

Nate glared at Ben Carter, fighting the growing urge to punch the lying man in the face. A broken nose would certainly erase his smug, self-satisfied smile.

"Do you really think we're that stupid? We have the pictures. We know what you're trying to pull."

Ben shook his head stubbornly. "You've got it all wrong, man. It wasn't supposed to be like this."

"It never is," Owen said drily. "Why not just admit that you're in over your head? Let us help you."

Ben's shoulders slumped as he finally dropped the overconfident act. He leaned forward to rest his head on the table with a quiet thud. "You can't," he said, sounding miserable.

Nate's patience snapped. "You know what? I don't care. I'm not interested in helping you. I just want to get Fiona back."

"I don't know why you think I can help you with that," Ben replied, sounding tired. "I certainly don't have her."

"Really? Because you have motive, means *and* opportunity," Nate replied, ticking each factor off on his fingers. "Let's review, shall we? You left the photos in Fiona's possession, and now that she doesn't have them, you want to punish her. That's what we call motive. You have a car, the means of transporting her. And you didn't work today, so you had plenty of opportunity to wait at her home and take her against her will."

"Why would I do that?" He sounded genuinely puzzled, but Nate wasn't buying it.

"Because now that the pictures are gone, you have no leverage over Big Sal. You're scared, and you want to take it out on someone. Fiona's the natural target. After all, she's the one who lost the pictures, right? She's the reason you're back in this mess."

Ben nodded, and a surge of satisfaction rose in Nate's chest. He was getting closer—Ben was just about to break, he was sure of it.

"You needed to punish her," Owen chimed in, his voice soft and soothing. "Who can blame you? She was just supposed to hold the pictures, not hand them over to us. How stupid can she be, right?"

"No kidding," Ben agreed. "She had no business going through those papers."

Nate bit his tongue, knowing any outburst from him would destroy the progress they'd made. He glanced at Owen, content to let his partner take the lead now. Owen was renowned in the department for his interrogation skills, and if anyone could get Ben to tell them where he'd stashed Fiona, it was him.

Nate slowly leaned back so Owen could establish himself as the center of Ben's focus. He just hoped that Ben would break soon so they could get to Fiona.

He thought of her, cold and alone, scared out of her mind. She was a strong woman—she'd proved that time and again over the past few days—but everyone had their limit. She'd already been through so much. He hated the fact that he wasn't there for her when she needed him most.

If she was even still alive. The dark thought made his stomach cramp, and he instantly denied it. She couldn't be dead. He refused to even acknowledge the possibility. He had to believe she was still out there, still waiting for him. He couldn't bear to think he'd let her down so spectacularly.

"She sounds pretty special," his dad had said. "We can't wait to meet her."

His father's words echoed in his head. Talking to his parents had been nothing like he'd expected—there had been no yelling, no recriminations. For the first time, his mother had seemed happy to hear from him. And Molly had been over the moon, her enthusiasm so contagious Nate had found himself smiling in spite of his worry for Fiona.

Talking to his family had made him realize Fiona had a point. He was a lucky man. And he wanted to share that with the woman he cared about. Once he found her, he was going to take her home to meet his family. His mother was going to love her, as was Molly. And he knew his father would approve. Hopefully, being around them would ease her loneliness.

If she even wants to be around you after this, he thought cynically.

After all, it was his fault she'd been abducted. He couldn't really blame her if she walked away and pushed him out of her life. It was the least he deserved.

The buzz of his phone cut into his thoughts. Owen shot him a look, and Nate rose and left the room, careful to shut the door quietly behind him. He took a second to watch his partner through the glass, noting how quickly Owen was able to redirect Ben's focus. *Keep it up, partner.*

"Gallagher," he said automatically, his gaze on the room beyond. Ben leaned forward, his expression earnest as he spoke. He was clearly trying to convince Owen of something, and Owen nodded reassuringly, urging him on.

"Please help me." The voice was barely more than a whisper, and Nate had to strain to hear.

"What? Can you speak up?"

"No, they'll hear me. Please just come."

"Who is this?" Goose bumps rose on his arms as he

tried to place the voice. It was clearly a woman, but it didn't sound like Fiona.

"The receptionist. From Mr. Salvatore's office. You were here earlier."

"What's wrong?"

"This man came in, dragging a woman with him. He threatened me with a knife and cut the phone line. Now he's in the office, and he and Mr. Salvatore are arguing." A series of loud pops followed her words, and she let out a stifled shriek.

"Oh, God, was that a gun?" Her voice cracked with panic, and she sounded as though she was going to pass out.

"I'm on my way," Nate said. "Get out of the building if you can. Otherwise, hide and don't come out until the police arrive."

"Please hurry," she said, obviously crying.

"Get to a safe place," he said, racing out the door. "Then hang up and call nine-one-one."

"Okay." She sucked in a breath. "I'll do that now."

Nate hung up and practically jumped into his car, tearing out of the parking lot with a squeal of tires. The bitter stench of burned rubber filled his nose, and he kept one hand on the wheel while he dialed with the other.

It took Owen a moment to answer, but once he did Nate quickly filled him in on the details.

"I'll meet you there," Owen said. "Just don't do anything stupid."

"I can't make any promises," Nate replied. He normally wasn't so reckless, but adrenaline pumped through his veins and made him a lot more willing to take chances. Especially if it meant getting Fiona back.

He slipped the phone back into his pocket and returned his focus to the road.

"Hold on, baby," he muttered. "Just hold on."

Fiona pretended to trip and threw herself to the ground. The gravel bit into the palms of her hands, but she ignored the pain. Sal bellowed with rage and kicked out, landing a solid blow to her ribs that knocked the breath from her lungs.

She curled into a ball to protect herself, gasping like a fish out of water. Sal towered over her, yelling and pulling at her, but the pain from his kick drowned out his words.

He pawed at her, trying to get a grip on her clothes so he could force her to stand. She writhed on the ground, avoiding his grasp, and watched his hands from behind narrowed eyelids. He couldn't get ahold of her with only one hand, which meant he was going to have to put down his gun…

There! He slipped the gun into his jacket and reached for her. Fiona let him grab her and draw her up, careful to maneuver herself so that she faced him as he pulled her to her feet. She only had one chance at this, which meant she had to do it right. If she tried to grab his gun too soon, he'd anticipate her move and block her. If she waited too long, her chance would evaporate.

She held her breath, trying to appear harmless. Waves of pain radiated from her side, making it hard to breathe, but she gritted her teeth and pushed the feeling aside. She could worry about her ribs later.

Sal pulled her close, shoving his face into hers. "I've had just about enough of you," he growled, giving her a shake that made her head snap back. "Don't push me."

Fiona shoved her hand into his jacket and groped wildly, her hand bumping up against something solid.

She wrapped her fingers around it and pulled, jerking the gun free of Sal's side holster. She pressed the barrel to his chest and glared up at him. "Let. Me. Go."

His eyes went comically wide, and his mouth dropped open in disbelief. His grip slackened, but his hands remained on her arms. Fiona took a step back, keeping the gun pointed at his chest. The thought of actually using it made her stomach cramp, but she had to put on a brave face so Sal wouldn't know she was bluffing.

The sirens grew louder, but Fiona kept her attention on Sal. His expression had shifted from shock to calculation, and she could tell he was trying to figure out how to gain the upper hand again.

She took another step back, out of his reach. He didn't move, but his eyes followed her and it was clear he was planning something.

"You should go," she said, proud that her voice was only a little shaky. "The police will be here soon."

He nodded, but he didn't seem concerned by that fact. "I suppose you think you've won?"

"It's not about winning. I just want to be left alone." It was the truth—she was tired of being a victim of circumstance, tired of being at the mercy of others. She just wanted to go back to her normal, safe life.

Sal shook his head, a cold smile curving his lips. "It's too late for that. You're involved now. I can't just let you walk away."

"Why not?" she cried. "It was just a bunch of pictures! Why can't you forget about them and leave me alone? I wasn't the one who took them anyway—this isn't my fault."

Surprise flickered in his eyes. "You really don't get it, do you?"

From the corner of her eyes, she saw a black-and-white police car tear into the far end of the parking lot, kicking up gravel as the driver skidded to a stop. When she turned back to face Sal, he was running in the opposite direction, heading back into the office.

Stupid of him, she thought, watching him enter the building. *Where's he going to go?*

Fiona tossed the gun on the ground as the police officer approached. "He's in there," she pointed. "I'm fine."

The man nodded at her and rushed into the building. Another car tore into the parking lot, the lights flashing so brightly it hurt to look at them. She turned her head and sank to the ground, feeling suddenly empty. The adrenaline that had kept her on her feet and functioning drained from her, leaving her shaky and uncertain. The pain from her ribs roared to life again, and she blinked back tears with every breath.

She should be thrilled to be free, but the situation felt *wrong* somehow, as if she was missing something. Sal's parting words had been cryptic, and she struggled to remember them, to try to make sense of what he'd said and why.

You really don't get it, do you?

What was there to get? What more was there for her to understand? He wanted the pictures back, but she didn't have them. Why couldn't he just let her walk away? Why keep targeting her?

Someone knelt beside her and spoke, but Fiona was too distracted by her thoughts to pay attention. She shook her head absently, the way she would brush away an annoying fly. She had to figure out what Sal had meant.

Her visitor spoke again, this time more insistently. Then he reached out and put a hand on her shoulder. Fiona instinctively shrank back from the touch, and the sudden movement sent fire down her side and into her abdomen.

"Did he hurt you?" Nate's face filled her vision, his expression a mixture of anger and concern. "Did that bastard touch you?"

Relief surged through her, making her feel light-headed. She drank in the sight of him, the feel of him, and relaxed for the first time in what felt like forever.

But what was he doing here? How had he found her? She didn't realize she'd spoken aloud until Nate replied, "The receptionist called me. It's a long story—" He was cut off by a series of loud pops that split the air.

Nate reacted instantly, pushing her flat on the ground and throwing himself on top of her to shield her with his own body. The sudden change of position and his unexpected weight made her ribs scream in protest, and she moaned. He lifted himself up a little, easing the painful pressure, and she sucked in a breath.

After a tense moment, shouts of "All clear!" came from the office. Nate eased off her. "We need to get you to a hospital," he observed, frowning at the way she clutched her side.

Fiona merely nodded, not bothering to argue. Hospitals had pain medication, something she desperately wanted right now.

Nate gently helped her stand and started to urge her forward. She caught sight of the gun lying a few feet away in the gravel and stopped, a horrible thought popping into her head. She had touched that gun! Her fingerprints were on it now, which meant they might think she had shot Joey. The realization sent chills through her body and made her stomach cramp.

"Sal shot Joey," she blurted out, pointing at the gun.

Nate nodded and gestured for another officer to mark it as evidence. "Okay," he said. "You can tell me all about it after we get you checked out." He tried to lead her away, but she dug in her heels. She had to make him understand, before they left the scene and the details of what had happened got jumbled in her mind.

"No, you don't get it. I touched that gun. I managed to take it from Sal, which is why he let me go. My fingerprints will be on it, but I swear, I didn't shoot Joey!" Panic made her voice rise, and she fought to control her emotions. The thought of going to jail for a crime she didn't commit was terrifying, especially now that it seemed the nightmarish ordeal was over.

Nate bent his knees until his face was at eye level with hers. "I know you didn't kill anyone," he said softly, reaching out to tuck a loose strand of hair behind her ear. "The evidence will prove it was Sal who fired the gun, so I don't want you to worry about it." He put an arm around her and they started walking toward the ambulance, which had arrived shortly after all the police cars. "For now, I just want to make sure you're okay."

Fiona relaxed against his body, grateful for his support. Sal's words still rang in her ears, but she couldn't focus on that particular puzzle right now, not with her side crying out for attention and her mind distracted by Nate. His presence was soothing, the first comfort she'd had since Joey had taken her. There was just something about him that spoke to her and made her feel calm and secure, the very opposite of her time with Joey and Sal.

She glanced surreptitiously at him as they walked, tracing the bones of his cheek and jaw with her eyes. He hadn't shaved since the attempted robbery at the store a few days ago, and his stubble was heavier, almost completely covering his cheeks. It made him look older and offset the normal playful twinkle he carried in his eyes.

"You look good with a beard," she murmured.

He turned to her and smiled. "You think so? I'm not so sure."

She nodded. "It suits you."

He rubbed his bristled chin against her cheek in a soft caress. "You suit me," he whispered.

A thrill shot through her at his words, but before she could determine if he was teasing her, they arrived at the ambulance and the EMTs pulled her away and helped her onto the gurney. One of the other officers approached Nate and spoke into his ear. Nate frowned and nodded, and the other man walked away.

Fiona tried to determine what the officer had told him based on his expression, but he gave nothing away. He stood at the end of the gurney, his eyes never leaving her as the paramedics performed their exam. She showed them where Sal had kicked her, and Nate sucked in a breath, his eyes narrowing and his fists clenching when he saw the dark red mark that was swiftly turning purple.

"You're going to need X-rays," one of the medics pronounced. "Is the scene secure?" he asked Nate.

He nodded. "Yes. There are no more injuries."

The other EMT raised a brow. "I thought I heard gunshots earlier."

"You did," Nate said flatly. "The suspect committed suicide."

Fiona's stomach dropped at the news. How was she supposed to figure out what Sal had meant by his parting words if she couldn't ask him about it? She had been counting on the police arresting Sal and interrogating him, but now that he was dead, she had no way to decipher his message.

But did it even matter now? Both Sal and Joey were gone—they couldn't hurt her anymore. She had nothing to worry about. Right?

It was the logical conclusion. So why couldn't she shake the feeling that something was still *off*?

Her distress must have shown on her face, because Nate moved to her side and slid her hand into his. "What's wrong? Are you in pain?" He looked at the medics questioningly, but Fiona shook her head.

"It's not that," she said. "I just can't figure out why Sal killed himself."

Nate shrugged. "Truth be told, I couldn't care less about him. I'm just happy you're safe."

"But don't you think it's odd?" she pressed. The medics wheeled the stretcher into the back of the ambulance, and Nate climbed in after it, sliding down the bench so he sat by her head.

"I suppose," he said. "Maybe he was freaked-out by the thought of going to prison. He decided he couldn't handle it, so he killed himself rather than go through the experience."

Nate's explanation made sense, but it didn't fit with the impression she'd formed of Sal. "He didn't seem like the kind of man who would suffer much, regardless of the circumstances," she said. "And I'm willing to bet he has the best lawyer money can buy on retainer. I doubt he would have faced a stiff sentence."

"What's this really about?" Nate eyed her thoughtfully. "Did he say something that has you worried?"

"Well, yeah," she confessed. "Just before he ran inside, he told me that I was involved now and couldn't just walk away. That sounds kind of ominous, don't you think?"

He frowned, mulling over her words. "Do you think he was trying to scare you?"

Fiona shook her head. "Why bother? If he knew he was running off to his death, why go to the trouble of trying to scare me? That's what I don't get." She winced as the ambulance took a bump particularly hard, jostling her against the rail of the gurney.

Nate squeezed her hand and leaned forward, his expression anxious. "Let's talk about this after you've been seen by a doctor," he suggested. He looked so upset that she said yes, if only to reassure him that she was fine. His concern was sweet, and she couldn't help but smile. Her mom was the last person to worry about her, and while at the time she'd found her mother's fears irrational, she now recognized them as an expression of her love. And while it was way too soon to be using the L-word when it came to Nate, the fact that he cared for her eased some of the loneliness she'd felt since the death of her mom.

He lifted her hand and pressed a kiss to her knuckles. "We're almost there," he said quietly.

If only, she thought wistfully. But as long as Nate refused to make family a priority, she had to protect her heart. She couldn't let herself fall for a man who didn't share her dreams.

No matter how amazing he seemed.

"You're very lucky." The doctor held up an X-ray film and pointed as he spoke. "You have two cracked ribs and some extensive bruising to the surrounding tissue, but it could have been much worse."

Fiona nodded, pretending to see what he was indicating. She could make out her ribs, but she didn't see the cracks he was describing. Of course, this was her first time looking at an X-ray, so her lack of discernment was forgivable. She glanced over at Nate, who seemed to be having an easier time making out the details.

"How long will it take to heal?" he asked.

The doctor lifted one shoulder in a shrug. "Probably about six weeks, give or take." He turned and met Fiona's eyes. "I'll prescribe some medication to help with the pain, and I need you to take deep breaths as often as you can." He saw her puzzled look and elaborated. "That will help prevent pneumonia from setting in."

"Sounds easy enough," Fiona replied.

"I'll go finish up your paperwork, and I'll have a nurse come in with your medication and an ice pack. We should have you out of here soon."

"Thanks," she called as he stepped out of the room.

She leaned back against the bed with a sigh, relaxing into the pillow. It was a far cry from the comfort of her normal bed, but compared to the one Joey had provided for her, it was pure heaven.

Nate sat at her side, staring at his hands. He was quiet, but not in a relaxed way. His shoulders were tense, and he looked like a man who had a lot on his mind.

"Everything okay over there?" she asked.

He cocked his head to the side, considering the question. Then he lifted his head and met her gaze, his eyes a deep, soft green in the overhead fluorescent lights. "I'm so sorry," he said, his voice rough. "This never should have happened. I should have done a better job of protecting you." He reached for her hand, his touch warm. "It's my fault you went through all this."

"Nate, you can't blame yourself. You had no way of knowing Joey was in my house, waiting for me. And if you had been there, things probably would have escalated and he'd have gotten violent."

"But I would have stopped him from taking you," he argued.

"Maybe," she said. "Maybe not. There's no way to

know what would have happened if you'd been there. He might have killed you to get to me!"

Nate didn't seem too bothered by that possibility, which made her shake her head in dismay. "What's done is done. You're going to have to let it go and move on. That's what I'm trying to do." It was the only thing she *could* do if she wanted to carry on with her life. She couldn't dwell in the past and focus on the bad. She had to pick herself up and think about her future—finishing her thesis, graduating, her career. It was a lesson she'd learned the hard way after her mom's death but one that had stuck with her.

Nate smiled at her. "That's what my dad said, too."

Fiona's eyebrows shot up. "You spoke with your dad?" When had that happened? The other night he'd seemed completely indifferent to his family's phone call. Had he had a change of heart? She sat up a little, hope dulling the pain of her injuries somewhat.

He dropped his head, looking sheepish. "I called him earlier. I was so upset about your abduction, I didn't know where else to turn."

She swallowed hard, trying to dislodge the sudden lump in her throat. "Did you talk long?"

"Long enough," he said. "I think I just needed to hear his voice, if that makes any sense."

"It does." She squeezed his hand, happy he had reached out to his family and found comfort in them. "I'm glad you reconnected."

Nate shrugged. "I don't know about that," he replied. "I think my mom is still mad at me over missing

Thanksgiving. But my dad seemed to understand, once I explained everything."

"It's a start," she said. "Maybe he can work to soften your mom up."

"Maybe." He paused for a moment, then glanced up, his gaze filled with vulnerability. "Would you like to meet them?" he asked shyly.

An electric tingle ran through her, making the fine hairs on her arms stand at attention. "You want me to meet your family?" she said, a little hoarse. Did he really mean it? That was such a big step, especially for someone like Nate who had trouble connecting with his relatives. The fact that he wanted to take her home to meet his parents and sister made her feel special, as though she occupied a significant place in his life.

Her earlier resolve began to crumble in the face of his offer. Maybe, just maybe, she and Nate *did* want the same things in life—a family, a home. A place to belong. Could she really refuse to take a chance on him if he was trying to change?

He nodded. "Yes. I think you'd like my sister. And my mom—she'd be nice to you. My dad, too, for that matter. They would make you feel welcome." He studied her carefully for a moment, then added softly, "I think you miss that."

His observation hit her like a blow, knocking the breath out of her. Was she really that transparent? Did her yearning for her parents come across in everything she did, everything she said? It was a depressing thought. She'd worked so hard to overcome her grief.

The idea that she hadn't really made progress after all was discouraging, and made her feel like a failure.

Or, her mind said, *maybe he just sees it because he's looked.* Nate wasn't like anyone she'd met before. He took the time to really talk to her, to go beyond superficial topics and get to know her. They'd spent a lot of time together over the past few days—was it any wonder she'd opened up to him and revealed things she hadn't shared with anyone else? He had truly listened, a rare quality these days. And one that she appreciated.

"I do," she replied. "I would love to meet your family."

He grinned and breathed out a sigh of relief. "Good. We'll get the investigation wrapped up first, and then I'll make the arrangements. It'll be nice to have you there. You can protect me from my mom. She wouldn't dare kill me in front of a witness."

Fiona shook her head, smiling at his flippancy. Maybe this upcoming visit would convince Nate his mother truly loved him, and that if she nagged him it was only because she cared.

A nurse entered the room, her hands full with paperwork, pills and an ice pack. Nate gave Fiona's hand a final squeeze and stepped back. "I'm going to call Owen. I'll be just outside—it won't take long. Then we can get your statement, and you can put all of this behind you."

"That sounds nice," she said with a sigh. The idea of moving on with her life was so appealing, it was almost intoxicating. Especially now that she knew Nate was trying to reconnect with his family. His apparent change of heart gave her hope that they could have a future together, something she had thought was out of her grasp. The possibility made her smile and sent tendrils of warmth through her limbs. But the moment was bittersweet, as well. What she wouldn't give for her mother to meet Nate! She would have loved him, that much Fiona knew. It made her a little sad to think the man she was growing to love would never meet one of the most important people in her life.

"Name and date of birth?" the nurse asked, jarring her from her thoughts.

Fiona replied automatically and took the pill she was offered. Despite her mixed emotions, she looked forward to getting to know Nate better and to see what their future held.

Together.

Chapter 14

It didn't take long to get back to the station. Since Nate had left his car at Sal's office, Owen met them at the hospital. He took one look at Fiona's pale face and the ice pack she clutched to her side and jumped out to help her into the car. Once she was safely inside, he shot Nate a quizzical look.

"I don't know all the details yet," Nate said, responding to his partner's silent question. "I told her to wait until we could take her statement, so she wouldn't have to tell the story a million times."

Owen snorted. "You know she'll have to do that anyway. It's never a one-and-done situation when it comes to witness statements."

"I know. But in her case, her abductor is dead and so is Sal. I know the evidence will show she didn't kill either of them, so I wanted to give her a chance to regroup before pummeling her with questions."

Amusement flickered across Owen's face. "So, in other words, you wanted to protect her."

"It was the least I could do, after letting her get taken in the first place!" Nate felt his cheeks heat and knew he sounded defensive. But he didn't care. Fiona might not blame him for what had happened, but it was going to take a long time before he forgot the sickening dread that had filled him at the realization she had been abducted.

Owen held up a hand in a gesture of placation. "Peace, man. I wasn't trying to give you a hard time. I know what it's like to see the woman you care about in danger." He shook his head, the shadow of memory passing over his face. "It's the worst feeling in the world."

Nate nodded in perfect understanding. "It is," he said softly.

Owen clapped him on the back. "Let's get this show on the road. The sooner we get back, the sooner she can start to rebuild her life."

Ten minutes later, they assembled in one of the interrogation rooms. "Can I get you anything?" Nate asked Fiona as she settled into one of the chairs. "Coffee? Water? Soda?"

She shook her head with a small smile. "I'm good, thanks. I'd kind of like to get this over with. How does it usually work?"

Sympathy welled in his chest, and he fought the urge to move his chair closer to hers so he could wrap his arm around her. But there would be time to comfort her later. For now, he was going to have to endure the torture of listening to the woman he adored recount her abduction and injuries, an experience he should have done more to prevent.

So he sat there, muscles growing tenser with every moment as she told her story. He tried to keep his face frozen so she wouldn't see how much her words upset him. She'd already been through enough—she didn't need to feel she had to comfort him. If anything, it should be the other way around.

Owen took it upon himself to steer the conversation, something Nate appreciated. He was in no frame of mind to do his job, not when it came to Fiona. He was too close to her to act as an effective detective when it came to her case, and he was grateful Owen hadn't pointed that out. There was no doubt his partner recognized this particular weakness, but he was too professional to overtly mention it, at least to Nate's face.

Owen was a master interviewer, asking Fiona pertinent questions in an unobtrusive way that didn't disrupt the flow of her story or jar her out of the moment. Thanks to his input, Fiona painted a more complete picture of her time with Joey and Big Sal.

She had just started telling them how Joey had dragged her into Sal's office when she was interrupted by a perfunctory knock on the door. The captain stepped inside, followed by two men sporting dark suits and white dress shirts. Their starched-shirt attitude screamed *Feds*, and Nate and Owen exchanged a loaded look. *What fresh hell is this?*

Nate glanced at the captain, whose pinched expression confirmed his first impression of the two newcomers. Captain Rogers looked like a grumpy basset hound, his thick brows drawn together and his mouth turned down in a frown that emphasized his jowls. "We have a problem," he said, his voice low and unhappy.

"What's going on?" Nate stood, not wanting to sit while the two suited unknowns towered over him.

The captain offered Fiona a small smile of apology and nodded at her. "Sorry to interrupt, Ms. Sanders."

She glanced at the new arrivals, her eyes growing wide. "Uh, that's fine."

Captain Rogers jerked his thumb at the other two men. "This is Agent Golightly from Homeland Security, and that's Agent Harmon from the DEA."

One of the men spoke up. "Actually, I'm Harmon, and he's Golightly."

"Whatever," the captain grumbled.

Owen rose, tucking his hands into his pockets. "What brings you to Houston, gentlemen?"

Golightly—or maybe it was Harmon—spoke up. "Someone in this unit recently uploaded a series of photographs to be analyzed by the facial recognition software. One of the individuals in those pictures is a known associate of Los Muerte, one of the largest and most dangerous Mexican drug cartels."

Nate and Owen exchanged another look. Big Sal was known for his gambling empire, and all the evidence they had suggested that he stuck to that line of work. Had he fooled them all?

"That still doesn't explain why you're here," Nate replied.

The agent gave him a thin smile. "We were notified of the hit, and dispatched to investigate. We need to talk to everyone involved in this case, to ascertain who knows what."

Nate couldn't hold back his scoff. "Well, unfortunately that's a low number. The man in the photographs is dead. And the man who originally had the photographs—"

"Is also dead," Captain Rogers put in grimly.

Fiona gasped softly, and Nate put a reassuring hand on her shoulder, squeezing gently to let her know he was still here.

"What?" Owen's incredulity was palpable. "How is that possible? I left him in a holding cell a little over an hour ago."

"He was given a sandwich, and he choked to death."

"Just like that?" Nate didn't bother to mask his skepticism. Ben Carson was a grown man who had spent a lifetime chewing his food before swallowing. It was highly unlikely he'd forgotten how to eat on today of all days.

Captain Rogers shot him a quelling look. "We're looking into it," he said gruffly.

Uh-huh. Something was definitely off here. First, Sal committed suicide for no apparent reason. Then Ben died under suspicious circumstances. And now two uptight Federal suits were butting in on the investigation.

The two men didn't look surprised at the news that

another possible witness connected to the case was dead. "It's starting already," one of them murmured.

"What's starting?" Nate asked sharply. He didn't like these men, he decided. With their arrogant, standoffish attitude and their expectation that Nate and Owen would hand their case over to them on a silver platter, they rubbed him the wrong way. It was time they started sharing what they knew—or thought they knew—about this investigation.

The two men remained stubbornly silent, which only served to further antagonize Nate. He felt his temper building and could tell from Owen's posture that his partner felt the same. It was time to take control of this conversation and show these two suits they didn't run things in this station.

"You know, you haven't told us who popped up in the image analysis," Nate said, striving for a conversational tone. "Big Sal is—or was, rather—one of our local treasures. He ran a gambling syndicate, but he wasn't into drugs. I can't imagine it was his picture that brought you vultures to our door."

The two agents shared a look but didn't respond.

"Are you thinking what I'm thinking, partner?" Owen asked.

Nate nodded. "They're not here for Big Sal," he replied.

"Nope." Owen's expression was friendly enough, but his eyes were cold. "They're here because of the woman in the pictures."

"She's your cartel link," Nate finished. He eyed the two men carefully. One of them had a decent poker face, but he caught the flash of subdued irritation that passed across the other man's features. *Gotcha*, he thought, the spurt of satisfaction he felt doing wonders to improve his mood.

He glanced at Owen, pleased to see his partner had noticed it, too. "I think it's time you shared what you know," Owen said quietly. "Otherwise, we can't help you."

One of the agents glanced at Captain Rogers, clearly expecting the higher-ranked officer to intervene. But the captain merely stared back, his expression pleasantly blank. Seeing they would get no help from that quarter, the two agents glanced at each other again. Some kind of silent communication passed between them, and finally one of them shrugged in acceptance.

"We'll tell you what we know," he said. Then he glanced at Fiona, seeming to register her presence for the first time. "But not in front of her."

"No." Nate rejected the offer swiftly, before Owen or Captain Rogers had a chance to respond. "Whatever is going on here involves her, and she has a right to know about it."

Fiona looked up at him, her eyes shining with gratitude. He acknowledged her thanks with another squeeze of her shoulder. She'd been through hell already and had come out a winner. If this nightmare wasn't over yet, she deserved to know why and what she was up against.

The agent—Nate decided he was Golightly—shot another look at Captain Rogers. The captain's jaw tightened, but he didn't overrule Nate's declaration. Nate made a mental note to take the captain out for a drink when this was all over. He could tell from the man's expression that he wasn't thrilled with Nate's pronouncement, but he was too loyal to his men to undermine Nate in the face of these strangers.

He caught his captain's eye and gave him a subtle nod of thanks. Captain Rogers returned the gesture. Then they both glanced at the two agents, who now wore identical expressions of pinched annoyance.

"Whenever you're ready, gentlemen," the captain drawled.

"The woman in the photographs is Isabella Cologne," one man said grudgingly. "She is the daughter of Cesar Cologne, who runs some regional operations for Los Muerte in Mexico." He stopped, clearly thinking he'd supplied enough information.

"So?" Nate prodded. "Why all the drama over the daughter of a Mexican mob boss?"

"She's not just his daughter." Golightly spoke through clenched teeth. "She acts as a recruiter for the organization."

"Meaning what?" Owen asked.

"She identifies potentially useful allies and sets out to align them with her father's interests. Using whatever means necessary," he finished, his emphasis on the final words leaving no doubt as to his meaning.

"It's a honey trap," Nate said, nodding slowly. It was one of the oldest tricks in the book—use sex appeal to trick a man into giving up secrets or doing what you wanted. It was a crude strategy but eternally effective.

Golightly nodded approvingly. "Usually, it works. And in this case, it appeared to be successful. We have reason to believe Big Sal was in negotiations to use his gambling connections and resources to launder money for the cartel."

Owen whistled softly. "That's actually not a bad idea."

"Like I said, the deal was all but done."

"Then why did he kill himself?" Fiona asked softly. Everyone turned to look at her, and her cheeks flushed a pretty shade of pink. She cleared her throat and spoke again, louder this time. "If Sal had such a great deal coming his way, why did he kill himself today? That doesn't make sense."

"I suspect he committed suicide to avoid answering to the cartel," the other agent said drily. "Once those pictures were out, Sal's links to Isabella and the cartel were no longer secret. That's something the cartel doesn't appreciate."

Nate realized with a growing sense of horror just what the other man meant. Without meaning to, he tightened his grip on Fiona's shoulder, making her squirm in protest. "So what you're saying," he began, speaking slowly to get the words out, "is that anyone who has seen those pictures is now a target of the cartel?"

Golightly's expression was deadly serious. "Yes. I'm afraid so." He turned to address Fiona. "We need to talk about getting you into protective custody, to make sure you're safe from the cartel."

Fiona went pale at his words, the color draining from her face so quickly Nate thought she might faint. "But why? No one else knows I've seen these pictures."

Golightly shook his head, dismissing her protest. Nate spoke up. "She has a point. Her name is not connected to these photographs. Why should she uproot her life when she's not a target?"

"Because she will be," Golightly replied. "It's only a matter of time before the identity of everyone who has seen the pictures is known. And the cartel will stop at nothing as it tries to employ damage control."

Nate frowned, the explanation sounding a bit off to him. "That doesn't make any sense. You already know Isabella tries to lure people into forming an alliance with her father. That means she's had unsuccessful attempts before, and someone lived to tell about it."

"Someone who is now in the witness protection program," Golightly interrupted.

"But I'm not a threat!" Fiona protested. "There's nothing I can do that will hurt these people, or their business. I don't understand why they would focus on me when my existence doesn't impact them at all."

Golightly shot her a pitying look. "These people don't care. To them, lives are cheap and disposable. And they'd rather snuff out someone who might one day turn out to be a threat than err on the side of letting them live."

Fiona looked up at Nate, her expression a silent plea. His heart ached for her and the fear he saw in her eyes. It was so unfair—she hadn't asked for any of this, and it was only through the selfish actions of her boss that she'd been pulled into this nightmare. He wished he could snap his fingers and make it all go away, but it didn't work like that. Instead, he was going to have to come up with a way to keep her safe, because he wasn't letting these two strangers load her into a black SUV and take her away from him forever.

"What are the options?" he asked. "For all of us."

Golightly frowned. "What do you mean, all of you?"

Owen piped up, his brows drawn together in a frown. "We've all seen the pictures. If what you say is true, then all of us are targets of the cartel."

"I'm only authorized to bring in one person today," Golightly said. "I'll have to talk to my superiors and explain that we need protection for an additional three police officers."

Nate nodded. "Why don't you do that now," he said, his tone making it clear it wasn't a suggestion. "Because I can tell you, she's not going anywhere alone."

Golightly shot him a disgusted look but stepped out of the room, his hand already reaching into his pocket for his phone.

Nate waited until the door closed behind the other man, then blew out his breath. "I don't know how you stand working with that guy," he said to Agent Harmon.

Harmon shrugged. "I don't really know him. This is the first time we've met."

Fiona stood. "Where's the bathroom?"

"End of the hall, last door on your right," Captain Rogers directed.

She nodded her thanks and started for the door. Nate followed her. "Are you okay?" he asked softly. "Do you want me to walk you there?"

"I'm fine," she said, shaking her head. "I just need a minute. It's a lot to process."

"Take your time," he said, briefly touching the small of her back. "We'll be here when you're ready."

She gave him a grateful smile and slipped out the door.

Nate turned to find that Owen had stepped closer. "Is it just me, or does something about this whole situation seem off to you?"

His partner nodded. "I was just about to ask you the same thing."

Captain Rogers drifted over, leaving Agent Harmon on the other side of the table. The man seemed oblivious, totally absorbed by the lit screen of his phone. Good. Nate didn't want his input on this conversation.

"I don't like this," Captain Rogers said as soon as he was close enough. "Something doesn't feel right."

"It's almost a little too perfect," Nate observed. "Their explanations for everything, I mean. And it doesn't match up with what we know."

Owen nodded. "If a major Mexican drug cartel was moving in, bodies should be piling up. We haven't seen that, and we haven't seen an uptick in the type of violence cartels are known for."

"Unless they're trying to keep a low profile," Captain Rogers said. "If they really are in the early stages of making a deal, they might not want to draw attention to it."

"That's possible," Nate allowed. "But I find it hard to believe the cartel would move this quickly. I scanned those photos into the system this morning, and you're telling me that in a matter of hours they saw them and dispatched goons to erase anyone who'd seen them? That seems awfully fast to me."

"It suggests they have someone working on the inside," Owen said, dropping his voice even lower. "What do you know about these two guys, Captain?"

The older man shook his head. "Next to nothing. I called their superiors, who verified they'd been sent. But that's all I know."

"Maybe it's time to do a little digging of our own," Nate suggested.

"Couldn't hurt," the captain agreed. "I want to hear what Golightly says first, and then I'll see what I can find out."

Nate tamped down his rising impatience. The captain knew what he was doing, and it would be good for all three of them to hear Golightly's report. He was glad he wasn't the only one who was uneasy about the situation. At first he'd worried that his growing feelings for Fiona were clouding his judgment, but knowing that his partner and his boss thought the same thing validated his suspicions.

Now if they could just figure out what was really going on.

Fiona splashed water on her face, the cool shock of it helping to refocus her mind. It was hard to think—her brain was going a mile a minute, churning out thoughts and worries so quickly she barely had time to examine one before another one jerked into view, vying for her attention. It was fear, she knew, that made her thoughts so chaotic and disjointed. If she could just conquer her fear, she could take a dispassionate, logical look at the situation and come up with the best solution.

She took a deep breath and closed her eyes, trying to block out the hum of the heater and the low buzz of sound from the people working down the hall. It took a moment, but finally she felt her heartbeat start to slow, to drop from a panicked gallop into a normal, relaxed rhythm.

It's too late for that. You're involved now.

You really don't get it, do you?

Sal's parting words now made sense, but she wished she could go back to a time when they'd still been a riddle. He had known about the danger—he must have, or else why had he killed himself? Had he been trying to warn her?

Not for the first time, she wondered what he would have done if she hadn't broken free. Traded her for the photographs? Or given her to the cartel in exchange for his own life? The possibility made her shudder. He'd probably thought to blame her for the pictures, and turn her over to the cartel for punishment. After all, Joey was dead and couldn't contradict that story.

"Thank God, I got away," she murmured. Although right now, she had to admit, she still didn't feel very safe.

If what the agent said was true, she still had a big, fat target painted on her back. And she'd read enough news articles to know that Mexican cartels weren't known for their restraint.

But what were the chances they would find her? Houston was a big city, and she was merely one out of two million people. Would they really comb every neighborhood in search of her, to snuff out the nonexistent threat she represented to their interests?

The federal agent certainly seemed to think so. He'd been quite insistent that she go into some kind of witness protection program, but Fiona wasn't sure she wanted to uproot her life like that. From what she understood, if she accepted his offer she'd have to move to a brand-new place, leaving behind her life here in Houston.

A few weeks ago, that wouldn't have bothered her so much. The only tie she really had to this area was her graduate program, and it was quite possible she could transfer to another university to finish her degree.

But now that Nate was in her life, Fiona didn't want to just walk away. The connection she felt with him was unlike anything she'd known before. And after spending the past several years putting herself last in her own life, she wanted to start living again, to see what the future held for her and Nate.

She reached for the paper towels and patted her face dry. Maybe she was being irrational, but she'd rather take her chances with the cartel than miss out on having a life with Nate.

Her mind made up, she turned to head back to the interview room. It might take some time to convince Nate, but once she explained her position, hopefully he would agree that she'd made the right choice.

She reached for the door handle just as it pushed inward. She took a step back to make room for the new arrival, but froze when the agent from the interview room walked in.

"What are you doing in here?" Had he really followed her into the ladies' room to continue arguing that she needed to go into the witness protection program? Talk about pushy.

"You need to come with me."

"No." She shook her head firmly. "I've thought about it, and I'm going to stay here. I'm not willing to uproot my life on the off chance I might be in danger." She moved to walk past him, but he held out his arm, blocking her access to the door.

"It's not a slight chance," he said, sliding his hand into his jacket pocket and withdrawing a gun. He pointed it at her, the fanatical gleam in his eyes telling her he was prepared to use it. "Now move."

For a half second, she was tempted to fight back. She'd had enough of men sticking a gun in her face and telling her to do something! But she could tell by the set of his jaw this man was crazy, and if he had to shoot her in the bathroom of the police station, he would.

"What's your plan?" she asked, taking a step forward. Maybe if people overheard him, they'd realize something was wrong…

"You and I are going to take a ride. And if you give me any trouble—" he jammed the gun into her side, making her wince "—I'm going to take a detour and kill your boyfriend first."

He would do it, too. She had a brief fantasy of being herded back into the interview room, where Nate and his partner could disarm the man and save her. But dread filled her stomach as she realized that if they went back, the gunman would start shooting with no warning. Nate wouldn't have a chance to react or defend himself—he'd be dead within minutes. And even though she was terrified and wanted nothing more than to see Nate's face one last time, she wouldn't be the cause of his death.

"I won't do anything," she said, swallowing hard to force down the lump in her throat. *Not here, anyway.*

This was it, then. She couldn't risk Nate's safety, or anyone else's for that matter. Better for her to go with him now and hope they could get out of the building without anyone getting hurt. She'd just have to figure out a way to escape later.

If it was even possible.

of his neck stood up and his muscles grew tense, his instincts screaming that something was wrong.

The man frowned slightly. "I'm Bill Golightly, from Homeland Security. I'm sorry, I thought my superior officer told you I was coming."

"*You're* Agent Golightly?" Owen said, his eyes going wide.

"Yes." The man reached into his pocket and withdrew his identification.

"Then who the hell is that other guy?" Captain Rogers barked.

Nate realized in a sickening instant what was going on. The other man was a plant, someone from the cartel sent to take out any witnesses.

And he'd probably seen Fiona head to the bathroom while he was in the hallway making his phone call.

Nate bolted from the room, leaving the other men to argue about who was real and who was not. He didn't have time to waste establishing identities. They could sort all that out later, as far as he was concerned.

He didn't see the man in the hall, but he hadn't really expected to. The phone call was a ploy, a way to regroup and replan when it had become clear that Nate wasn't going to let Fiona just walk away with a stranger. Had he cornered her in the bathroom? Were they still there now?

He forced himself to slow down as he approached the bathroom door. If he busted in, guns blazing, he could very well spook the man into hurting Fiona. It wasn't a chance he was willing to take. Instead, he forced himself to take a deep breath and pushed gently on the door, easing it open until he could see the room clearly.

Empty.

He stepped inside and checked all the stalls, just to make sure. No one was here. No window, either, which meant they'd had to leave using the door. But where would he take her?

The garage. That had to be their destination. The man wouldn't want to draw attention to himself by killing Fiona in a public place. Better for him to take her someplace remote. And the only way to do that in a city like Houston was to drive.

Nate raced out of the bathroom and nearly ran into Owen. "Garage," he said shortly. Owen nodded and fell into step beside him.

They hit the doors together, shoving them open with such force that the sound ricocheted through the parking garage like a gunshot. At this point, Nate no longer cared about the element of surprise—he just wanted to find Fiona and get her back safely.

He glanced around, hoping to catch a glimpse of movement or some other clue that would tell him where they'd gone. The parking garage at the precinct wasn't terribly large, but there wasn't enough time to search car by car.

"You don't have to do this." The words were faint but clear. Nate nearly cried out in relief. She was still here!

He glanced questioningly at Owen, who nodded. He'd heard it, too.

Keep talking, he silently urged. He took a careful step in the direction of the sound, hoping he'd picked the right trajectory. It was hard to be sure, the way noise echoed in this place. But if Fiona would continue to talk, he could find her.

"I'll just pretend I never saw the pictures," she said, her voice getting louder as he moved. His heart pounded a steady rhythm in his ears as adrenaline and anticipation surged together in his blood. He was getting closer!

Owen touched his arm, forcing him to stop. His partner made a few gestures, indicating he was going around so they could close in on the man from both directions. Nate nodded, then resumed moving forward. Now that he'd heard Fiona's voice and knew where she was, he wasn't going to stop until she was back in his arms.

Where she belonged.

"Shut up," the man grumbled. Fiona made a soft, pained sound that had Nate seeing red. Had the man just hurt her?

"Stop pulling my arm," she said, sounding a little testy. Nate couldn't help but smile at her feisty attitude in the face of certain danger. *That* was the woman he knew and cared about. Maybe even loved.

The thought brought him up short, but he dismissed the shock of it almost instantly. Yes, he was well on his way to loving her. Now he just had to get her back so he could tell her and show her how he felt.

"Move faster!"

"No!" He heard sounds of a struggle, as if Fiona was pulling away and the man was scrabbling to get ahold of her again. "I'm not getting into a car with you."

"You don't have a choice!"

"Yes, I do." Fiona's voice was stubborn. "If you're going to kill me, just do it now. Why draw it out?"

"This isn't the place," he said, sounding a little desperate.

"Well, I'm certainly not going to make it easy for you!" she snapped.

Nate crept closer, holding his breath. He was happy she was stalling her abductor, but if she pushed him too far…

There was a faint beep, as if the man had remotely unlocked a car. They must be getting close.

"Get in the car," he ordered.

"No," she replied.

A muffled thump sounded, followed by Fiona's faint cry. Unless he missed his guess, the fake agent had just hit Fiona and was trying to manhandle her into his vehicle. It was too much.

He couldn't wait to see if Owen was in position. He had to move, now, before Fiona was hurt any more by this psycho.

Keeping his head down, Nate rushed around the corner in time to see his worst nightmare brought to life. The man, whoever he was, had his hands on Fiona and was trying to force her into the backseat of a dark sedan. She was putting up a good fight, but his greater strength and anger was slowly overcoming her resistance. Nate watched in horror as the man drew back his fist and landed a blow to Fiona's ribs, right in the spot where Big Sal had kicked her earlier.

The breath gusted out of her on a choked moan, and her body went limp. Taking advantage of this new opportunity, the man hefted her into the back of the car, bending to sweep her feet inside.

Nate waited until she was safely behind the closed door of the car before making his move. It was risky, but if bullets started flying, he wanted her behind some kind of cover.

"Freeze!" he shouted, advancing quickly with his gun held out.

The man jumped, clearly surprised to find he wasn't alone. He tried to make a dash around the trunk of the car to reach the driver's side door, but Owen approached from the opposite direction, his gun also up. "Don't move!"

Fiona's abductor stayed in place while his head swiveled back and forth between Nate and Owen, as if he was trying to decide who was the greater threat. Apparently feeling Nate was the bigger problem, he turned to face him and stepped forward.

"This ends here," Nate said, struggling to keep his voice calm. The logical, cool side of him recognized he needed to talk this guy down, to arrest him and question him and have him sent to trial to answer for his crimes. He clearly worked for the cartel; there had to be blood on his hands, and he should be made to pay.

But Nate's emotional, angry side kept replaying the sight of this man punching Fiona in the ribs and stuffing her limp body into the backseat of a car. His finger itched to pull the trigger, to end this now and make sure this man could never hurt Fiona again.

In the end, his training won out. As satisfying as it would be to avenge her, he knew that it would only serve to make things worse. He couldn't very well have a relationship with Fiona if he was behind bars. She deserved so much more than that.

"It's over when I say it's over!" The fake agent was growing increasingly agitated, a fact that made him unpredictable. While Nate wasn't worried about getting hurt—he knew Owen would cover him—this guy was still too close to Fiona. If he snapped and started shooting into the backseat, there was little Nate could do to stop him before he hurt her again.

"This doesn't have to end badly," Nate said, inching forward as he spoke. He kept his gun up but made eye contact with the other man, trying to show his sincerity. "You can put your gun down, and we can go back inside and talk some more."

The man shot him a disbelieving look. "You must think I'm an idiot."

Nate shook his head. "No, I don't. What's your name?"

While he spoke, Owen crept ever closer to the backseat. If Nate could keep the perp distracted, Owen could grab Fiona and get her out of there. It took everything in Nate's power not to focus on his partner's progress. He kept his eyes locked on the man in front of him, knowing that if he looked distracted, it would tip the assailant off that something was going on behind him.

"No." The man shook his head firmly.

"No?" What was that supposed to mean? "I don't understand."

"I don't care if you understand, Officer. I'm not going to play your game."

Nate's brows rose. "What game? There is no game here. I'm trying to help you."

The man let out a humorless laugh. "Sure you are. You want to know my name so you can start to personalize the conversation. To get me thinking of my family, my friends, my life. Then you'll try to make me see that if I don't cooperate with you, I'll never see them again. You want me to surrender peacefully so you can go back to your desk and pat yourself on the back for a job well done."

Nate blinked. Well, yeah, that was pretty much the gist of it.

"And above all," the man continued, "you want to keep me talking, to distract me from the fact that your partner is inching closer to the door of my car in a futile attempt to rescue my hostage." At this, he withdrew a second gun from the waistband of his pants and took a step back, so that he now had both Nate and Owen in his sights.

Damn, damn, damn! They'd been played, and they hadn't even seen it coming.

Owen froze, his jaw clenched so tightly Nate could practically hear his partner's teeth grinding together.

The man smiled arrogantly, enjoying the turn of events. "It seems we're at an impasse."

Nate glanced at his partner, who nodded subtly. They might both have guns pointed at them, but even the best shooter had to focus on one target at a time.

"I don't see it that way," Nate replied smoothly. "There's still two of us, and only one of you. By my count, we still have the advantage."

"That's where you're wrong." His smile didn't waver, but he did take another half step back, betraying his insecurity. "You want to live through this. And you want to save the hostage. Me? I know the cartel will punish me if I don't complete my mission. And I would rather die in a hail of bullets here than live to experience their justice." He laughed softly, the sound echoing eerily in the cavernous garage. Goose bumps broke out along Nate's arms as he stared at the man, recognizing him for the fanatic that he was.

"My only goal is to kill my target. And there's nothing you can do to stop me."

Fiona clamped her jaw shut, determined to stay as quiet as possible. Every breath triggered an avalanche of pain, but she refused to release the whimpers building up in the back of her throat. If she made noise, she couldn't hear what was going on outside the car, and she had to make sure her timing was just right...

Nate was here! She'd heard his voice just after her captor had landed that incapacitating punch to her side. She'd recognized his voice and had wanted nothing more than to break free and run to his side, but her body just wouldn't cooperate. The ribs that hadn't been broken by Sal's earlier kick were most certainly fractured now, and she was reduced to lying in the backseat of the car, taking shallow breaths and trying to move as little as possible.

From what she could gather, Nate wasn't alone, a fact that filled her with relief. She didn't doubt Nate's abilities or competence, but she was happy there was someone with him to watch his back and keep him safe. Besides, two against one made for much better odds.

The man who'd taken her was speaking again, and she could tell by the tone of his voice that he thought he'd gained an advantage. Moving carefully, trying not to draw attention to herself, Fiona pushed herself up and risked a quick peek outside. Her abductor was standing near the door, his back to her. Nate was facing him, several feet away. She hadn't seen anyone else, but based on the way the bad guy was pointing his guns, someone else was approaching from the other side of the car. A classic standoff pose.

If they could only get the man to shift a little, Fiona could hit him with the car door and throw him off balance. That would give Nate and his friend a chance to move in and gain the upper hand. But she couldn't waste the opportunity. If she tried that stunt now, the door would completely miss him. No, he had to change his position first.

She silently willed Nate to press onward, hoping that if he took a step forward, her assailant would take a step back. Just a little bit farther, that's all she needed to help turn this around!

She was focusing so hard on getting the bad guy to move that she'd stopped paying attention to his speech. But the word *kill* broke through her concentration, and she realized with a sudden, icy shock that he was talking about her.

Of course, she thought wryly. Nate's appearance had made her forget she was still in danger. After all, normal people didn't try to continue committing their crime when they were faced with two armed police officers. She'd assumed that Nate's presence guaranteed her safety and all that was left was to work out the formalities of surrender.

That probably would have been the case, too, had the man who'd taken her not been a fanatic. It was clear he was willing to die here, in this dirty police parking garage, as long as he took her down with him.

Anger swelled in her chest, burning away the pain of her injured ribs. She would not die in the backseat of an unmarked car, only a few steps away from the man she cared about! It simply wasn't an option.

Make him move! She silently shouted the thought in Nate's direction, repeating it over and over again as if that would somehow make a difference.

"I won't let you hurt her any more." Nate's voice drifted in, muffled but determined. She smiled, despite her concentration. His protective claim made her feel cherished, and for a split second, she had the urge to cry. *Not now*, she told herself, blinking hard to dispel the prickling sensation of tears forming in her eyes. If she started crying now, she'd miss her chance.

"You act as if you have a choice," the man said. His voice was louder, but he hadn't moved closer. Not yet...

"What's to stop me from shooting you now?" Nate asked. He sounded calm, but Fiona could detect the note of strain in his voice.

No, Nate. Don't do it. Fiona's heart beat hard against her chest, and she held her breath. She didn't particularly care about her abductor, but she did care about Nate. Deeply so. And she knew that if he shot a man who wasn't posing an immediate threat, he'd never forgive himself. While Nate's concern for her safety was touching, she didn't want to be the reason he punished himself for the rest of his life.

"You can't." The man's voice was openly mocking now, and Fiona bit down hard on her lip to keep from screaming. "If you shoot me now, you will lose your career. I know all about the rules you must abide by in order to do your job. I have no such hindrances."

"You might want to brush up on your reading," a second voice piped up. Was that Owen? It had to be. "You're threatening two officers with a weapon. We are well within our rights to defend ourselves, using deadly force if necessary."

"Then why don't you? Go ahead, pull your triggers. End this now." He sounded cajoling, even a little persuasive.

Fiona frowned. Why was he goading them?

"I know why you hesitate," the man continued. "You want to take me alive. You hope to question me, to find out how I am connected to the cartel, what else I have done for them." He made a clucking sound with his tongue. "I won't tell you."

There was a beat of silence, and then Nate spoke again. "Well, if you're sure about that…" She heard a shuffling sound and imagined Nate stepping forward. The man moved back reflexively, into her line of sight. It was now or never!

Fiona drew back her legs, reached for the door handle and pulled. Then she kicked out with all her might, sending the door flying open. There was a satisfying thud of resistance as the door met flesh, and the man let out a startled "oof!" as the breath was knocked out of his body. Fiona allowed herself a split second of satisfaction and grinned fiercely.

Then all hell broke loose around her.

Chapter 16

What on earth?

Nate barely had time to register the sudden movement of the car door before it made contact with the perp's body, slamming into him and sending him careening to the side to crash into the car next to him.

Fiona, he thought, pride filling him at the fact that she'd waited until the guy was within range to make her move. She was clearly trying to help, and while he appreciated her efforts, he really wished she'd stayed out of it. Her actions had introduced another element of unpredictability into the equation, and she'd made herself a target again.

The man realized it, too. He pushed against the car to right himself, then turned to point his guns at Fiona.

"Don't shoot!" Nate yelled, rushing forward to disarm the man.

For a terrible second, it seemed the man hadn't heard him. He remained focused on Fiona, anger tightening his jaw as he stared down at her. Time seemed to slow as Nate lunged for him, desperate to deflect his aim so he couldn't hurt her. At this range, the guy couldn't miss.

At the last second, the perp pivoted on his heel, turning to face Nate. He brought his guns up, now training them on Nate's body. A satisfied gleam lit his dark eyes, and Nate realized he'd been played. But he couldn't stop now. His forward momentum had taken over, and he was going to run into the man, like it or not.

Nate braced himself, tensing his muscles as he prepared for the shots he knew were coming. And the bad guy didn't disappoint. He fired, the sound of his guns echoing in the garage like cannon fire. Nate closed his eyes as he plowed through twin plumes of smoke, and the sharp tang of cordite filled his sinuses.

He heard a second barrage of shots coming from somewhere behind and off to the side. Owen. His partner was trying to cover him.

Feeling no pain, Nate opened his eyes and saw a look of panic cross the perp's face. Evidently, he'd expected his shots to stop Nate, and the fact that they hadn't scared him. Had they the time, Nate could have explained it to him—he was protecting his woman, and nothing and no one was going to stand in his way.

He tackled the man with all the force of a pro linebacker, driving him to the ground in a tangle of limbs.

The back of the man's head hit the concrete hard, bouncing off with a painful-sounding thud that made Nate's skin crawl. He went limp for a moment, clearly dazed. Seeing his chance, Nate quickly flipped the man over onto his stomach, and, keeping his knee pressed into the bad guy's back, he made quick work of disarming and cuffing him. Only when he was satisfied the man was no longer a threat did he stand and allow Owen to take over watching him.

He turned to the car to find Fiona peering out, her eyes wide and her face pale. Her hair was a tangled mess on top of her head thanks to the perp's manhandling, and there was a dark pink mark on her left cheek where the man had obviously hit her. She clutched her side, plainly feeling the effects of her rude treatment, and he could tell by the way she pressed her lips together that she was in pain.

Despite all that, she was the most beautiful thing he'd ever seen.

She met his gaze, and he saw the reflection of his relief and something more in her eyes. He started toward her and she climbed out of the car, moving to meet him halfway. He wanted to pull her into his arms, press her against his chest and never let her go. He reached for her, but remembered her ribs just in time and stopped himself from grabbing her.

Heedless of her own injuries, Fiona practically threw herself at him, her arms wrapping around his neck and squeezing so tightly that he had trouble breathing. It was worth it, though, to feel her solid and warm against him again.

"You scared ten years off my life," he murmured into her ear, her hair tickling his lips.

She let out a weak laugh. "That makes two of us."

"What happened?"

She relaxed her grip and leaned back slightly so she could make eye contact again. "He came into the bathroom and pointed a gun at me."

"Why didn't you yell for help?"

Her brow lifted. "And risk having him shoot anyone who came to help? I don't think so."

Nate nodded in acknowledgment of her point. "Fair enough."

She snuggled back into his embrace. "It doesn't matter now. You're here."

"I am." And he was never letting her go again.

"What happens now?"

He sighed, knowing reality was about to intrude on their moment. He glanced over her head and met Owen's eye, and his partner gave him a meaningful nod. "You have to give your statement," Nate said, knowing he sounded unenthusiastic about it. "And we should probably get you checked out at the hospital again, to make sure you didn't exacerbate your injury."

"Okay." She nodded, the gesture rubbing her head against his chest. "But after that, we can leave?" She sounded so hopeful, he couldn't help but smile.

"Absolutely." He pressed a gentle kiss to the top of her head. "After that, I'll take you anywhere you want to go."

Fiona stepped into her house with a sigh, feeling her muscles relax as the familiar, comforting scents of home enveloped her. Nate quietly shut the door behind her, then moved and put his hands on her shoulders. She leaned back against his chest, drawing comfort from his solid strength and warmth.

"Better?" he asked, his voice a low rumble in her ear.

She smiled. "Much."

He wrapped his arms around her in a loose embrace, and they stood there for a moment, simply enjoying each other's touch. She could have stayed like that forever, but Slinky chose that moment to let out an indignant howl.

Nate laughed softly, his chest vibrating against her back. "Sounds like someone else is happy to be home."

"I'm sure he is." Fiona put the gym bag on the floor and unzipped it. Slinky poked his head out and sniffed, then jumped free of the bag in one elegant motion. He immediately set about investigating the room, rubbing his cheeks up against the furniture to renew his claim on everything.

She heard the smile in Nate's voice when he spoke again. "He's a resilient little guy."

Fiona laughed. "Little? Are you sure we're talking about the same cat?"

"Okay, you have a point. Still, I can see why you love him so much."

She rested the back of her head against Nate's shoulder, taking comfort from the simple touch. "He's my baby. For the past several years, it's just been the two of us." A lump formed in her throat, and she swallowed hard to push it down. Now was not the time to feel sorry for herself.

"You've been lonely." It wasn't a question—Nate stated it as a simple fact. But there was no judgment or pity in his voice. He seemed to understand how difficult it had been for her, how hard it was to feel truly alone in the world. Probably because, for so long, he'd felt the same. Even though their circumstances were different—she'd lost her family, while he'd pulled away from his—the end result was the same.

But they didn't have to be alone anymore.

"Yes," she said quietly. She took a deep breath, gathering her courage. "You have, too."

He was silent for a moment, but he tightened his arms around her stomach, letting her know he'd heard her. "That's true," he admitted finally.

"Nate?"

"Hmm?"

"I'm tired of being alone."

She felt the change in his body the moment he realized what she was really saying. His muscles tensed and he grew unnaturally still behind her, his breathing going from a deep, regular rhythm to shallow, rapid breaths, almost as if he was afraid any extraneous movement would scare her away. She could feel his heart beating against her shoulder blades, quick, hard thumps that betrayed his reaction.

"Are you sure?" His voice had changed to a deep, gravelly rumble that caused the fine hairs on the back of her neck to stand up. She fought the urge to shiver, not wanting Nate to interpret the gesture the wrong way.

Fiona nodded firmly, then twisted in his embrace until she faced him. His eyes were the deep, vibrant green of a forest after the rain, and as she met his gaze, she saw a mixture of hope and concern warring in their depths.

"I'm sure," she told him with a smile. "I've felt a connection to you from the moment I saw you, and after the events of the past few days, I'm tired of waiting for the 'right' time. Life is too uncertain for that."

"But your injuries," he protested, gently touching her side.

She shrugged. "I'm fine." It was true. The doctor hadn't been thrilled to find out she'd aggravated the injury, although to her surprise, another round of X-rays had shown no additional ribs were broken. He'd loaded her up on pain medication and told her to take it easy, and Nate had quickly promised he would take care of her. Normally, Fiona would have been annoyed at the idea that she needed a babysitter, but she knew Nate spoke up because he cared and was worried about her. Besides, the thought of him taking care of her was rather appealing.

"I don't want to hurt you," he hedged.

If she hadn't known better, she'd think Nate was stalling because he wasn't interested in her. But she could feel the evidence of his desire pressed against her hip. He was genuinely concerned and wanted to do the right thing, a fact that made her love him all the more.

The realization drew her up short. Love? Could she really say that, after knowing him for only a few days? Her rational mind whirled, searching for a reason to scale back her emotions. But her heart piped up, taking control. Yes, she really did mean love. They hadn't known each other long according to the calendar, but the experiences they'd shared had been intense and emotional. She'd seen Nate at his best and his worst, and he'd shown his true colors. He was a kind, decent, thoughtful man with a great sense of humor and a strong sense of honor and duty. *Love* was the perfect word to describe how she felt about him, and she refused to stress about the implications of that powerful word.

Her emotions must have shown on her face, because Nate's expression changed to one of awareness. His features softened, his concerned frown relaxing as his brows rose slightly and his lips formed a small *O* of surprise.

"Oh," he said, his tone reverent.

Fiona smiled and he swallowed hard, his Adam's apple bobbing under the golden skin of his throat. She lifted her finger and traced the line of his neck with the edge of her nail, pleased to see goose bumps pop up on his skin in the wake of her touch. It was a heady sensation, the realization that she affected Nate so strongly. He projected such a powerful physical presence, it was easy for her to assume he had no weaknesses, that nothing could break through his armor.

Except, it seemed, for her.

Nate closed his eyes and inhaled deeply through his nose, causing his chest to rise and connect with hers. He wrapped his arms around her and pulled her in close, until their bodies were flush against each other. Heat poured off his body, seeping into hers. The combination of her desire and his warmth caused her muscles to melt, and she clutched his shoulders for support.

His eyes searched her face, as if looking for any sign that she had changed her mind. Fiona reached up and cupped his cheek with her hand. His rough stubble tickled her palm, sending tingles of sensation up her arm. She nodded ever so slightly and saw an answering heat flare in his eyes.

He dipped his head, his lips brushing over hers in a gentle caress. Then he let out a sigh that might have been her name, and his mouth took full possession of hers.

He kissed her as if he was staking a claim, branding her as his own. Not that she was interested in going anywhere—she had no desire to be anyplace but in Nate's arms.

Did he realize what he was telling her, that his lips and teeth and tongue communicated his feelings better than any words? She marveled at the intensity of his emotions, amazed that he had managed to contain such fiery passion behind a calm exterior. What other hidden depths did Nate possess? It was a puzzle she had to solve, and the thought of getting to know him, the *real* him, filled her with a delicious sense of anticipation.

She wrapped her arms around his neck and returned his kiss, putting all the joy and enthusiasm she felt into it. Communication went both ways, and if Nate could share his feelings, she could share hers back.

She didn't know how long the kiss went on. It could have been minutes, it could have been hours—it was hard to keep track of time when her whole focus was on the man in front of her and the feelings she could finally express.

After spending so much time on her own, devoting herself first to taking care of her mother and then to her graduate program, there was something almost intoxicating about allowing herself to *feel* again. Her emotions were a dizzying concoction of sensations that set her blood on fire and rushed to her head, clearing it of all logical thought. She was reduced to a mass of nerve endings, each one exquisitely sensitive to the touch of Nate's hands, his mouth, the solid lines of his body against hers.

She clung to his shoulders for dear life, loving every minute of the experience and praying it would never end.

Chapter 17

Nate could hardly believe his luck.

Fiona was here, in his arms, kissing him back with all the enthusiasm and eagerness he'd only dreamed about.

Seeing her being dragged through the parking garage by that cartel hit man had nearly made his heart stop. For the first time in his life, he'd felt genuine fear.

Oh, he'd been scared before, of course. As a police officer, he'd faced his share of dangerous situations. But even when he'd been shot as a rookie, he'd never actually thought about his own death. Maybe he'd just been naive, or maybe he'd been lucky. Either way, he usually didn't stop to think about the potential consequences of his job.

Until now.

He'd been so used to compartmentalizing his life and his relationships that he'd never really allowed someone all the way in. He had his work friends and his family, and he liked keeping the two categories separate. Now, for the first time, he recognized that he'd been shortchanging himself. He'd put so much time and effort into his job that he'd neglected the life part of the work-life balance.

Fiona had changed all that. She'd given him a reason to focus on life again. And while he'd focused on work to make sure he could provide for his family later on, he wasn't going to have much of a family left if he didn't invest the time in them now. That realization was her gift to him, and it was priceless.

She was such an amazing woman, and she didn't even know it. The way she'd stepped up to care for her mother, the way she'd urged him to connect to his own family—she'd opened his eyes to his mistakes without any judgment or censure. She'd merely served as an example, showing him in her own, unique way how things could be.

And he loved her for it.

He wrapped his arms around her, pressing her even closer. She clutched his shoulders, a fine tremor running through her body as she kissed him. He could feel her heart beating against his chest, galloping out a rhythm to match his own. The knowledge that her eagerness matched his only served to heighten his arousal, and he had the sudden, all-consuming need to *feel* her, to remove the barriers between them and touch her skin. He needed to have that unrestricted contact between their bodies, to revel in the sensations that only her skin could provide.

He gave the hem of her shirt an experimental tug, silently asking permission. He didn't want to rush things between them, but if he didn't get his hands on her soon, he felt like he would die.

Fiona broke the kiss, pulling back enough that he could see the flush on her cheeks and the shine of her eyes. She moved to take off her shirt but paused with her arms halfway up, wincing.

"Help me?"

The sight of her pain hit him like a cold shower and Nate bit his lip, shaking his head. "Maybe we should wait until you've recovered."

Fiona pursed her kiss-swollen lips and lifted one eyebrow, her expression determined. "I told you before, I'm fine. Now, am I going to have to cut my shirt off, or are you going to help me?" Her mouth curved up in a wry smile that sent a zing of sensation straight to Nate's stomach.

"I'd hate for you to ruin such a nice shirt," he murmured, reaching forward to take the hem in his hands. He lifted it slowly, gently, taking care not to jostle her or disturb her side any more than was necessary.

He'd meant to fold the shirt and place it on the sofa, but the sight of her pale, albeit bruised, skin transfixed him and he dropped it carelessly to the ground. If Fiona noticed, she didn't seem to care. She looked up at him from under her lashes, seeming suddenly shy.

"You're so beautiful," he breathed, running his gaze over the dips and slopes of her body.

"Really?" She sounded hopeful, as if she wanted to believe he was telling her the truth.

He stepped forward and traced her collarbone with the tip of his finger. Goose bumps rose in the wake of his touch, and he traced the line of the bone with his tongue. She shivered and let out a low moan.

"Really," he said, tipping her head up so she met his gaze.

Her eyes softened and she nodded, giving him a small smile. "Your turn," she whispered.

Nate set a land speed record tugging off his shirt, and his ego was rewarded by the sight of Fiona's eyes widening in appreciation. "Very nice," she said, her gaze tracing over his chest and stomach to linger on his belt buckle. Her hand lifted, a tentative gesture of intent. He stepped forward, taking her hand in his and pressing it to his chest. "You can touch me anywhere," he assured her.

Her fingers curled into the hair on his chest, sending a bolt of pleasure straight to his groin. She brought her other hand up to roam across his torso, stopping to explore the ridges of muscle and trace the line of hair that bisected his stomach. Nate was content to let her take the lead—his body wanted nothing more than to speed things along, but he was determined not to rush Fiona. Not for their first time. He wanted her to set the pace, and so he gathered every ounce of his self-control and ignored the needs of his body.

But then she put her mouth on him, and all logical thought flew out the window.

He groaned and stepped back, needing to break

the contact before he did something he'd regret. Fiona glanced up at him, confused and a little uncertain. "I'm hanging on by a very thin thread," he told her, his voice so hoarse he barely recognized it as his own. "I don't want to rush you into anything."

Her lips curved in a seductive smile, and her eyes warmed. "Let go," she said, her voice sultry. "I'll catch you."

He watched in silence as Fiona deftly worked the button of his pants. He wanted to warn her, wanted to tell her he wasn't going to last, but his brain simply would not work. Then she touched him, and his consciousness short-circuited into a million sparks of light.

He was vaguely aware of movement, of Fiona taking him by the hand and leading him somewhere. Then he fell into softness and realized they were in her bedroom. Fiona stood over him, tugging on his pants. He helpfully lifted his hips, and his pants slid free of his body in one smooth motion. The cool air of the room felt good against his heated skin, and the shock of it pulled him back into the moment.

He sat up and reached for Fiona. She came willingly into his arms, pressing herself against him with a sigh of pleasure. He leaned back, bringing her with him until they both lay on the bed, their limbs entwined. He rolled until he was over her, careful to keep his weight on his arms so he didn't crush her ribs further.

Fiona's hair spread out on the bed in an auburn halo, and the familiar scent of lemons he'd come to associate with her grew stronger as he bent to kiss her again.

She moved under him, her hips lifting in a silent plea he was only too happy to acknowledge.

He skimmed his hand down the silky softness of her side until he reached the waistband of her pants. Then it was his turn to rise up and tug, peeling the pants from her body and exposing her legs inch by provocative inch. Her skin glowed in the soft light of the bedside table lamp, a pale, luminous shine that made it look as if she'd been painted with a silvery gilt. So lovely. He took a second to appreciate the sight, pushing down the demands of his body lest he miss out on something. He certainly didn't plan for this to be the only time they were together, but he wanted to remember everything about their first encounter so he could savor it later.

Fiona apparently didn't share his patience. She reached for his hand and tugged, pulling him down on top of her and kissing him. He relaxed his muscles, his body melding around hers as they moved together. After a few moments, she pulled away, tearing her mouth from his on a gasp.

"Wait," she said, sounding a little breathless as she moved under him.

Nate rose up on his knees, pushing down his disappointment. She'd changed her mind—maybe her side was hurting her more than she wanted to admit? He glanced down, his jaw tightening at the deep purple marks that marred her skin. No wonder she wanted to stop. Breathing alone had to be painful enough.

Fiona wriggled out from under him and turned to her bedside table, reaching for the drawer. It took him a second to realize what she was doing, but awareness dawned on him when she turned back and handed him a small foil packet. His face must have betrayed his relief, because she took one look at him and laughed.

"Did you think I had changed my mind?"

He lifted one shoulder in a shrug, feeling his cheeks heat. "It's okay if you do," he said. He traced a finger over her bruises, but she shook her head.

"Not on your life. Now get back here."

He was only too happy to comply. He took care of business and was welcomed back into Fiona's arms, and then into her body. She let out a sigh of satisfaction that was echoed in his soul, and as they moved together, Nate felt like he was coming home.

Sometime later, Nate tightened his grip on Fiona, pulling her even closer as he wrapped his body around hers. She made a small, inquisitive sound, and he nuzzled her hair.

"I'm just not ready to let you go yet," he whispered.

He heard the smile in her voice when she responded, "That's okay. You can hold me as long as you like."

His mind drifted over the events of the past few hours, playing back their interlude as he recalled every moment. The look on her face. Her sounds of pleasure. The feel of her skin against his. He'd had his fair share of lovers before, but nothing had ever been quite like this. He chuckled softly as realization hit.

"What's so funny?" She sounded a little drowsy, as if she'd been pulled back from the edge of sleep.

Nate debated for a second, then decided he might as well confess. He was tired of keeping people at arm's length, and Fiona deserved to know exactly how he felt about her. Even though they'd only known each other a few days, he had a feeling she would understand.

"I was just thinking," he said, nuzzling the shell of her ear. "Everyone talks about 'making love,' and I've never really understood that description. I thought it was just something a marketing guru made up to sell cards or chick flicks. But now—" he pressed a soft kiss to her earlobe "—I actually get it."

Fiona stopped breathing, and Nate felt a flicker of fear. Had he said too much? Maybe he should have played it cool. The last thing he wanted was to scare her away!

"Are you saying what I think you're saying?" she asked, her voice very small.

Nate's gut twisted into knots, but he couldn't back down now. Better to tell her the truth than to lie and pretend otherwise. He wanted them to have a life together, and he refused to build the foundation of their relationship on lies.

"Well. Yes. I think I am."

She turned in his arms until she was facing him. Her eyes were wide and luminous, and as he watched, a sheen of tears formed. She blinked them away, but he'd seen them. Great—he'd made her cry.

"Fiona," he started, trying to find the right words to apologize. This was not going well at all. "I'm—"

She shook her head and pressed a finger to his lips, silencing him. Then she smiled, and it transformed her face. "You have no idea how it feels to hear you say that."

"Oh?" So those weren't sad or scared tears after all. His worry evaporated, and a sense of relief enveloped him. He hadn't screwed up the moment!

"And just so you know," she continued, leaning forward to kiss him. "I feel the same way about you."

Her words hit him right in the heart, and for a second, he could only stare at her in wonder. It was one thing to imagine she had feelings for him. Hearing her say it, though, was quite another, and it took him a moment to process it. Her confession triggered a waterfall of emotions, each one racing by so fast he didn't have a chance to grab hold before another one passed by.

The sheer joy he'd felt as a kid on the first day of summer vacation. The pride from graduating the police academy. The bliss of a lazy Sunday afternoon at the ballpark. The stomach-churning anticipation at the top of a roller coaster, right before the first plunge. The fizzy, blood-tingling effervescence of sipping champagne. So many sensations, and yet none of them did justice to his current feeling.

After a moment, he realized Fiona was studying him, a small frown on her face. "Are you okay? Is it too soon to talk about this?"

He laughed, the sound one of unbridled joy. Had he ever laughed like that before? Had he ever had a reason to?

"I've never been better," he assured her, pulling her close again. "And we can talk about anything and everything. I don't care what we talk about, as long as you're with me."

She melted against him, her body going limp and

liquid around his. "Oh, good," she said, her breath hot against his skin. "But what do you say we hold off on conversation for a bit? There are other ways we can communicate." She punctuated this statement with an intimate caress that made him see stars.

"Later is fine, too," he managed to choke out, right before he lost the ability to speak.

Epilogue

One week later

Nate pulled to a stop and cut the engine before turning to look at her. "Ready?"

Fiona twisted the hem of her shirt in her hands and bit her lip. "Are you sure about this?"

He smiled, but it did little to reassure her. Her stomach was full of butterflies, and she couldn't remember the last time she'd felt so nervous.

"Are you having second thoughts?"

She shook her head, but his question had hit close to the truth. "I just don't know if this is the best idea. Your family hasn't seen you in months. They're going to want to spend time with you, not with some random girl you've brought with you."

Nate's brows drew together as he regarded her. "First of all," he said, taking one of her hands, "you are not some random girl—you are my girlfriend, and I love you." He punctuated this with a squeeze, and she was forced to smile. She'd never get tired of hearing him say those three words. So simple, and yet so powerful.

"And second of all, they're excited to meet you. I've told them all about you, and they're thrilled by you already."

"But it's Christmas! Surely this is a time for your family traditions, and I don't want to intrude."

He leaned over to brush a stray strand of hair behind her ear. "Do you honestly think I'd leave you alone on Christmas? Not on your life. Like it or not, you're part of my family now, and that means you get to be included in all the celebrations. Besides, we've already started making our own traditions." He waggled his eyebrows at her in an exaggerated leer and she laughed, the memory of their morning celebrations making her cheeks go warm.

It was hard to deny his logic. Still, she couldn't help but worry. What if Nate's mother took one look at her and hated her? What if she thought Fiona was taking away her baby boy? What if his sister, Molly, didn't like her? Nate was just starting to reach out to his family again, and she didn't want to do anything to jeopardize the progress he was making.

"I can practically hear you thinking," he said drily.

Fiona opened her mouth to respond, but a flicker of movement caught her eye. The curtains hanging in the front window of his parents' house had moved. Their arrival had been noted—it was too late to make Nate take her back now.

The front door opened, and a young woman barreled down the walk, almost tripping over her shoes in her excitement. She ran up to the car and began tapping insistently on the driver's side window, her face split into a wide grin.

Nate waved at her, then turned back and pressed a quick kiss to Fiona's mouth. "You've got this," he whispered. She smiled and nodded, and he gave her hand one final squeeze before opening his door and climbing out of the car.

Fiona emerged slowly, her eyes never leaving Nate as he wrapped his sister in a bear hug and picked her up off the ground to spin her around, eliciting delighted squeals of laughter.

"You came! You came!" she said, her eyes shining as she stared up at her big brother. "I've been waiting all day! I woke up really early, which made Mom and Dad grumpy. But they're not mad anymore," she clarified.

"I'm glad to hear it," Nate replied. "And of course I came. I couldn't miss seeing you at Christmas."

Fiona shut the car door, and Nate's sister turned to look at her. "Hello," she said with a smile. "My name is Molly."

"Hi, Molly." Fiona took a few steps forward until she was standing next to Nate. He put his arm around her shoulders and drew her in close to his side. "I'm Fiona."

Molly's expression melted into one of transfixed fascination. "Were you named after the princess in the movie?" she breathed.

Fiona laughed and shook her head. "No, but I really liked that movie. What about you?"

Molly nodded enthusiastically. "It's my favorite. I like it that she's green. Green is my favorite color."

"Mine, too," Fiona told her.

Molly grinned, then grabbed Nate's hand and started to pull. "Let's go inside. Mom made a turkey, and she said we have to wait to eat until you get here. I'm glad you came, because I'm hungry."

Nate laughed, but resisted his sister's tug. "Give me just a minute, okay? Fiona and I have some things to carry inside."

"Like presents?" Molly sounded so hopeful Fiona couldn't help but chuckle softly. Nate winked at her and then turned back to his sister.

"Exactly. Go ahead and tell Mom and Dad we're here. We'll come inside in just a minute."

"Okay." Molly nodded happily and ran back inside the house, yelling for her parents the moment she crossed the threshold.

Nate glanced down. "Doing okay?" he asked, his tone solicitous.

Fiona smiled up at him. "She's wonderful."

"She is," he agreed. "And not at all scary, right?"

"Right." She let out a sigh of relief, feeling a little lighter. His sister seemed to like her. One down, two to go...

"Ready to meet Mom and Dad?"

"Yes," she said, gathering her courage.

Nate's green eyes were the color of a Christmas tree as he smiled. "They're going to love you. Just like I do."

"I hope you're right," she replied.

He opened the back door and retrieved a basket of brightly wrapped packages. They had spent the past week shopping for gifts, something Nate claimed he'd never done before. He had wanted to give everyone gift cards, but Fiona had insisted on buying real presents for his family, and Nate had humored her. Fighting the crowds hadn't been fun, but she had enjoyed spending the time with Nate and learning more about him.

"Let's go meet your new family," he said, nodding at the walk.

Fiona blinked back tears as they started toward the house. Oh, how she hoped he was right! While no one could ever replace her parents, it would be so good to feel like part of something again. She wasn't lonely with Nate by her side, but it would be nice to experience all the joys of family again.

The door opened before they reached the porch, and Nate's parents stood just inside the house, smiling at them. His mother's eyes were wet, and she reached out and cupped Nate's face, pulling him down for a kiss. "It's so good to see you!" she exclaimed.

Nate's father patted him on the back and smiled. "Glad you made it."

Then they turned their attention to Fiona. "You must be Nate's girlfriend," his mother said.

Fiona nodded and tried to smile. "It's nice to meet you." She offered her hand, but his mother merely stared at it in confusion, as if she didn't understand the gesture. Fiona felt the beginning flutterings of panic set in. Had she committed a faux pas already?

"My dear, you're family. Family doesn't shake hands." The older woman reached out and pulled Fiona into a bone-crushing embrace. "Family hugs in this house."

Fiona returned the hug, feeling an empty part of her heart fill at this ready acceptance. After a moment, Nate's mother released her, and his father stepped in to enfold her in a second, more gentle embrace. Their simple touch immediately made her feel welcome and accepted, and the last of Fiona's worries dissolved like sugar in hot tea.

Nate's mother beamed up at them, looking fit to burst with pleasure. "Now it's really Christmas," she said, reaching out to lay a hand on each of their arms.

"Welcome home."

* * * * *

ROMANTIC suspense

Available December 1, 2015

#1875 CONARD COUNTY WITNESS
Conard County: The Next Generation
by Rachel Lee

When his late wife's friend Lacy Devane discovers her bosses' corrupt activity, recovering war veteran Jess McGregor insists on protecting her from possible retribution. As life-threatening danger crosses their paths, neither Jess nor Lacy is immune to peril—and love...

#1876 HIS CHRISTMAS ASSIGNMENT
Bachelor Bodyguards
by Lisa Childs

Ex-cop Candace Baker has never understood other women's weaknesses for bad boys...until she falls for reformed criminal-turned-bodyguard Garek Kozminski. But when Garek takes an undercover assignment to catch a killer, he's risking not only his life, but also Candace's heart.

#1877 AGENT GEMINI
by Lilith Saintcrow

Amnesiac spy Trinity—aka Agent Three—is fleeing the government agency that infected her with a virus. But before she reaches freedom, she must dodge the agent on her tail. Cal knows he and Trinity are two halves of a whole, and he intends to make her realize it—if he can catch her.

#1878 RISK IT ALL
by Anna Perrin

When PI Brooke Rogers is targeted by the Russian mafia, FBI agent Jared Nash rescues her. As the two embark on a mission to search for Jared's missing brother, they fall deeper and deeper into love—and into danger.

Shock rippled through him, but not enough to completely
erase his desire for her. Man, she'd probably have nightmares
if she saw the stump of his leg. It would inevitably
destroy the mood. Then there was Sara, a woman they
had both loved. He'd feel as if he was cheating on her, and
he suspected Lacy might as well, ridiculous as that might
be. Loyalties evidently didn't go to the grave.

Jess sighed and reached down with his free hand to
rub his stump, as if it could free him from the pain he had
never felt when he was hit, pain that his body evidently
refused to forget.

"Can I help?"

"Nah." Oh yeah, she could. With a few touches she
could probably carry him to a place where nothing but the
two of them could exist. But afterward... Hell, he feared
the guilt that might follow. He could ruin a perfectly good
friendship by getting out of line with this woman.

He and Sara had once had a serious discussion about
the possibility that he might not return from one of his

deployments. Just once, but he remembered telling her to move on with life, that he'd never forgive himself if she buried herself with him.

She'd cocked a brow in that humorous way of hers and asked, "Do you really think I'm the type to do that?"

"Just promise me," he'd said.

It was one of those rare occasions where she'd grown utterly serious. "I'll promise if you'll promise me the same thing."

Of course he'd promised. It had never occurred to him he might be the lone survivor. But that didn't mean he wouldn't feel guilty anyway. Maybe he had some more demons to get past.

He realized that Lacy had unexpectedly dozed off against him. Smiling into the empty night, he removed the mug from her loosening grip and put it on the side table. He guessed she felt safe with him, but he wasn't at all sure that was a good idea.

That note. It hung over him like a sword. What the hell did it mean? He stared into the fire, uneasiness joining the pain that crept along his nerve endings and the desire that wouldn't stop humming quietly.

Turn your love of reading into rewards you'll love with
Harlequin My Rewards